A
Change
of
Scenery

The
CAÑON CITY
CHRONICLES
4

DAVALYNN SPENCER

A Change of Scenery © 2021 by Davalynn Spencer

Wilson Creek Publishing

Print ISBN: 978-1-7350741-1-5
Ebook ISBN: 978-1-7350741-2-2

Scripture quotations are from the King James Version of the Bible.

The characters and events in this book are fictional, and any resemblance to actual persons or events is coincidental.

Cover design by ebooklaunch.com

BOOKS BY DAVALYNN SPENCER

Historical

THE CAÑON CITY CHRONICLES SERIES

Loving the Horseman - Book 1

Straight to My Heart - Book 2

Romancing the Widow - Book 3

The Cañon City Chronicles – Collection books 1-3

THE FRONT RANGE BRIDES SERIES

Mail-Order Misfire - Series Prequel

An Improper Proposal - Book 1

An Unexpected Redemption - Book 2

An Impossible Price – Book 3

Novellas

Snow Angel

Just in Time for Christmas

A High-Country Christmas – two-novella collection

The Snowbound Bride

The Wrangler's Woman

As You Are

Contemporary

The Miracle Tree

Sign up for my Quarterly Author Update
and receive a free historical novella!
http://eepurl.com/xa81D

A
Change of Scenery

Davalynn Spencer

Wilson Creek Publishing

~

For man looketh on the outward appearance,

but the Lord looketh on the heart.

—1 Samuel 16:7

~

CHAPTER ONE

Cañon City, Colorado
June 5, 1911

The gun shot rooted Ella to the concrete sidewalk.

Chest tight, unable to breathe, she clutched the folded shirt to herself until the truth twisted through her, loosening her muscles and her fear.

It wasn't gunfire. Not in today's civilized world of unlikely things moving on their own accord. Things like pictures and carriages.

Air squeezed from her lungs, and her lips parted to aid its escape.

The motorcar passed and she continued on, black leather low-cuts tapping an irregular beat from the Hotel Denton to the corner of Seventh and Main.

At the curb, she paused for another choking contraption in full complaint of its early morning errand. Here to stay, as much as she despised them, at least the automobiles were more easily observed than ridden in. Somewhat.

The dust and her apprehension settled a second time and, stepping into the intersection, she smoothed the recently mended shirt draped over her arm. She'd been early to work every morning since arriving in town three days ago, and she intended to maintain the habit.

Another backfire, another sudden stop.

1

A horse screamed in the next block. Frozen halfway across the street, Ella watched it rear in its traces. Break free. Bolt down the street with its buggy.

Grounded as surely as the hotel on the corner behind her, she stood unable to move. Someone yelled. Men rushed into the street, shouting and waving their arms. Wild-eyed and panicked, the horse charged straight for her.

A lone rider came up behind the buggy, gaining on the flailing contraption. He leaned low along his horse's neck, his hat brim plastered back in his speed.

Jockey-like, he passed the runaway. Ella raised her hands to her face—and flew into the air. The wind crushed from her as the rider swung her up against his leg.

Dirt and gravel kicked into her face. Store fronts and people raced past.

Dangling like a trick rider at a Wild West Show, she squeezed her eyes shut against the bizarre parade.

The rider tightened his arm around her waist and leaned to his left.

"Whoa!" His leg flexed beneath her as he held his seat in a racing turn. Hoof beats muffled, and her eyes flew open as his horse charged across a city park. Crowded into the wide turn, the buggy nag slowed on the grassy surface. Its winded gasps warned of collapse.

The rider's pace slackened to a trot, and Ella's insides bounced like the empty, rattling buggy behind them. He reined to a jarring stop. "You all right, ma'am?"

She twisted to look up at eyes blue as the sky behind them and creased at the corners. His arm relaxed but didn't release her.

Grit coated her lips. Her stomach rolled. Oh Lord, no. She was going to be sick.

~

Snatching featherbrained females off the street was not the way Cale Hutton had planned to spend his morning. But some people didn't have sense enough to get out of the way of a runaway horse.

The gal weighed little more than a sack of flour, though she smelled a sight better. Her short-cropped hair reminded him of a roached-mane filly. She clapped a hand over her mouth and her brown eyes grew dollar-round. Either he'd scared the living daylights out of her, or she was going to—

She heaved behind her hand and her thin shoulders bounced forward.

"You gonna . . ."

She bobbed her head.

He let go of Doc's reins and gripped her around the waist with both hands. When her feet hit the grass, instead of running off to the nearby bushes, she collapsed. Doc stepped gingerly away just as she let loose.

Cale coughed and looked away. Some things were best done in private, but the gal didn't seem to care at the moment. He rode to a shade tree where the runaway stood quivering, then dismounted. His legs wobbled as if he'd been the one to cheat death and not that willow of a woman. He pulled in a lung-full and tugged at his shirt front, then checked the buggy's harness and lines, making sure nothing had torn loose.

Daring a glance over the horse's back, he found the gal still kneeling in the grass, a piece of clothing wadded up beside her.

Guess he'd be heaving too after a stunt like that, now that he thought about it. Though he'd once seen his sister Grace do nearly the same thing on purpose.

Several men rounded the corner at a run and made for the park, one apparently the buggy owner.

"I can't . . . thank you . . . enough." The gent stopped before him and braced his hands on his knees as he sucked wind.

"She can't . . . tolerate those . . . confounded devil wagons . . . when they start shooting like dadblasted fireworks."

"There ought to be a law," another fella offered, wiping his brow with a handkerchief and settling his derby.

Cale pried his hat off and reshaped the brim. There ought to be a law against buggy drivers not carrying a buggy stake. "Next time, leave the halter on her with a lead rope and tie her to the hitching rail. If she jerks it out of the ground, at least it'll slow her down." He set his hat. "Or you could carry a hitch weight."

The owner, still a might sallow, offered a weak handshake.

Cale gathered Doc's reins and returned to the woman. He stopped a respectable distance away, figuring she might need help back to wherever she was headed. She wasn't from around these parts, that was for sure. Not in that getup. Her boy's haircut said she was likely from the East and made her own mind up about most things.

He huffed out a breath and shook his head. Beat all he'd ever seen.

Circling around to stand before her, he offered a hand.

She gathered the crumpled shirt, gripped his fingers with surprising strength, and pulled herself up quicker than he'd expected.

As soon as she straightened, she let go. "Thank y—"

Her leg buckled.

He reached for her again. "No wonder you didn't get out of the way. You shouldn't have been out in the street without help. Or a cane—"

She jerked her arm free and fired from eyes as deep and dark as a cannon barrel. "I am *not* an invalid."

Snake-bit, he stepped back at her venom. "I didn't say you were. Just that—"

"I know what you said. There is not one thing wrong with my hearing." She tossed her head and a forelock fell across her eyes. She pushed it aside.

He studied her a minute—the way she stood all stiff, tilted to her left. She hadn't fouled herself or her funny-looking shoes. One fine-boned hand smoothed the front of her pink skirt and she stuck her chin in the air.

He'd always considered himself a Christian man, but it suited him fine if that was the way she wanted things. He stepped up on Doc and turned for Main Street, tipping his hat in her direction. "You're welcome."

CHAPTER TWO

Ella focused her stare to a pinpoint on the cowboy's vested back, determined to bore a hole through him. How dare he tell her how to cross the street.

The sensation of his iron grip still belted her waist, and her hand shook as she fumbled in her jacket pocket for biscuits the hotel's cook had given her. Two of them, now flattened like pancakes.

She hadn't been atop a horse in a year and a half. With a shake of her head, she shoved the biscuits back in her pocket and took a tentative step forward. The man had not even offered to help her back to the studio. As if she would have accepted his help anyway.

He saved your life.

Guilt, these days, had acquired a voice remarkably similar to her dear Nana's.

All right. He had saved her life. She plucked an ornery grass stem from her stockings. He'd also insulted her. And who was to say that she might not have side-stepped the charging horse and buggy had he not been in her way?

She imagined Nana Elizabeth's eyes rolling heavenward at such ingratitude, and an uninvited image imposed itself—her own trampled body in the street, buggy-wheel tracks marring her rose-colored suit.

Three men approached, one with a bowler in his hand and regret on his face.

"Miss . . ."

"Canaday."

"Miss Canaday, please, may I offer you a ride back to town?" The bowler indicated the buggy, horse twitching in the traces. "I do apologize for any injury or danger resulting from my mare's nervous condition."

Nervous indeed. But not as much as Ella would be if she accepted his offer. Though her walk to the studio was blocks farther now than usual, she couldn't trust that animal to remain calm at the next choking automobile, and it seemed more of them crowded the street now than before.

"Thank you, but no. I believe I'll walk." She gave a polite smile and angled away, her limp more pronounced than ever. As it turned out, *she* was the one who suffered the searing burn of someone staring a hole in her back.

Rounding the corner at Main Street, she ducked away from her audience and leaned against the store front. She couldn't stop trembling, whether from anger or fear she didn't know. So much for a change of scenery and observing the rumored West before it vanished. Perhaps she should have stayed in Chicago on the Canaday estate and filled her days with tatting and china painting and tea with spinsters whose ranks she would soon enough join.

Her now-empty stomach rolled, and a moan escaped. She'd completely humiliated herself in that cowboy's presence. Not only had he seen her weakened condition, but he'd also seen her sick. She closed her eyes and leaned her head against the brick, pressing a hand to her midsection until her insides settled. At lease she had no call to face him ever again.

The ache in her leg spread downward from thigh to calf, but she waited for passersby to do just that before kneading her fisted knuckles into the scarred thigh muscle. The building that supported her housed a grocer, one of three she had seen in town so far, advertising locally grown vegetables and fruit in season. A shame that early June was not the season for that fruit.

Jed Barr's gabardine shirt looked as if it had been run through a wringer. She inspected it for tears but found only wrinkles, which could be remedied provided she had the time. She pushed off the wall and peered ahead for her destination, though it was completely out of sight. The Hotel Denton rose two blocks from where she stood, and the Selig Polyscope studio was three blocks beyond that. By the time she arrived, she would be even sorer—and sorely late—providing yet another arrow for the leading lady's artillery.

Nearing the Denton's stately four stories, she wanted nothing more than to stumble upstairs and into a hot bath, but she pressed on. Urgency tempted her to hurry, but she took her route slowly, accommodating her leg by strolling rather than rushing.

A baker's enticing aromas wafted into the morning, as did a spicy concoction from the Ceylon Tea Store's open door. The small town preened beneath her perusal, boasting a millinery and ladies' clothing store, the *Cañon City Record* newspaper office, two drug stores—one with a soda fountain—as well as a hardware store, paint store, and a church.

The walk had dissipated most of her tension and loosened her tight nerves. Her leg, however, was another matter.

She stopped at the corner of Fourth and Main, looked both ways for signs of nervous horses or cacophonous motorcars, and then successfully crossed the street for her final stretch to the studio.

The dignified Raynolds Bank peered down as she passed, but she focused on resisting her leg's painful throbbing and almost missed a visitor waiting at the studio—the very horse that had carried her to safety. In a manner of speaking.

Her neck prickled at the fresh memory of a man's iron-like grip and pillared leg that together served as what really carried her from certain death, or at least further maiming. Pushing away those troublesome sensations of the cowboy's powerful presence, she considered his equally powerful mount that waited calmly in front of the studio, reins dangling to the dirt.

He was a beauty with his fiery coat and fine head, two qualities she had failed to appreciate while flying down Main Street.

She cushioned her approach with a soft greeting. "Hello, you handsome fellow. And thank you for coming to my rescue earlier."

The horse flicked an ear and nuzzled her jacket pocket.

She angled her right hip away, but rubbed the animal's velvety nose, careful to keep her fingers from its supple lip. "Sorry, but they might be all I'll have time to eat today."

Dark eyes regarded her with a calm and understanding gaze. She leaned into the strong body still overly warm from its run. A good brushing and a bag of oats were what he needed. She drank in the familiar scent of horse, leather, and sweat, not surprised that it still held the power to console and depress her at the same time.

"You truly are a beauty."

He dropped his head and rumbled a deep-chested thank-you.

"I prefer handsome."

The bass tones jerked her around to the cowboy shadowed in a notch of the building. Unbalanced by the sudden move, she tilted against the horse's shoulder, embarrassed by her awkwardness and peeved by a man who would not make himself known immediately. So much for never seeing him again.

The horse stood solid. Its owner moved toward her slowly, as if he didn't trust her and hadn't recently yanked her from the ground in as daring a stunt as any Jed Barr and Mabel Steinway staged. His expression was guarded and hardened, lacking the concern that had earlier drawn his brows together and kept her clutched in his protective hold. No staged scene, *that*. No director or cameraman, costumes or makeup.

A chill fluttered through her like winged truth, and her breath caught at the enormity of what she had been so quick to dismiss simply because she believed he thought her an invalid.

She straightened and faced him squarely. "Thank you for your assistance earlier today. What you did was quite . . ." *Heroic?* "My comments were less than appreciative. Please forgive me."

His eyes narrowed almost imperceptibly, and his head turned a degree in that way that people did when doubting what they perceived.

She deserved that.

Standing so close to him without the wind tearing against her, she detected an earthy scent similar to his horse, minus the sweat. More like hay and sunshine, not at all in keeping with his previous manner. But if manners were in question, hers had been less than exemplary. "I am Ella Canaday."

"Cale Hutton." He touched his hat brim with his left hand in a perfectly natural and unaffected way. Jed Barr could learn a thing or two.

He extended his other hand, and she accepted it, not in the least surprised by his strong grip. Azure eyes had a similar hold. Creased at the edges but clear as the morning, they took her in with unpretentious candor.

Rescuing her hand, she buried it in her skirt pocket. "Are you expecting to meet someone, Mr. Hutton?"

"Cale."

People here were quite casual with strangers, she'd learned, and Mr. Hutton was no exception, though she was hardly a stranger. Her half-nod revealed nothing of her determination to *not* be so familiar—a response she'd used countless times in the family parlor with any number of her father's hand-picked suitors.

Mr. Hutton spread his stance and crossed his arms, apparently accustomed to controlling every situation he encountered.

She held back a sniff.

"Do you work for the studio?"

Rather inquisitive for a first meeting. Well, second meeting. "I am in charge of costuming." A nervous tremor shifted through her at the lofty title, but it was none of his business what she did.

Ruing such a boastful answer rather than evading his query with a pithy reply, she smoothed an obvious wrinkle in the piped yoke of Jed's shirt.

He dipped his head. "That getup for Mr. Barr?"

"It is." *Drat.* Had she no resistance to a penetrating, sky-blue gaze?

His cotton shirt and woolen vest quietly contested the fancy attire on her arm, and his wide shoulders carried a collar band a bit longer than Jed's, by her estimation. She doubted the shirt she held would fasten across Mr. Hutton's chest.

Surprised by the thought, she sidestepped him to get to the door.

He moved with her.

"I've come to see Robert Thorson about leasing my stock. He and Jed Barr were out to the Rafter-H the other day, and I told him we'd think about his offer."

"I see." She recalled their long absence and her relief that she hadn't been required to accompany them. Working behind the scenes had its advantages. "Well, did you see him?"

"The door's locked."

At this hour? She dug the key from her skirt pocket, and when he held his place, she challenged him. "Excuse me, please."

He watched her for an extra beat before stepping aside.

Brash. It might do him well to wait outside. But she had spent her allotment of rudeness on this man, if such a thing were possible. "Mr. Barr will not be in, but Mr. Thorson should be here soon if you care to wait."

He followed her indoors and removed his hat from hair as dark as her thoughts. Turning on the lights, she gestured toward a chair. "Have a seat if you'd like."

He folded himself into a curved-back captain's chair, where he braced arms on legs and twirled his dusty hat between his knees. If Thorson used him in a scene, the man would dwarf Jed, though with his fair eyes, he'd likely be nothing more than a background character.

11

The camera's blue-sensitive film would give him a ghostlike appearance if his eyes met the lens.

But her pocket Kodak was another matter altogether. For a moment, she considered what lighting would best aid her in capturing the cowboy's rugged features.

Caught by his glance, she abandoned her musing. With slow and deliberate steps, she crossed to the clothing rack and hung Jed's shirt with the other costumes. Once her cotton twill jacket was on a coat hanger, she smoothed her matching rose-colored skirt.

For the second time that day, she burned with an unsettling awareness of uninvited eyes on her back.

~

Ella Canaday was as puzzling a female as Cale had ever met. Unlike any rancher's daughter, that was for sure. Not like his housekeeper, Helen, or his brother's deceased wife, Jane. Not even like their little sister, Grace, who was a breed to herself where women were concerned. No, this gal wasn't like one single woman he could think of, with her flimsy shoes and opinionated little chin.

And to think he'd held her in his arms. Make that *arm*. He snorted.

She jerked her head his way, hair swaying like fringe on a surrey.

He drove his gaze off in another direction. She hadn't capped her name with a *Miss*, but her ringless finger said enough. No surprise there.

He leaned back, crossed one boot over his knee, and took in the room. Or saloon or hotel lobby, depending on where he looked. Movable canvas walls bore painted-on windows and doors and staircases, and all the furniture looked like it'd been rode hard and put away wet.

He'd seen a couple of flickers, but everything had looked better on the screen than all this did. Even Jed Barr had looked a little less than himself up close, compared to his nickelodeon posters.

A door closed at the back of the building, and heavy footsteps brought Thorson around the end of a saloon wall and into the clutter of scattered furniture.

Cale stood.

"Mr. Thorson, Cale Hutton is here to see you about some livestock." Miss Canaday flicked her dark eyes his way.

"Hutton," Thorson bellowed as if Cale was hard of hearing. "Good to see you this morning. You considered my offer?"

"Yes, sir."

"Good, good." The director swatted the air with each word and strode to a desk pushed against the wall. "I have a contract right here that I hope you will find adequate, and we can complete the transaction immediately."

Thorson signed with a flourish and dusted his signature with fine sand from a small pot, then handed the paper and pen to Cale and stabbed a finger at a blank line toward the bottom.

A careful read of the small print satisfied Cale that no ambush awaited, and he added his name. Two hard winters, rustlers, and renegades—whether man or beast—had cut the herd in half. The Rafter-H wasn't the only spread on Eight Mile and the high parks that needed outside cash to cover losses. This could be just the ticket.

Thorson gave him a second paper identical to the first, and Cale signed it as well. After the signatures dried, he folded his copy and stuffed it inside his vest. From the corner of his eye, he caught Miss Canaday watching the proceedings with interest. Or watching him. Something akin to dread darted through him like a startled quail.

Thorson corked the ink pot. "When can you have the cattle corralled for filming?"

"I've got twenty head bunched at the lower pens and horses at the ready. My brother will ride along as well, but your men need to be able to horseback, or those ponies'll turn out from under 'em."

Thorson guffawed.

Cale flinched, grateful the man didn't trail cows with him.

"I assure you, Mr. Hutton, Jed Barr can handle whatever you throw at him. So can the other three men who will be driving out to your place tomorrow."

"Only four coming?"

"Several more than that, I assure you. At least two touring cars, maybe three. Actors, cameraman, seamstress, technicians, myself. There will be quite a group."

Cale picked up his hat and frowned at visions of city folk trampling the pastures and riling the animals. Doubt tripped up the dollar signs prancing through his head. Was it worth the risk?

"Don't worry, son." Thorson laughed again and slapped Cale's shoulder. "We won't be tearing anything up or down on your ranch. Just show us where to leave the automobiles when we get there. We all know how to stay out of the way."

He cut a look at Miss Canaday, someone who *didn't* know how to stay out of the way. Sure enough, she'd drown in the rain with her nose in the air like that. But five dollars a day for himself, another five for Hugh, and more for their cattle and horses would help stop the bleeding.

"Tomorrow, then." He shoved his hat on and tugged the brim. "Miss Canaday."

She gave a bare nod. From the way she rode herd on that rack of costumes, he'd wager she was the seamstress. He'd also wager she had no business around livestock.

He walked outside and gathered Doc's reins. If Ella Canaday didn't watch where she was going at the ranch, this whole affair might end up more risk than he'd bargained for.

14

CHAPTER THREE

"Get out of my way, you cripple."

Ella clenched her jaw and stumbled aside into the clothes rack rather than be trampled by the flouncing actress. Unbalanced, she reached for a side table and dislodged a coffee cup. It hit the wooden floor and shattered.

Mabel Steinway glanced over her retreating shoulder with a snicker. "Come on, Jed. All this racket grates on my nerves."

The studio door banged shut behind the couple and Ella inhaled, dragging air through her teeth. Pain splintered through her leg, as sharp as the jagged edges of the broken cup. Coffee dregs puddled on the hardwood while impatience pooled in her heart.

Would she never regain her former strength?

Falling into the nearest chair, she fingered the narrow depression in her right thigh, kneading the misshapen muscle with little resistance from her cotton skirt and thin petticoat. The unseen vise eased its grip, and she straightened her leg, flexed her ankle, and drew a deep breath through her nose.

Mabel had the manners of a cow.

Ella leaned over and picked up the broken stoneware, noting that the costume rack leaned dangerously askew, threatening to tilt its contents onto the floor. If Mabel's clothing acquired a coffee stain, Ella would never hear the end of it.

Pushing to her feet, she reminded herself of the importance of keeping her job. Her father had threatened to withdraw his support if she took a position with a moving-picture company.

And so he had.

She dropped the broken cup in the waste basket, and with a rag from the makeup box, toweled the spilled coffee with her foot to avoid kneeling. Avoid curious eyes that always watched when she pulled herself up on the furniture. Avoid pitying whispers.

Pity nettled her more than Mabel's open scorn. It insinuated doubt in her abilities—the exact impetus that set her at odds with her father. She kicked the wet rag beneath the rack and sorted costumes for mending.

In contrast to her father's warning, Nana's comforting voice wove through her memory on a silken thread.

You will recover, Ella. And someday you will love again if you choose.

Now, that thread snagged. Ella had already chosen, and she'd believed that the match was of the Lord's making. Charles—with his laughing gray eyes and fun-loving manner—had also chosen, and he'd chosen her over the flamboyant Mabel Steinway.

The *soiree* at the riverside home of her father's business partner two years ago had been held in the wake of Chicago's explosive enjoyment of what the newspapers called *moving pictures.* Even film studio owners, George K. Spoor and "Bronco" Billy Anderson had attended, as did an up and coming actress, Mabel Steinway.

And the beauty wasted no time in flaunting her talents under the noses of every eligible bachelor in attendance, particularly Charles. For some reason, he piqued the actress's interest more than the others. And for some reason, he failed to return that interest.

Instead, he chose the only daughter of Patrick Canaday III, of all people. In spite of her advanced twenty and five years.

Ella shoved women's blouses to one side of the rack, the cowboys' shirts to the other, leaving Jed's wrinkled gabardine between them. Gilmore's Laundry across the street opened in twenty minutes. They'd make light work of the wrinkles from this morning's escapade.

Like an arrow from a drawn bow, pain shot from her heart to her leg. She doubled over, gripping the chair as she crumpled into it. Minutes passed until her breath came evenly and the sting subsided.

With a clear view of the front door, she sagged against the chair's wooden arms and unwrapped her breakfast, clearly aware of what her father would think of Clara's handiwork, flat or not.

Though crushed, the soft bread melted in Ella's mouth, its goodness unharmed by the morning's ordeal. Misshapen, yes, but it survived. She tore off another bite and popped it in her mouth.

Fate had been cheated a second time today, if one cared to view it that way.

In her youth, she would have declared Cale Hutton a heaven-sent salvation, whisking her from death's dismembering hooves.

Now, she saw his appearance as mere chance.

What more could it be? For if she'd truly had a choice, she would not have been in the street this morning. She would have redone that long-ago stormy night's drive with Charles the same way Robert Thorson re-filmed a chase scene or a bar-room brawl. Charles would be alive, and she would be his wife, at home in the security of his arms—not mending costumes or freezing in front of runaway horses in a dirt-street town.

She tore the remaining biscuit in two, relishing its buttery flavor that contrasted sharply with her emotions. One did not walk well after a life-altering injury and fifteen months of idleness. Nor did one drag death—real death—off life's set in a scene change.

Hence, the only choice she truly had was where and how she would deal with her loss. And even that was infringed upon by another. How could she have possibly known that Mabel Steinway would leave her former production studio and go West with the Selig Polyscope Company?

17

At nine o'clock she took Jed's shirt from the rack. Thorson was in a full-blown argument with the cameraman about the day's set arrangement, and she hurried out the door to the laundry, praying that Jed Barr did not show up early for once.

"Morning, Miss Canaday." Mr. Gilmore's thick neck bulged over his tight collar and his puffy eyes left Ella guessing at his previous night's pastime.

She laid the shirt across his counter.

"Would you have time to press out this crease in the next thirty minutes?"

"I'd be happy to." Mr. Gilmore ran a hand across the creamy fabric and traced the piping-edged yoke with a thick finger. "Nice work. Did you make this?"

"Oh, no. This shirt came special order from Chicago. I simply mend and tailor the clothing to fit, though I do make a few things."

"Well, from what I've seen so far, you are quite good at what you do." He picked up the shirt and held it at arm's length, scrutinizing it with an expert eye. "If you ever need something to keep yourself busy, I'd be happy to give you some of my tailoring overload."

Ella rubbed her temple at the suggestion, forcing a gracious smile and tilting her weight to her left leg. "I shall keep that in mind, Mr. Gilmore. And I will be back in a half hour. Thank you."

He raised a hand as he headed for the back. "My pleasure."

She looked both ways before crossing the now busy street, giving steady regard to the west, the direction Cale Hutton had taken out of town. The state penitentiary walls rose cold and impenetrable at the end of the street where travelers jogged to the left and down a small hill. Quarried locally, the pale stone blocks were not meant to keep people out, but to keep criminals in.

Laying a hand at her throat, she paused before the studio, her heartbeat pushing against her own self-imposed barrier. For what purpose had she raised such an impenetrable wall? To keep others out or herself imprisoned?

More than three hours later, Mabel and Jed laughed through the studio's front door, faces aglow with private levity. The *femme fatale* for all Selig Polyscope's moving pictures, Miss Steinway could bat her kohl-rimmed eyes into nearly any man's good senses, especially Jed Barr's. But he was a fool if he thought she cared a whit for him.

Ella's stomach and the biscuits tumbled at the smell of fried chicken clinging to the couple's clothes as they hurried through to the back. Mr. Thorson, who did not care to be left waiting for anything or anyone, had called a meeting for eleven-thirty. She checked her lapel watch. Mabel and Jed were an hour late.

"Miss Canaday!"

The director's megaphone voice boomed over the flimsy saloon partitions and bar dividing the temporary store-front studio.

She limped to the makeshift doorway, praying he'd not insist she shuffle closer with the entire troupe watching.

"Are costumes ready for this afternoon?"

Of course they were. "Yes, sir."

Mabel snickered and elbowed Jed with a stage-whispered, "She's a real *hobble*-skirter."

Flush with visions of stitching the woman's lips closed, Ella cocked one hand on her hip and raised her chin. Mabel wasn't the only one who could act.

"Good, good." Thorson dismissed her with a wave. "We leave in a half hour."

Ella spun on her left foot, a move she'd practiced countless times in the last six months. Gritting her teeth, she ordered her right leg to not give way and made it out of sight just before it folded like a paper fan. The loud slap of her hand on the bar shuddered up her arm and into her shoulder, reminding anyone with ears of her less-than-sound constitution. At least she'd caught herself.

The afternoon promised a tenuous trek across the river-spanning foot bridge at the Hot Springs Hotel, and rough terrain at Grape Creek. Ella hoped for a stolen moment of relaxed massage before it all began, but scraping chairs and raised voices announced the meeting's end much sooner than Mr. Thorson's estimated thirty minutes. Time to film Jed and Mabel's signature ride into the make-believe sunset after a save-the-lady scuffle for Jed.

If only Ella's ride in an automobile were not required.

She gathered chaps and shirts, her satchel and her resolve, and hurried outside to the touring car parked nearest the door. By securing a seat in the back, she dodged yet another painful situation. It seemed as if avoidance filled her days, consuming much more of her concentration than she had anticipated when she took the seamstress job.

But sitting in the front robbed her breath and wrecked her fingers. Even the short drive to the Hot Springs foot bridge was long enough to cramp her hands from gripping the leather seat's edge.

~

Cale left the ranch road and loped Doc across the open field toward the lower corrals. Hugh's hammer rang like he was driving steel through a railroad tie.

Reining in, Cale thumbed his hat up and leaned on his saddle horn. "The deal's done and they'll be here tomorrow. A whole crew."

His mirror image pulled off a sweat-ringed hat and dragged his sleeve across his forehead. "And they're driving out in those rackety tin cans, aren't they?"

Cale nodded.

Hugh spit. "Blasted invention." He threw his weight against the new cedar pole. "They'll spook the cattle and rile the horses."

"They'll also ease our woes at the bank and buy us a few extra head."

Hugh picked up the box of nails at his feet and spit again.

"Appreciate your sunny attitude." Dust from the ride home coated Cale's grin, but as the younger twin by a minute, he felt it his duty to keep the banter going. Never let it be said that he'd allow sixty seconds to stand in the way of a little jawing.

Hugh sliced him a cold look and trudged off to the barn.

Cale set Doc to an easy walk around the back of the house, mulling over what had his brother's tail in a tighter knot than usual. He scoured the yard, the corrals, the swing in the big cottonwood tree, looking for the boys and whatever trouble they might be in.

Maybe Helen had them scrubbing floors or picking berries. If anyone could wrangle them, she could.

In spite of the clear, sweet-smelling day, a sad note hummed heavy in his gut. Helen had come to their aid early on. She'd taken to Jane at church and did for her what she'd never been able to do for her own brood since there'd not been one. But when Jane took sick and died, Helen swept those boys up and moved in. Cale didn't remember who asked her, or if anyone had. She'd just been there.

He did his part too, but he and Helen couldn't take the place of a loving woman whose smile never failed to soften his brother's sharp edges. Nowadays, those edges cut against everything Hugh came in contact with, including his sons.

Truth was the whole situation had put the whoa on Cale as far as a wife was concerned. Not that he didn't want a bride of his own. But loving a woman and then losing her was a proposition that set his teeth on edge. Besides, he hadn't found the right one yet, and he was creepin' up on thirty.

The image of a hot-blooded, bob-haired filly circled the back of his mind. Something about that gal whetted his curiosity. Just what he didn't need—distraction.

With a snort to make Doc proud, he kicked for the barn.

Six of their best horses stood swishing their tails in the corral. They'd have a rodeo for sure if those city boys couldn't ride. He stopped outside the barn where Hugh was banging around in the tack room. "I'm gonna drive down those twenty head we corralled up the draw."

His brother stepped out and squinted up at him. "Why? The flicker crew will be here tomorrow."

"My gut tells me someone—or something—else might be here tonight."

Hugh's spit hit the dirt like a bullet. "Want help?"

Doc danced sideways, picking up on Cale's sudden tension. "I've got it. Finish what you're doing here."

Hugh pulled his gloves off and slapped them on his chaps. "We've got enough saddles if those stall-fed dudes can stay in 'em."

"Thorson says Barr knows his way around. Word is he worked for an Oklahoma spread, him and the other three fellas he's bringing with him. Can handle himself on about anything, I hear."

Hugh cut a side glance. "Care to make a friendly wager?"

"And take your hard-earned money?" Cale shortened the reins and shifted his weight. "I'll pass. Besides, I'll skin him at the rodeo in a couple weeks, if he enters."

Hugh looked out across the yard. "They can park their rattle traps in the lower pasture. I'll have the boys out there early tomorrow, directing 'em away from the fence."

That meant Kip, Jay, and Ty would be out of Hugh's hair. So long as one of them didn't get run over. Cale wasn't especially fond of automobiles himself, and this morning's close call deepened his dislike. They cut down the time spent traveling, but it was a toss-up as to what a fella valued more: time or peace.

Or his life.

He again saw the stark fear on Ella Canaday's face as she stood frozen in the street, and it sent a chill up his neck. He'd taken a mighty big chance with that running grab—he'd be the first to admit it. The good Lord had saved his hide again. And hers.

He turned toward the draw that cut north from the house and barn, watching the dry trail for sign. Juniper peppered the air with its pungent smell, and a blue bowl hung above it all, not a cloud in sight. That fact alone concerned him. Whatever was taking their cattle did so more often during the dry spells. Easier for a man to cover tracks.

But a bear?

Some ranchers claimed a renegade was stealing their cattle. A descendant of that rogue grizzly, Old Mose. Cale wasn't convinced. Only thing for certain was there'd been no rain for a week, and the Rafter-H couldn't afford to lose one more steer.

The twenty he was driving down were marked for a Cripple Creek butcher and his hungry gold miners. A quick run through the draw tomorrow shouldn't take much weight off the cattle, though Hugh was right about it being easier to leave them up there tonight.

Trouble was Cale's gut was right more often than not, and his gut said bring 'em in now.

At supper that evening, Cale hung his hat on the hall tree and swallowed a snicker. The boys were still as crickets under a courtin' moon. Tough being their age, all full of spit and vinegar. Helen had her hands full, he'd give her that. But Hugh could jerk the slack out of his sons by cocking a sharp eyebrow, which he did as soon as Helen bowed her head. She'd laid down the law—they'd give thanks or they wouldn't eat. Cale obliged her, as did Hugh, but not without fighting the bit.

Cale peeked at the portraits gazing down on the table from the back wall. His mother was of like persuasion as Helen. It showed in the soft lines flanking her mouth. His pa had cowboyed this spread and passed it on to Cale, Hugh, and Grace when he died. They all favored their mother, aside from her light hair. Even Hugh's boys carried their grandpa's darker look. Jane had something to do with that too, Cale supposed, seeing as how her near-black hair had matched that of her sons. What was it about those dark manes that drew the Hutton brothers' attention?

"Where are you, Cale?" Helen caught him wading through his thoughts.

He'd missed the *amen*.

"Beg pardon?"

She offered him her peach preserves and a biscuit. He took two. Old enough to be his and Hugh's ma, Helen kept them all fed and cared for, but Hugh still wore the same look he carried just after Jane's death. Devastation. Suppertime seemed to pull it out of him, and Cale usually hurried through the meal and escaped to the barn.

"What are they plannin' to do out here tomorrow?" Hugh shoveled his food and tore a biscuit in half to sop the bowl, frowning more tonight than usual.

"Thorson said they want ranch scenes. Herding, branding, chasing."

The last word stopped Hugh's soaked biscuit halfway to his mouth. "Chasing?" A swear word took the sop as Hugh growled out his displeasure, rousing Helen's disapproval. "I'm not running the weight off the cattle, that's for d— " Her warning glare cut the word from his throat. "That's for sure."

The boys kicked each other under the table, squirming like worms on a hook. Helen eyed them over her coffee cup. "Whose turn is it to wash tonight?"

Two heads swiveled toward the oldest.

"Aw, Miss Helen." Ty screwed up his eight-year-old face, and his brothers snickered.

"No complaining, Tyler Jonathan Hutton." The woman plated her flatware and handed it across the table. "Jay, you'll be clearing the table and putting the dishes away after Kip dries them."

All three faces fell. Cale shoved his coffee cup against his lower lip and drowned a laugh.

A garbled mumble rolled across the table and landed within range of Helen's hawk-sharp hearing.

"What was that, Jay?"

"Nuthin'."

"Speak up." Hugh's hard edge straightened his middle son's back.

"That's woman's work." Two dark eyes stared at the pile of plates while his siblings shed him like thick hair in summer on their way to the kitchen. Lightning was about to strike.

Helen set her cup in its saucer and cleared her throat with a lady-like cough. "If you'd like, son, I can parcel out some woman's work for you tomorrow while your brothers help your father and uncle direct our visitors and their motorcars."

She leaned back in her chair with a far-off look, fingering the gray at her temples. "Now that I think on it, I have a lot of washing to do. And there's the kitchen to mop, rugs to beat, beds to strip, and chickens to pluck. And after that, I can show you how to darn your brothers' socks that sprout holes quicker than weeds grow in the garden."

Cale's own collar tightened. He should be bedding down. Morning always showed up early.

"Sorry."

"What was that?" Hugh bore into the youngster with a blue stare.

The boy's head popped up. "Beggin' your pardon, Miss Helen. I meant no disrespect." His dark eyes shimmered with his effort to keep the tears corralled.

"Thank you, Jay. I know you didn't." Helen's shoulders softened, and she leaned toward Jay with a lower tone. "Now don't keep your brothers waiting. They won't be able to finish their chores without your help." Glancing toward the kitchen, she raised her voice a notch. "Heaven forbid I have to find something extra for them to do because they dilly-dallied."

A shy grin capped off a forgiven "yes, ma'am," and never did two short legs carry a body out of a room quicker.

Cale scooted back from the table. "Thank you, Helen. We've got an early start tomorrow."

"You're not having any of my rhubarb cobbler?" She scooped a large helping onto Hugh's plate and a smaller portion for herself. "I baked it fresh this morning."

He was tempted, but he wanted to put some thought into tomorrow. The way he fell asleep after one of Helen's desserts, he'd be lucky if he got his boots off first. Tonight he'd pass.

"More for me," Hugh growled around a spoonful.

On his way out, Cale looked over his shoulder, remembering the way Jane used to lean against his brother's arm and say something to pull a grin across his grumpy face. Now he just sat there and ate his rhubarb in silence.

Hang fire. If he could, Cale would order him up a bride, but folks didn't do that anymore. Pity.

The moon lit the yard like near day, exposing Cale's own hidden longings. Hard to admit he wanted his own close table-talks with a woman, one who'd spread a smile in his heart and a quilt on his bed. But a fella didn't always get what he wanted—or keep it—and he was old enough to know the truth in that.

The blue-gray night settled around him, and an owl called from the cottonwood. Tug padded up and shoved his cold nose in Cale's hand. He rubbed the old spotted dog's head and thanked God again that they didn't live in town.

At the barn, he stopped in the wide doorway long enough for one of the cats to lace herself around his legs. Her long back arched beneath his hand, and he caught four wide-eyed kittens watching from a dark stall.

Satisfied the cattle were settled in the corral, he made for the far end of the house and the stone stoop marking a back door to his father's old study. Helen's arrival required he give her his former room, and he'd shoved the big desk up against one wall and set a cot against another.

Inside, he closed the door with a quiet click. Moonlight spilled through the window and across the narrow bed. He kicked his boots off, dropped onto the cot, and closed his eyes against the intruding moonlight.

Might as well try sleeping at high noon.

CHAPTER FOUR

That evening, Ella sank into the copper tub until her shoulders slipped beneath the silky water and her bobbed hair teased its surface. She had not expected such luxury so far from Denver, particularly the Hotel Denton's running cold *and* hot water. Steam coated the gilded mirror on the wall next to the tub, obscuring her reflected image and confirming her over-indulgence.

She toed the lever, sighing as warmth swirled beneath her legs and back. After a day of stumbling around boulders at Grape Creek and tripping on loose, flaky rock the locals called shale, she wanted nothing more than to stay in the tub all night.

Her leg ached. Her heart ached. All of her ached, but the heat was helping—exactly what she'd heard about the Hot Springs Hotel. Evidently people came from far and wide for the springs' curative powers. But if she wanted to take the waters there, she'd have to hire a hack or entrust herself to an unknown local automobile driver.

Her shudder sent ripples dancing across the water.

A knock at the bathing room door shot her upright, and water splashed onto the floor. "Just a moment."

She pulled the plug and carefully climbed out to a towel-draped chair scooted against the tub. After drying off, she tightened the sash of her dressing gown, gathered her slippers and room key, and opened the door to find no one waiting.

Her jaw clenched. Who would play such a cruel trick?

One name came to mind, but Mabel's room was on the floor above. Surely she wouldn't come all the way down to torment Ella after hours.

Surely she would.

Ella flicked off the electric light switch and made her way down the hallway's lush carpet runner. She let herself into her room, careful to turn the key in the lock behind her. Taking a seat at the dressing table, she brushed her bob, appreciating how little time it took to care for, other than a few curls crimped around her face with a marcel iron. Much to her father's distaste.

She pulled the hairbrush through again and puffed an indignant breath. He did not spend hours twisting knots and teasing long strands into pompadours that called for combing out and fluffing up day after day. Good riddance to both.

Her reflection reddened, and she quickly refocused her anger on the knots and pompadours, not her father. As much as she'd fought to flee his controlling presence, "honor thy father and thy mother" lay firmly planted in her soul, a hedge she found herself snagged in more often than not where her father was concerned. Unfortunate for her that she had not been a male child, though she possessed the pluck necessary to tear away from the hedge. When he'd first threatened to cut her off, she'd beaten him to it with a pair of fabric shears.

Émilie Bouchaud had done the same and managed to survive society's scandalized response. Ella would as well. Charles had loved her long hair, and she had loved Charles. With one gone, why not the other?

She shook her head and the unfettered fringe brushed against her face. *Unfettered*—such a lovely word. And so reflective of the coming styles in hair and dress for this new century. Women continued to break out of traditional roles and molds, and she fully intended to follow suit.

She laid aside her dressing gown, switched off the light, and slid between the cool cotton sheets, drawing her knees up beneath her shift. Escaping her father's world had landed her in a sea of strangers making moving pictures of robbers and villains and heroes saving damsels in distress. Yet for the life of her, she did not know why Selig Polyscope's leading damsel continued to hate her so. They had both lost Charles, though in truth, Mabel had never possessed him. Yet she seemed to enjoy taunting Ella. Mr. Thorson showed her no favors and was as exacting on her as he was every other member of the troupe.

A niggling memory flickered briefly, as outrageous as the incident that spawned it. Jed Barr had been exceptionally welcoming on Ella's first day with the company, going so far as to lean over her hand and brush it with his lips in a very uncowboy-like way.

Mabel had seethed like a boiling kettle, her charcoal eyes flashing nearly green.

But that was weeks ago, before the company boarded the train to Colorado's Rocky Mountains. In plenty of time for Ella to back out after learning that Mabel had joined the company.

Which, of course, she did not.

Ella stretched her legs out and rolled to her back. Faint light from the streetlamps painted the ceiling gossamer gray. An errant automobile clattered by, intruding upon the night's calm and her conscience. She must write Nana. The dear woman would worry if Ella didn't let her know she'd arrived safely and was in secure surroundings.

Or she could telephone. The Denton boasted of telephone service to the outside, but that would dip into her meager earnings and she needed to save every penny. Perhaps tomorrow she'd have time to write and post a letter, describing to her grandmother the peculiarities of the fabled *West*.

Her eyes drifted shut, and with a silent prayer, she offered thanks for constant work and its attendant fatigue that kept the nightmares at bay. Waking from dreamless sleep was a blessing she'd not been afforded back home in Chicago.

~

Cale bolted upright. The room was dark and still, no moon in the window. His heart hammered. Had he really heard the bellow or was he dreaming?

Outside, Tug yelped like a rustler was on him with a hot iron.

Cale dashed for the gun cabinet in the dining room, knocking over chairs and making as much racket as was going on outside. Hugh ran down the hall for the same purpose, and they both sprinted out the kitchen door.

The cattle bunched at one end of the corral, clacking horns against each other and kicking up dust. Tug growled and barked, frantic after a shadowed hulk at the opposite end.

A rail snapped like a rifle shot, and the shadow took off with a bawling calf.

Cale raised his gun and fired. Hugh followed suit, but the moon was long gone and they saw only the flare from their weapons. They heard no cry, no fall.

They'd missed.

Cale called Tug. Whimpering, the old dog skulked to him, dropping to the ground at his feet. He knelt and rubbed a hand over its body, and a wet sticky spot on one hip drew a yelp. Tug pressed into him as if he'd let his master down and was begging forgiveness.

"You did good, boy. We'll get you fixed up."

"Bear or man?" Hugh's voice ripped the night like an iron rasp.

"Hard telling with no light. Could be a claw mark on the dog, could be knife." Cale stood, his eyes adjusting to the dark, and realized he was barefoot. "Whatever it was, it was good-sized. We probably shouldn't have shot blind."

Hugh's spittle hit the ground. "Doesn't matter. Nothin' has the right to steal our cattle."

Cale agreed, except it did matter. "I'll get a lantern. But first, I'm gettin' my boots."

The top pole was snapped clean as a whistle, and when he returned, they wired a board across the break by lantern light.

Hugh pulled against the mend. "That'll hold 'till morning, unless we get a return visit."

Cale grabbed the light, and they made for the house. "It got away with one of our calves, so I doubt it'll come back tonight. I'll ride up the draw at daybreak, look for a trail."

In the kitchen, he cleaned and salved Tug's wound, relieved to find only a shallow gash and no torn muscle. The dog had gotten away from something sharp, but he wasn't sure what. It could have been a lot worse.

Cale let Tug curl up on the rag rug by his bed, and he listened to every snore and rabbit-chasing escapade before giving up and dressing in the dark. His own sleep escaped as easily as the marauder, and when gray hit the eastern horizon, he was mounted and riding up the ravine. Even in the thin pre-dawn, he could make out the drag trail.

Not long after, in clear light, stench and buzzing flies drew him to the kill covered with leaves and brush. The back of his neck crawled. Doc blew against the smell of death, his nostrils flared, his neck arched and tight.

Cale pulled his Winchester from the scabbard and stepped down, keeping tight hold of a rein. He kicked away the brush until a leg showed. Warming to the task, he found a heavier branch and cleared the brush for a better look.

His blood chilled. It wasn't a calf this time, and the other ranchers might be right.

No little black bear hauled off a thousand-pound steer and left if half eaten. Neither did a man.

But a grizzly could.

~

Ella bit down on an empty thread spool and squeezed her eyes shut, envisioning herself kneading bread. Her fingers probed as pain slid from beneath her lashes. The muscle twitched and then tightened, waking in full rebellion from the night's dormant state and yesterday morning's long walk. If she clenched her teeth much harder, she'd either dislocate her jaw or fill her mouth with splinters.

Her breath staccatoed over the sting until the muscle yielded. As it relaxed, she traced the pink scar running nearly to her knee. This time when she bent her leg, it didn't burn. She opened her mouth and the spool dropped into her hand. Progress came at a high price.

Gingerly she stood, testing her weight, then smoothed the bedclothes and her cheeks. Self-pity was a price she refused to pay.

Morning spilled through the window, brightening another of Jed's gabardine shirts hanging over the back of a small rocker. Should someone enter her room, they would think the worst of her. A sharp laugh cut against her sore ribs as she transferred the garment to a wooden hanger and fastened the top button. Had things gone differently, the shirt could have belonged to Charles and not served merely as proof of her skill with a needle.

As it was, Jed would not notice her repair of the ripped seams from yesterday's faux skirmish. But Mabel would. Ella rolled her lips to squelch an unkind remark. The woman noticed everything. Not that she approved, she simply noticed.

A split riding skirt, also newly mended, draped the footboard, and Ella folded it over a hanger. It was the second skirt Mabel had torn that week. She seemed bent on discrediting Ella's abilities.

So be it.

Ella had not joined the company to make friends but to make a living, as meager as it was. She fingered the tatted edge of her camisole, the delicate lacework her most recent attempt at copying Nana Elizabeth's fine stitches. "Mended tears and tatted edges beautify one's life," she'd often reminded Ella. One of her *pearls,* as Ella called her grandmother's sayings.

Sadly, Nana was the only person she missed from home.

Ella buttoned her heart beneath her blouse, belted her own split skirt, and pulled on her boots. Not that she intended to ride. Heavens, yesterday's fiasco of dodging horses at the river was far closer than she had ever intended to come to it. But since she could not get out of going to the ranch, she did not want to be hindered by her good shoes or a suit. And there could be snakes.

Her pulse raced as she tidied the room and picked up the mended clothing and her satchel, camera tucked safely inside. She'd not felt such anticipation in months. Fifteen to be exact.

Her room door shut with a quiet click, and she turned the key. No sense waking other hotel patrons in her pre-dawn trip to the studio. The burgundy carpet runner swallowed her uneven footfall, and at the stairs she glanced at the elevator. So much easier.

And noisier.

She grasped the railing and continued down.

A sharp left turn at the bottom sent her straight across the elegant dining room and through the kitchen door, following her nose to another of Clara's marvelous concoctions. The woman could make a wooden Indian's mouth water.

"You've ruined me for going without breakfast." She stopped next to the buxom cook, drinking in the conflicting aromas of cinnamon and sausage. Flour clung to the woman's dark hands and dusted the front of her starched apron snugging a long-lost waistline.

Clara reached for a rolled napkin lying at the back of the massive stove and offered it with a firm decree.

"Put some meat on those skinny bones."

Clara's motherly scolding warmed Ella from the inside out, and she wanted to toss the clothing in the corner, sit down at the worktable, and gorge herself on biscuits and gravy.

And pour her soul out at the older woman's feet. Though they'd met only a few days ago when the company arrived in

Cañon City, she sensed Clara's compassion was as big as her girth, if not bigger. "You're a dear."

"Pshaw." Clara waved her off. "Don't you be late. We can't have Mr. Barr fussin' about his fancy clothes."

Clara—and half the town—might not swoon over the leading man if they knew he didn't arrive at the studio until ten o'clock, though he'd better be early today. But Ella refused to distort moving-picture dreams with harsh reality. The locals loved their *reel* cowboy hero.

And she loved the play on words.

"We're going out to the Rafter-H Ranch today."

Clara's rhythmic kneading halted a half-second as she spun the dough a quarter turn and flopped it over on the flour-covered board. "If I'd known you'd be up before the chickens, I'd had a picnic ready for you." She raised a brow at Ella's skirt. "Mmh-mmh-mmh," she chided, punching each syllable with a shake of her head. "You're not planning to ride one of them wild mustangs are you?"

A small dart of fear pierced Ella's breast. "Heavens, no. But I cannot hobble around out there in my low-tops now, can I? A girl has to be ready for anything."

Clara clapped flour from her hands and planted them on her hips with a pointed look. "Like you was yesterday?"

Stunned, Ella balked against the stone in her stomach. "How did you know?"

Humph. "Know? Whole town knows, honey. It's not every day that handsome Cale Hutton charges down Main Street on that fine horse o' his and snatches hisself a gal out from under a runaway wagon."

Ella's gasp sent chuckles rippling through the woman's bosom as she raised a dusty finger. "I knows everything that goes on in this town. And I knows he was at the studio yesterday mornin' talkin' to that director o' yours."

35

Ella studied the stove pipe that disappeared into the high white wall and drew a deep breath through her nose. If Clara really knew everything, why didn't she know they were leaving early?

"It was a buggy, not a wagon. And it wasn't quite as dramatic as you make it out to be."

Another *humph.* Clara reached for an empty baking powder tin, swirled it in flour, and pressed it into the puffy dough.

Flummoxed, Ella followed her nose to the counter where a line of fruit pies sat cooling. The closest one was still warm to the touch. "My goodness, Clara. How early do you get up in the morning?"

"Early enough to bake two extra pies for you."

Pricked by the tender voice close behind her, Ella turned to see Clara offering a cloth-covered basket full of something that smelled deliciously like baked apples and nutmeg.

"One for you and one for your Mr. Hutton."

"He is not *my* Mr. Hutton."

Clara's black eyes snapped with glee, and she squeezed Ella's arm. "Make sure you get a good-sized piece. Can't have you wastin' away and breakin' in half."

Ella felt as if she'd already done just that, but she'd die right there before admitting it. She dropped a quick kiss on Clara's cheek and was promptly turned about and ushered toward the door.

"You don't wanna get left behind and miss a whole day out on the ranch with that handsome cowboy."

With a flush crawling her neck, Ella limped through the lobby, past the front desk, and out the Denton's grand door, escorted by Clara's fading laughter. Obviously, the woman had a spy, some urchin who hid under tables and chairs and reported back with every bit of scandalous gossip in town.

She peeked beneath the white linen napkin, and her traitorous stomach twisted in anticipation. A heart-to-heart talk later would set the "handsome cowboy" matter straight, but right now she needed to focus on the day ahead.

If she'd had a third hand, she would have brought a kettle of Clara's coffee, which she far preferred to the bitter brew Mr. Thorson delivered each morning. Honestly, Jed probably dropped one of his horse's shoes in the pot when no one was looking.

The town was awash with morning. A fresh start. A new beginning, as if every mistake were swept away. In spite of her injury and emptiness, she'd not completely rejected her childhood habit of viewing each new day as a gift.

And then she saw them.

Three rented motorcars in front of the studio, crouched like hungry green tigers waiting to devour their victims.

Her limp became more pronounced. Her palms dampened, and her temples pulsed at the idea of riding in one even farther than she had to the Hot Springs Hotel.

The Horses of Disaster plunge in the heavy clay. She shuddered against the taunting line from a favorite poem and squeezed her eyes tight against a flashing scene. Halting on the sidewalk, she clutched at her collar, clawing for air.

It isn't night. It isn't raining. The roads are dry.

Truth swept through her on a quivering breeze, and she opened her eyes to bright morning, trading memories for reality. *Thank you, Lord.* Setting out again, she sought distraction from beneath the linen napkin, and the homey aroma lifted her spirit.

The pies. Focus on the pies.

At the 300 block of Main, she stepped into the street. If she took the pies inside, they would never make it to the ranch, and at the moment she did not feel that generous.

She stopped at the nearest car and set the basket in the back seat. Nothing Mr. Thorson had ordered from the café would half compare to Clara's talents. With this hungry crew, Cale Hutton would be lucky if he got a single slice of apple pie for himself.

After gathering additional costuming for the day, Ella waited near the door, and at the first sign of departure, hurried to her chosen car. She slid in next to the basket and covered it with shirts and scarves and hats. Warmth seeped into her thigh, a delightfully distracting sensation.

"Something smells powerful good," said the fellow who climbed in at her left.

"That'd be your mustache, Slim."

Slim punched the jokester who sat ahead of them, and everyone laughed as the driver maneuvered the coughing contraption into the street. Mr. Thorson, the cameraman, and technicians took the next automobile, and Jed, Mabel, and other actors took the third. Ella had not asked how far it was to the ranch, but she prayed it wouldn't be more than an hour, reasoning that it couldn't be if they intended to get any filming done while they still had good light.

Leaning her head against the back cushion while the men jabbed and joked, she marveled at the blue Colorado sky. No smoke or haze as she was accustomed to in Chicago. And exactly the color of a certain cowboy's eyes.

CHAPTER FIVE

The wind shifted, ruffled through the ridge-top grass, and trailed Cale's face like a woman's fingers. His saddle creaked beneath him, and he tilted his hat brim to the lip of land where the sky burned gold.

Since boyhood, he'd had a need to see the sun break over the hills, watch it bleed fire across the mountains and leak down into the valleys and parks. But this morning, a flame curled in his chest, flickering stronger as dawn chased the shadows. He rubbed a spot beneath his vest, a familiar burn, the longing he thought he'd broke with for good.

Doc tossed his head and nickered, and the rumble traveled through Cale's legs and up into his gut.

Morning's breath licked around behind him and whispered against his neck – *she's close.*

An hour after sunup, Cale strung a picket line along the west end of the near pasture, and another at right angles on the north edge, bemoaning the effort it took to corral horseless carriages. Nearly as much as it took to corral cattle, but he had to keep the rattletraps away from the animals. No telling how rowdy those moving-picture folks were, and he couldn't afford any accidents.

Satisfied with his work, he headed back to the barn. The parade would arrive any time now. Hugh's boys were itching for excitement and jostled each other as they ran to meet him.

"Are they here yet?" Ty hollered over the back of the middle boy who outran him with his longer legs. As the oldest, Ty had drawn the short straw on height, but he made up for it in grit.

"Not yet." Cale handed the middle youngster the hammer. "Take this to the tack room and hurry back. I've got a job for three good men."

Jay dashed to the barn and halfway back by the time Cale shoved his hat up and squatted to address his nephews eye to eye.

"Wait for me! Wait for me!" The youngster had a hard time stopping his feet, and he slammed into Kip, who hollered like a scalded dog.

Cale helped the littlest boy off the ground and dusted his britches, then soothed his bruised pride with a hand on his shoulder.

"I need a good lookout to let me know when those clackety ol' wagons turn onto the ranch road. You know anyone fit for the job?"

Arms shot up like firecrackers in July.

"I knew I could count on you three." Cale straightened and reset his hat. "Ty, you're in charge. Make sure you all stay together—no one goes off by himself. Take Tug and watch for rattlers. And when you see dust on the road, hightail it back here and let me or your pa know. Understand?"

Three heads bobbed, and the youngest would have gotten away if Cale hadn't snagged his shirt collar. "Hold on. You all need your hats. Kip, you grab a canteen. Jay, see if Miss Helen has any leftover cookies to take along."

He chuckled at the wild bunch headed toward the house. What he wouldn't give for energy like that nowadays.

As usual, Tug knew something was up. He peeled his old, sore self from the shady spot by the barn and stood at the back door until the boys stampeded out and down the road. The dog trotted along behind them like the good nursemaid that he was, a slight limp in tow.

Cale spent the next hour picking hooves and saddling horses with Hugh. Helen commandeered them both into hauling crates and nail kegs to the yard, and directed the placement of each makeshift seat in what, by mid-day, would be the shade of the big pine on the west side. The kitchen table came next, dressed with a checkered cloth for Helen's lemonade and gingersnaps. He tossed a cookie to Hugh and sampled one himself. Those city fellas were in for a treat.

He cut back to the barn, gathered Doc, and rode for the ridge south of the creek bottom.

Pine jays scolded. Magpies flagged across the trail and jabbered from the scrub oak. Cottontails dashed to the tree line and froze as Doc scaled the ridge. Cale filled his lungs with mountain air, the purity of it and the peace. Would those city folks notice it? Would she?

He scratched the itch. Not likely.

At the crest, Doc slowed to a standstill, familiar with the routine. The western range bared its rocky spine to a clear sky, and a long narrow valley rolled out at its feet. The Rafter-H claimed most of the cedar and grass-covered country, and around the shoulder of two lower hills stretched the neighboring Crossett Ranch.

He'd grown up with old man Crossett's daughter. She loved this life, even rode like a man and worked the roundups. Cale shifted in the saddle, considering how he'd tried to take a liking to her. George Harper's daughter too. She was pretty and smart. Knew her way around the cattle business. But neither one suited him for some reason that escaped his cowboy sense of what fit and what didn't.

All he knew was he'd not settle for a mismatch in a horse, and he refused to settle on a mismatch for a wife. Now he was almost too old.

He nudged Doc along the ridge. Cedar perfume escaped at the brush of his chaps against the dark blue berries. It'd been easy for Hugh. He and Jane were sweethearts back when they all grew out of the desks in that old one-room schoolhouse on Crossett's place. Maybe that's why Jane's death still pained his brother so. He'd been sweet on her his whole life.

Cale, on the other hand, knew cows better than anything, and until lately, he'd been content to work 'em. Especially after watching his brother shrivel into an angry old man right before his eyes.

A clattering cough scattered the jays, and Doc's ears perked toward the valley. Less than a mile away, three automobiles crawled ahead of a dust cloud like ants on the march. They'd soon be at the turnoff, and three little boys would be running to tell him the moving-picture makers were coming.

He reined Doc around and worked his way down the ridge and back to the barn, anticipating and dreading in equal parts the sight of Ella Canaday climbing out of one of those rattletraps.

~

Ella gripped the edge of the leather seat, regretting that she hadn't brought her duster with her from Chicago. But she'd not expected so much *touring* to accompany a seamstress job. The track was not much more than a wagon trail, rutted and pitted and bent on jarring every bone in her body, including the weakest one.

Slim didn't look much better than she felt, and once they slowed in the ranch pasture, he jumped from the car before it came to a standstill. The engine choked to its death, delighting three small boys who bounced around the automobiles, waving their arms and yelling directions. The sight surprised and cheered her, for she'd not expected children. Of course that was silly. How else would ranchers get future ranchers if not by raising their own?

Discomfort shivered up her already sweaty neck, and she glanced around for sight of Cale Hutton, whose clear image had prompted the blush to begin with. Such thoughts, when she wanted nothing to do with the man and his man-handling ways.

Quickly she draped the folded costumes over the back seat, climbed down, and lifted the basket. A piercing stab buckled her knee, and she dropped the basket to grip the running board. Tucking her chin, she drew in several deep breaths and all her determination to not throw herself on the grass and weep. *Oh Lord, help.*

Pulling upright, she regarded the remainder of the brutal track that lay between her and the ranch house where everyone was headed. Could she make it that far?

Scuffing in the grass behind her set her heart to fluttering. Please, *please,* not Mr. Hutton.

"Can I help you with that basket?"

A dark-haired boy with squinting eyes and a dirty face stood a pace away, one hand raised to shield the sun.

She could have kissed him.

"Why, yes, you can." Forcing herself to her full height, she gave a bit of her weight to her right leg while holding the door's edge. "What a gentleman you are."

A shy grin escaped before the boy bent to heft the load and visibly gulped in the spicy fragrance. He lifted his gaze with a hopeful question. "Is this here apple pie for *everybody?*"

Laughter eased her grip on the door, and she took a shaky step. "The answer is yes, again. Do you like apple pie?"

He grinned more fully and threw his shoulders back. "Sure do." He eyed her feet and scoured her from toe to head with the purest of childish curiosity and worldly wisdom. "Can you walk all right, or do you need me to get somebody bigger to help you?"

Somebody bigger? Like his father? She would walk or die. Another step forward and she grimaced but took another, then another. "With you by my side, I think I shall make it, young man. Might I ask your name?"

"Jay Hutton, ma'am." He jerked his chin toward the house, where the other two boys were darting through the crowd. "Them's my brothers, Kip and Ty. I'm in the middle but I'm the tallest."

So Cale Hutton had three sons. Perhaps he'd used his daring rescue stunt before, sweeping his children from harm's way. She rubbed her leg and continued to match the boy's short strides. "I'm so glad you are, Jay. You are the perfect size to help me with the pies. My name is Ella Canaday, but you may call me Miss Ella."

By now they were across the road with a grassy patch ahead that hemmed the house and spread beneath a giant pine at the far end. An older woman stood behind a table with a red-checkered cloth, filling cups from a large crock and handing them to those who stood nearby.

"Is that your grandmother at the table, Jay?"

"Grandma's dead." He blinked and his footsteps slowed. "So's my grandpa and my ma."

An ache passed through her. So much death in a young life.

"That's Miss Helen. She cooks for us, our pa, and our uncle, and makes us wash behind our ears." Stopping, he looked up and wrinkled his nose into a question. "You don't got no behind-your-ears, do ya?"

In spite of the ache, laughter bubbled again at the boy's straightforward speech. "Well, if you can keep a secret, Jay, I did not voluntarily wash behind my ears either when I was your age."

His eyes rounded in disbelief.

"But I do now. Always." She nodded to strengthen her statement, and he must have decided to believe her, for he dashed off to the table and lifted the basket to Miss Helen. The woman looked Ella's way with a welcoming smile and set the basket beside the stoneware crock.

Ella had never been thirstier.

She quickened her pace to near normal. Blue sky draped the giant pine where Mr. Thorson stood, his booted foot planted atop a wooden keg as he leaned toward the actors and others fanned out around him. Pete jotted notes in his little camera book that was always with him, and Mabel twirled a long curly lock around her finger, looking completely bored and put out.

"Hello, dear. I'm Helen."

Ella turned her attention to the woman behind the table.

"So glad you made it out with everyone." Helen offered a tin cup of cold lemonade and a warm smile.

"Thank you." Ella grasped the cup in one hand and the sturdy table's edge with the other. Perspiration clung to her neck beneath her bob, increased by her trek from the car. "Exactly what I needed."

Helen flicked a concerned gaze over her, then met her eyes with a lowered voice. "Are you all right, dear?"

No, I am not. "Yes, quite." The tin cup kissed her lips with cool relief, rescuing her from further explanation. She did not want accommodations. Merely a moment to regain her strength. Too many months of a sedentary lifestyle were costing her dearly.

Helen lifted the napkin from the basket and leaned over, drawing in a deep breath. "My, but these pies smell delicious. Did you bake them?"

"Oh, no. I'm renting a room at the Denton, and the cook there, Clara, sent them with me this morning."

Helen's obvious curiosity brightened her kind gray eyes, urging Ella on.

"She thinks I'm too thin." She let out a self-conscious laugh and eased along the table's edge until she stood directly in front. "What can I do? I won't be needed during the filming, so I'd be happy to help you set up for the noon meal."

Helen lifted the basket. "Many hands make light work, my mother always said. Follow me before one of those fellas discovers what you've brought and tucks into them without us getting a chance to divvy them up for everyone."

Excited voices drew Ella's attention as the troupe and cowboys made for the corrals. Several horses stood saddled and waiting, including Mr. Hutton's. He was not in the crowd. She ducked her head and patted the back of her hair. No sense staring after someone who wasn't there. A clearing throat drew her around to three stair-step boys whose scantily concealed mischief brimmed in their eyes.

She straightened, reminding herself she was the grownup in the current setting.

"May I help you?"

Jay elbowed the boy in the center, who took a step forward and jerked a thumb at the elbow's owner. "Jay says you got two apple pies from town. That so?"

Ella pinched back a smile and folded her arms at her waist. "Well now. Would your brother tell you something that wasn't so?"

Jay added a couple of inches to his stature and a confident smirk lifted his mouth.

She held a hand out to the speaker. "I'm Ella and you are . . ."

A small, grimy hand took her fingers. "Ty. I'm the oldest."

"And I'm Kip," said the smallest boy, shoving his hand out with a gap-tooth grin. "I'm six going on seven."

"Next year," Ty scoffed.

Her heart melted. "I believe there will be a piece of pie for any boy who has helped me."

Jay nearly popped the buttons on his shirt and his two brothers visibly deflated.

"Since Jay helped me carry the heavy basket, perhaps you— and you—can bring to me the clothing that is in the back of the dark green motorcar. Wait, they're all green. Check the one in the middle."

Dust stirred like storm clouds as the two pushed away to run for the cars.

"But"–Ella raised her voice, and they skidded to a stop— "No pie if the clothes are wrinkled or have been dragged in the dirt."

Again the youngsters tore out for the automobiles in the pasture, and Ella looked squarely at Jay. "Do you think they can do it without ruining the costumes?"

"Maybe I better go make sure."

"I will be in the kitchen with Miss Helen." She muffled a laugh as Jay's long legs carried him across the yard toward the pasture, so full of boundless energy. Heading in the direction Helen had taken, she stopped at the sound of a fray at the corrals.

Mabel snatched at the chestnut's bridle, and the horse tossed his head viciously, his ears pinned back, forelegs stamping. His displeasure was enough to send the leading lady skidding away, and Ella covered a chuckle with her hand and hurried around the back of the house.

Mr. Hutton's horse was indeed a very intelligent animal.

Helen met her at the back screen door with a table knife and an extra apron.

"After you wash up, slice each pie into eight sections. I normally don't cut such scant pieces, but this way when the men ask for a second helping, they'll think they're getting something." Her eyes sparkled with merriment equal to that of the boyish trio.

A small table beneath the kitchen's back window boasted a half dozen berry and custard pies in addition to the two Clara had sent. Ella donned the ample apron, wrapping the strings around her waist and back again and tied them into a long bow. A white pitcher of daisies brightened the sideboard, and a hand pump delivered icy water to the sink, not surprising so far from town. She'd also spied the privy set back among the scrub oak. A more primitive atmosphere than what she was accustomed to— and with no electric lights, she guessed. Oil lamps perched on sideboards, unneeded now in the bright sunshine pouring through the window.

Apparently, few modern comforts found their way to a mountain ranch, but a nearly tangible peace looped itself into Ella's apron strings and snugged around her.

The large kitchen appeared to be as wide as the house, added onto one end where a rough log wall had no doubt been the outside of the original cabin. Now a long sideboard stretched its length with cabinetry above and below, interrupted by a doorway into a dining room appointed in lovely fashion. While drying her hands, she noted a fine cherry-wood table taking up most of the low-ceilinged room, framed with matching high-back chairs, and cushioned by a floral oriental rug of deep burgundy and muted blues. Never would she have guessed such a room offered hearth and home between the time-worn logs of a ranch house.

Helen squeezed lemons and added the juice to a sugar-syrup base. "I've no ice for the lemonade, but our water's always a bit nippy and should wet their whistle plenty."

Ella's hands still tingled from the cold wash. "Everyone will be happy to have something other than Mr. Thorson's coffee to wash down the box lunches." She looked around the kitchen but didn't see any boxes. Cookies, pie, and lemonade would be scant lunch for the troupe after today's filming. Surely Mr. Thorson had not forgotten.

"Oh, I'm glad you mentioned that. I forgot to make more coffee."

The screen door popped against the outside wall, and Jay bounded through, his hands clutching two large hats stuffed with belts and scarves. Kip and Ty were right behind, arms draped with shirts and trousers and a riding skirt.

"Didn't drop a one, Miss Ella." Kip clutched one of Jed's shirts that was bigger than he was, pride shining from his little face. Ella could steam out the wrinkles with Helen's kettle.

She took the hanger hook from Kip, gathered what Ty had carried in, and motioned to Jay to set the hats on a chair. "You

boys did a fine job, thank you. But I have one more favor to ask."
What she considered a painful chore, they might find a lark.

Again they lined up, hands behind their backs, eyes on
Helen. Well trained, at best.

"There are twelve small paperboard boxes in the automobiles—lunch for the actors. If you each return with four boxes, I'm
sure Miss Helen and I can find a tasty reward for your efforts."

Helen's mouth twitched as she wiped her hands on her
apron and queried Ella. "Do you think they'll earn a piece of
pie?"

Three little chests expanded.

"I believe so, but we'll have to wait and see."

She bent at the waist, hands on her knees. "You were so
careful with the costumes. Can you be that careful with the box
lunches and not drop even one?"

The trio nodded in unison and scrambled out the door.

No sooner had Ella sliced the final pie, they stampeded onto
the back porch, through the door, and into line again. One of
Kip's boxes bore dirt around the edge and a bent flap.

"Thank you all. Please put them on the board over there."
She indicated the long surface fronting the log wall.

Assignment accomplished, they lined up again.

"Shall we let them choose?"

Helen wagged her finger at the boys. "Don't be makin' a
mess in my kitchen. Take your slice and eat outside."

All three crowded the table and reached for the nearest apple
pie. They made it out the door with only two apple chunks hitting the smooth wooden boards. Ella knelt to clean the spills with
her apron, then gasped as she pulled herself up on a chair.

Helen threw her a questioning look.

"They're good boys." Good enough, Ella hoped, to run a
conversational decoy to what was obviously on Helen's mind.

"They are." The woman resumed her lemon squeezing.
"When they aren't in trouble, that is."

Laughter sparked again, its long-forgotten pleasure becoming the mark of Ella's day. How often had Nana told her that a merry heart bore medicinal effects? The memory rose like a vapor nearly forgotten, smothered by more recent, unpleasant realities.

"Would you grind the coffee for me, dear, while I finish up these lemons? We've plenty of time to cook a pot before everyone comes back to eat."

Happy to busy her hands, Ella found a sack of coffee beans where Helen's finger pointed and filled the large mill near the stove. What she wouldn't give for a stout cup of tea with milk.

"Then, if you don't mind easing a nosy old woman's curiosity, you can tell me all about that leg of yours."

CHAPTER SIX

Cale and Doc led the band of mounted dandies away from the home place, across the north pasture, pushing twenty head toward a draw that stretched into a canyon a half-mile back in the breaks. Hugh flanked the herd on the east side.

Thorson rode up, bouncing in his saddle. "You plan to run the cattle back down this draw?"

"Yes, sir." But this was no circus where ponies trotted around in show rings. Every steer carried near forty dollars on its head, and Cale had no plans to litter the canyon with money. "Have your camera fella pick out a spot on our way up, because I'm running them down only one time. Can't be burning weight off 'em."

Thorson dropped back, and Cale turned in the saddle to see if he understood. Sure enough, the kid riding Scout, a snorty bay, seemed more than happy to cut off to the side.

Cale shook his head. They'd picked the wrong horse to pack that camera contraption. Scout shook his head and chewed his bit, and the little bounce in his hind quarters looked like he'd as soon toss the whole kit 'n caboodle into the scrub.

Cale should have warned them.

Or not.

Everyone else seemed to be holding their own. Jed Barr and a woman rode mid-pack, but he didn't see the seamstress. Suited him fine. The less trouble he had today, the better.

Around the shoulder of a hill, Hugh sat sentinel, one leg cocked up over his saddle swells, his shoulders slumped in that "missing Jane" attitude. Their approach raised his head, and he drew his leg back, reined around, and trotted over to Cale.

"This everybody?" Icy eyes took in the riders.

As much as Cale felt for his brother's predicament, he also wanted to beat the stuffin' out of him. Moping around and seeing the bad side of everything was no way to run a ranch or raise his boys.

"Don't forget we're marked men." That drew Hugh's attention. "Five dollars a head every day for each of us and our horses, plus what Thorson's givin' us to use our cattle." His brother couldn't argue with cold cash and he knew it.

Hugh indulged his habit again. He didn't chew—just spit when he was mad, which lately was dang near all the time.

Cale turned Doc to face the approaching riders bringing up the tail end of the small herd. Riding drag probably wasn't in their plan, but they'd look more the part with a good coat of dust. Jed Barr and his friends faired best of all. At least some of the bunch would know what they were doing. Thorson and Barr broke from the group and rode over.

Cale jerked his chin toward the draw. "We'll hold them around the next outcropping until you give the word."

Thorson shifted in his saddle, obviously unaccustomed to hard leather.

"Good. Good." His hands were busy holding the saddle horn. "We'll film a stampede today, and if we have time afterward, a runaway scene with Mabel."

Cale cut a look at the woman who flashed him an eye-batting smile and considered the finer points of his brother's bad habit. "Runaway *what?*"

"Horse, if you've got one."

Oh, he had one, but Snake could drag her to death. She wasn't a hand like his sister, Grace, and he wasn't about to risk some highfalutin woman's neck.

Hugh had other ideas. "She done a runaway before?"

Thorson's belly bounced with a laugh. "No, but Slim has. We throw a wig on him and dress him like Mabel, and you'd never know the difference. Then we film her before and after the danger's over."

Figured. More play-acting.

Cale pointed to a flat boulder jutting into the shallow draw. "That'd be a good spot for the camera. Tell your man to stay high. You don't want him run over."

Thorson barked another laugh. "Excellent. Excellent! Pete can handle himself." He jerked his horse around and joined the cameraman trying to dismount his jittery horse. They might have a runaway right this minute, whether they wanted it or not.

Barr heeled his horse forward. "You want me and the boys to chase 'em down?"

Over Barr's shoulder, Hugh was shaking his head. "We'll cover it."

At least his brother hadn't told the leading man to stay out of the way. Cale coughed against the back of his gloved hand, grateful for small miracles. "Probably best if you and your men position yourselves along the top of the draw in case some of the steers try to break out. We're not runnin' this stampede more than once."

Barr quirked a half-hearted agreement and turned back to the others, who split off, a couple of them taking each side of the wash.

Pete found the ground and, stiff-legged, hefted his equipment to his shoulder. Thorson showed him where he wanted him, then followed the fella to the top. That left Mabel and another man.

She kicked her mount forward and stopped close to Cale, her painted eyes fluttering between him and Hugh.

"I certainly didn't expect *two* handsome cowboys out here in the wilderness. What's a girl to do?" She held out a gloved hand. "I'm Mabel Steinway. I'm sure you've heard of me."

Prodded by memories of their ma's teaching to treat a lady with respect, Cale shook the end of her fingers, hoping that counted. "Ma'am."

Hugh huffed and turned Shorty toward the draw, leaving Cale with a woman fit to be tied.

~

Ella wiped dirt from the box Kip had dropped on his way to the house. He'd been so proud to match his older brothers' efforts that she hadn't the heart to point out the bent corners and dust. But looking inside, her stomach clenched at a thick slab of beef embraced by two pieces of day-old bread, both amply spread with butter.

No watercress and minced-chicken tea sandwiches here.

If the men and Mabel were hungry enough, perhaps they wouldn't notice the less-than-delectable offering. An apple, two cookies of questionable content, and a pickle rounded out the meal.

She re-wrapped the sandwich in its waxed paper, tucked it back in the box, and folded over the flimsy top. There could be an ugly confrontation involving wooden spoons and rolling pins if Clara got wind of this fare.

As if Clara's scolding and cosseting weren't enough, now Ella had a second mother hen to deal with, completely opposite in her approach. Clara boasted that she knew everything that went on in town. Helen unashamedly demanded to be told one's personal history. It was none of her business, but how did one put off such an obviously caring woman's bold inquisition and avoid an uncomfortable day working side by side?

Ella ordered the boxes into a neat line, much like the Hutton boys' presentation, and toyed with the idea of escaping to the yard. She could sit on a crate and stay out of the kitchen, leaving Helen to serve alone. They would never see each other again, but that fact didn't allow for such unkindness. Nana's lessons had not fallen on deaf ears.

A scraping chair and breathy *oomph* behind her announced Helen's seated position. Ella joined her hostess, who lifted a coffee cup to her lips. Another steaming cup, filled near to the brim, waited before a second chair at the pie-covered table.

Resigning herself to a partial revelation, Ella sat, grateful at least to be off her feet, and sorted through what she would share and what she would not. Where to begin?

"At the beginning, dear." Helen dabbed her brow with her apron hem. "Start at the beginning."

Surprised, Ella fidgeted with her belted skirt waist. Did the woman read minds? No wonder those three little urchins were so well mannered.

"It's not every day I get womenfolk to visit with out here on this ranch full of men—tall ones *and* short ones." A soft chuckle betrayed her affections. "So pardon me if I cut past the chit-chat. But what happened to your leg? Help yourself if you want a piece of pie. Or is it your hip or ankle that pains you?"

Trying not to picture herself in a courtroom, Ella stalled as she sipped the hot coffee. Not as bitter as what Mr. Thorson brought from the café, but strong enough to strip paint. She glanced around for sugar and cream and finding none, chose to apply the old adage, *when in Rome.*

She had not discussed her condition, nor its cause, with anyone. Everyone she knew also knew what had happened, and therefore they did not ask. Her family, their physician. Charles's family. Even Mr. Thorson hadn't mentioned it.

Her throat tightened and she drew a deep breath through her nose. "I was in a motorcar crash involving a horse . . ."

Helen swirled her coffee and shook her head. "Those infernal things will be the death of us all."

"My fiancé was killed."

Helen's shock bled into regret, for she leaned across the corner of the table and took Ella's hand. "Forgive me, dear. I've no intention of re-opening wounds or prying into your business." She leaned back. "Just thought you might benefit from talking it over some. About your leg, that is. And how you hired on with a moving-picture company when moving about is, well, difficult for you."

Helen's curiosity, guised as concern, was stronger than her sense of propriety. But maybe her homey recipe for "talking it over" was worth trying. Appreciating her play on the word moving, Ella swallowed a second sip of unsweetened coffee more easily than the first. "I needed a change of scenery."

Helen nodded, eyes trailing over the assorted pies. The soft line of her mouth and her silence invited Ella to continue.

"A change in scenery is easily managed with a moving-picture company." Ella's mouth tipped in a wry smile. "They use portable backdrops."

Helen puffed gently against her coffee cup. "You've got me there." Her eyes smiled with her. "As clever as you are, do you write the stories for the pictures?"

"Oh, no." Feeling as though she'd escaped a firing squad, Ella warmed to the change of topic. "I've copied script onto a few title cards, but I don't write the storyline. Mr. Thorson, our director, does most of that. I'm just the seamstress." A much less boastful explanation than what she had given Helen's employer.

The woman visibly straightened from her relaxed posture and focused her gray eyes on Ella as if learning she was a moneyed heiress. "Is that right?"

"I look after the costumes, mend tears, tailor pieces for proper fitting. And make sure accessories are readily available during filming."

"Do you sew as well?" Helen eyed Ella's simple blouse.

"I've made some of my own clothing and reworked a few costumes."

That seemed to satisfy the woman, and an eager light entered her eye. "If you have the time, could you look at a pattern and a dress length I bought last summer and give me a few pointers? I haven't got around to doing anything with it, what with feeding these men and looking after their needs." She pushed to her feet and refilled her cup, offering to do the same for Ella.

"No, thank you. I still have plenty." Ella cradled her cup away from the looming coffee pot. "But I'd be more than happy to look at what you have."

A distant rumble drew Helen's attention to the screen door, and she stood squinting through it quite like Clara, one hand on a robust hip. "They'll be comin' 'round the mountain." Her shoulders bounced with a chuckle.

Ella joined her, following Helen's gaze to a pale dust cloud trailing into the brilliant sky. Though far removed, it was churned by numerous hooves, and the faint roar stirred the same sensation that had frozen her to Main Street's dirt course. Suddenly dizzy, she stutter-stepped back, bumping against Helen's empty chair.

"Are you all right?"

The second time the woman had inquired about her well-being. Was Ella that transparent? "Y-yes, thank you."

She gripped the table's edge for support, working hand-over-hand until she reached her chair and fell into it, tight-chested and faint.

"Honey, what's wrong?" Helen set the coffee pot on the table, and with one hand on Ella's shoulder, bent to look into her eyes. "You're trembling like a leaf."

Ella raised a hand to her temple, confirming Helen's observational skills. Disgusted with herself, she crossed her arms and leaned against the chair back.

"Did you eat breakfast this morning?"

Eyes closed, she slowly shook her head.

The clatter of a plate and utensil alerted her to Helen's remedy. She and Clara were cut from the same cloth.

A stronger scent of cinnamon and sugared apples tainted the air, and Ella peeked with one eye to a plated slice before her and a fork dangling from Helen's fingers. Both were supported by a visual command that brooked no argument.

"I'll get you a glass of milk to go with that."

Ella took the plate and a bite. She didn't like milk, but that was a moot point. Pie and milk beat passing out on the kitchen floor. Maybe Clara had been right all along, and she didn't eat enough.

~

Surprisingly revived, Ella pushed the screen door open with the toe of her boot and carried out a tray of boxed lunches. With pie and lemonade and Helen's snappy ginger cookies, the meal might be a success.

A cooling breeze danced past the back porch and around the massive pine, carrying the whoops and hollers of mounted men. Thick dust rose from a gap beyond the house, and a half dozen riders thundered around the base of a rock outcropping, as if fleeing the grim reaper himself. Ella held the empty tray against her waist, drawn by a childhood memory of the wind lashing her face and whipping her hair—and the luscious sense of power and strength beneath the saddle that spread into her legs and arms and dreams.

The screen slapped, and she whirled. Helen carried the refilled lemonade crock. Ella's feet stuttered in her quest for balance, and she fairly danced to Helen's side. No more whirling.

"Looks like they're hell-bent, pardon my language." Helen set down the crock and swiped her apron corner across her forehead. "Do you mind filling the cups? We'll bring the pies out after they eat whatever's in those boxes."

Ella could only hope. "I don't mind at all."

"And send everyone round back to wash up first. Don't let them get by without it. 'Specially those three boys." Her gaze shifted over Ella's left shoulder. "They'll try you, so watch out."

She followed Helen's frown to see the boys dashing for the yard. They must have been hiding out in the barn, waiting for their father and everyone else to return.

Father. Cale Hutton.

She snatched the ladle from the red-checkered cloth and in her best Clara imitation, aimed it in the direction of the wash-stand behind the house. The little urchins didn't even stop at the table, just cut to their left, dragging their enthusiasm along with them.

Most of the company had ridden themselves weary. Horses plodded around the barn and up to the corral, where their riders dismounted and unsaddled. At least those who knew to do so. Mabel slid down and pulled her hat off, tossing her dark mane as if she didn't know every man there was gawking at her. Fame gave her license to let someone else tend to her horse.

Ella rolled her lips and ladled cool lemonade into a tin cup. One of Jed's friends unsaddled Mabel's mount, all the while gazing after the woman like a lost pup as she sashayed to the yard.

Pete was first to the table, poor man. He looked like he'd carried his horse rather than ridden it. Swabbing hair off his forehead with his sleeve, he lifted a cup, closed his eyes, and drank it dry in one long draw.

"Wash first, then you can eat."

Pete's eyes opened slowly, as if resenting the effort.

She pointed toward the house. "In the back." He dragged himself that way only to meet up with the Hutton herd. They slid to a stop in front of the table and their heads wagged like curious kittens before Ty uttered what Ella knew they all were thinking. "Where's the pie?"

"Pie? You mean you want *more?*"

Shoulders slumped at her tease, and they eyed the boxes.

"Your lunch is inside, boys. These are for the company actors and crew." At their disappointed droop, she leaned across the table with a stage whisper. "What Helen fixed for you is *much* better than what the grownups have to eat."

A visual consultation among the three decided the matter, and they bolted for the back porch. Did they never walk?

"I'll have another."

She knew the voice without raising her eyes to its owner. "Of course, Miss Steinway." Ella took the proffered cup and refilled it with a polite smile. "Please help yourself to a box lunch. Dessert will follow."

Mabel peered down her nose at the lunches, snatched one off the table, and turned on her booted toe.

Pete returned from washing, looking the better for it, and stepped in front of a cowboy reaching for a cup. "Wash first. Over there."

The man frowned, glanced at Ella, and stomped off to the chore.

"Thank you, Pete." She handed him a full cup and a box. "How did the stampede go?"

"Nearly got trampled is all, but I got the film."

"Saved us a lot of money, I might add." Thorson's hearty voice drew Pete up with a start, or maybe it was his thumping hand on Pete's bony back. "Earned your keep today, son."

Ella peered into the crock to hide her notice of the snarl on Pete's face.

"Wash, Thorson. Back there." Pete jerked his thumb over his shoulder and headed for the tree.

The director inspected his hands and turned away shaking his head. "Come on, you rowdies." His heavy arm flagged the air and the troupe followed.

All but Cale Hutton who strode to the tree and groused at the boys for not staying out of the way.

Ella's heart plummeted. So he *was* their father. She drew herself up and promised to see the boys had an extra piece of pie. Even if it meant that Mr. Hutton had none.

He turned away from his sons and with a hard stride, crossed the yard and stopped before the table. A frown marred his striking features. Abrupt and distant, he grabbed a box and dismissed Ella with a surly glance, as though she were a distasteful morsel.

Stricken deeper than she would have expected, she fingered the collar of her blouse and forced her stinging eyes elsewhere. He'd been kinder at the studio. With renewed fervor, she added a stony layer to her emotional blockade and busied her hands rearranging boxes, ladling lemonade for thirsty cowboys, and serving thin slices of berry and apple pie that Helen brought to the table.

Until Mr. Hutton came back.

Angered by his reappearance, she steeled herself against his good looks. Did he think her feather-headed and easily fooled, too dimwitted to observe his different vest and hat? She tugged at her apron and ignored his heavy presence, standing there waiting, as if in need of her notice. Well, she did notice. It was her job to regard such details. Even his belt was different.

She looked up. The same blue eyes took her in but without scorn. Clearer, this time, with no frown cutting between the brows. Her breath caught at an unlikely possibility. Searching the crowd, she spotted Mr. Hutton straddling a log and eating like a heathen.

But that was impossible. He was standing right . . .

Her gaze shifted back to the tall cowboy calmly waiting, a dimple stitched into one cheek as he held out his empty cup.

"Oh my." She dunked the ladle. Warmth crested her cheeks at the laughter rumbling from his throat as she filled his cup.

"Thank you."

"Mr. Hutton."

"Cale."

"Indeed." She dropped the ladle in the crock and lemonade splashed a spot onto her flaming face. She dabbed it with a corner of her apron, too embarrassed to meet his gaze, but he reached across the table and touched her arm ever so lightly. Her traitorous eyes responded.

"Younger by a full minute." A near smile.

He tipped his head toward the giant pine where his carbon copy sat stuffing his mouth. "And the better-looking of the pair, don't you think?"

A soft laugh bubbled out, and she pushed at the fringe on her brow. Relief loosened a block in her barricade, and she took note that it was his left cheek that dimpled. She must remember that if she was to keep the two brothers straight.

CHAPTER SEVEN

Relief sucked the air from Cale's lungs. Quicker than lightning, Ella's temper changed from stormy rebuke to sunshine.

"Don't take it personal. Hugh's been surly since his wife passed a few years back. Right after Kip, their youngest, was born."

Again she fingered the forelock that hung at her eyes. No rancher's daughter wore her hair like that.

"We're as different as lard is from butter, and I'd like to—"

"And which might you be, cowboy? Lard or butter?" The syrupy voice coiled around his arm with fingers that pulled him close against a woman's body. Miss Steinway ducked her head, then looked up with rounded eyes and dragged him from the table. "Come on, you handsome thing. How is little ol' Mabel going to tell the difference between two strapping cowboy brothers?"

Fighting the urge to shuck her off like a bothersome fly, he ground his teeth and let her pull him down to a crate, where she squeezed in next to him. Yeah, he'd hired himself out to Thorson, but lettin' the leading lady ring his nose and haul him off wasn't part of the deal. He glanced around for Hugh, who'd made himself scarce. Miss Canaday remained behind the table, handing out pie with a smile for every taker. A pretty smile.

"Tell me, Cale. It is Cale, isn't it?" She rubbed a bold finger against his jaw.

He flinched. "Yes, ma'am. Miss Steinway."

"Oh, you must call me Mabel since we'll be working so close together." She pressed herself against him, and he reacted like any red-blooded male would this side of the cemetery.

Prattling on about how he was a *real* cowboy, she linked her hands around his upper arm. "Why look at that, Cale honey. I can't even get both hands around your arm. You're so big and strong!"

He yanked out of her grip and stood, nearly toppling her from the crate. Respect was one thing, but he wasn't some prize bull to be pawed over. City fellas might fall for her empty peach-tin ways, all fancy label with nothing inside, but he didn't take to her kind. He lifted his hat and set it down hard.

"Nice visitin' with you, ma'am. But I got chores to do." Before she could close her gaping mouth, he high-tailed it to the barn to lose himself in some place she couldn't find. And if he ran into Hugh, he'd be giving him a piece of his boot for leaving him as bait for that female.

His hands clenched and unclenched, aching to take hold of something or someone. The first thing he came to worth grabbing was a saddle hanging on the corral instead of in the barn. He hefted it over his shoulder and made for the tack room. Hang fire, he had more important worries than staying shy of some painted-up gal with no shame.

He hung the saddle on a rack and laid the blanket on top, then stood there a minute to slow his pulse and gather his wits. After tugging his neckerchief loose, he wiped his face and neck, then walked to the barn door.

Ella Canaday stood by the corral with Doc hanging his head over the rail and lipping apples from her palm. Before one was chewed, she pulled another from a pocket in her skirt and balanced it on her hand, fingers flat.

Took horse sense to know to do that.

She leaned against the poles, seeming to favor her right leg with all her weight on the left. Cale re-tied his scarf and headed out.

Doc saw him coming and swiveled his ears. She followed the signal, and her eyes locked on Cale like a wary yearling, not sure which way to run. He checked his feet to an easy pace and stopped close enough to reach Doc's muzzle but still keep a polite distance from Miss Canaday.

~

Certain it was Cale who approached, based on the vest and hat and the gelding's response, Ella watched for signs of resentment for feeding his horse.

He stopped on the other side. Not ready to relinquish the close contact of such a genteel animal, she continued rubbing beneath the horse's forelock until its eyes closed and a contended whiffle escaped. Comfort seeped into her from the horse's familiar smell and restful power. She hadn't been this close to one since—

"He likes you."

Cale Hutton's deep voice slid over her skin like a soft woolen coat on a cold day.

She failed to restrain a smile. No wonder Mabel had drawn him away to herself. Where was she, anyway? Ella glanced toward the crew gathered around Mr. Thorson. Mabel watched from a stump, alone and sullen, no doubt concocting hateful barbs to throw Ella's way.

The horse had not endured Mabel's hands on him that morning, yet here he stood nearly asleep beneath Ella's touch. And Mr. Hutton? What had he thought of the leading lady's forward ways?

"Would you like to try him?" The dimple flashed and disappeared just as quickly, and he seemed to take a keen interest in her answer.

She shifted her weight onto both legs and stepped back, wiping her hands on her skirt. Flustered, she sought refuge in the rocky ridges beyond the barn, their pine-draped slopes so unlike the rolling farmland of Illinois. "I don't ride." *Anymore.*

He leaned forward. "Beg pardon?"

Addressing the horse instead of its owner, she edged her reply with finality. "No, thank you." Mr. Hutton's blue scrutiny was palpable, and she retrieved the last apple from her skirt pocket.

"Doc's a good horse. Best I ever had." His voice softened. "I'll help you."

His gentle confidence unsettled her, but she could not trust a stranger who knew nothing of her background. She shook her head, swinging hair against her cheeks. Only Helen knew her story, and that a mere slice of the whole. The thought of explaining her condition to Mr. Hutton dredged up emotional pain she'd worked hard to overcome. Her leg began to throb.

She offered Doc the apple at arm's length, and Mr. Hutton's offer drifted away like the few cottony clouds above them. He planted a foot on the bottom pole and leaned against the top with Doc's head between them. His sense of propriety was refreshingly clear as the air, unlike that of Jed Barr, who always stood too close.

She eased forward and through the rails, stroked Doc's burnished neck, breathing in his scent. How she'd missed the smell of strength under control, a hair-and-hide awareness of power beyond her own feeble body.

"You have a natural way with him."

She peeked around the horse's muzzle. Perceptive, this earthy rancher. Unexpectedly so, in light of their first frenzied meeting. Hope and doubt nibbled two corners of her heart. In this setting, with this gentle horse, dare she reach again for what had once been a passion? She could certainly testify to the animal's faithfulness. And to its owner's.

She drew her hand back and folded her arms. It'd been nearly a year and a half since she'd ridden. And fifteen long, frustrating months of fighting pain and sorrow in equal portions. She'd endured countless doctor's visits and recuperative exercises, yet her strength had not returned to its former proportions. She'd be a fool to try.

More than her thigh muscle had torn. More than her femur had broken. She'd lost a great portion of her heart as well. The dread of losing her bearings if she remained an invalid in her father's home had driven her to this job with Selig Polyscope. The bold move was her bid for freedom and forgetfulness.

But a third, uninvited element quashed her hope. Stark fear shot to her throat with a twist. She couldn't take such a chance in spite of this cowboy's proven ability and offer to help her ride. Regardless of his sky-blue promise to—again—keep her from harm, she couldn't trust him.

~

He'd heard her the first time, though it was nigh on a whisper.

Cale expected more from a gal with such fire in her eyes, and he figured fear must ride her hard. Had something to do with her gait and the way she favored her right leg, he'd bank on it. But plain as spots on a fawn, she had horse sense.

He looked her up and down. "So why'd you dress like that if you didn't intend to ride?"

"I beg your pardon?" Her shoulders squared stiff as a singletree.

"Well, you're all gussied up in fancy high-top boots and a riding skirt. I figured you wanted to ride, not just strut around like a peacock."

Not exactly how he meant to put it.

With one sharp look, she skinned and quartered him, then marched off-kilter to the big pine.

Thorson waved him over.

Confound it all. He yanked his hat off and slapped his leg, wanting to join the group about as much as he wanted to whack a bee tree with a hatchet. He took his time getting there, shying away from both the seamstress and Miss Steinway, who sat scowling like a wet polecat, and ambled around to the other side.

Thorson wiped his brow with a handkerchief and stuffed it in his pocket. "We've got enough film to keep us busy, so we'll head back to the studio and write script tomorrow. The plan is to come back the day after for a branding." He turned to Cale. "We'll do that runaway scene I mentioned then too. That work for you, Hutton?"

Hugh stood with his back against the house, a boot planted on the wall behind him, his expression blank.

Cale gave a two-finger salute. "That'll work."

"Good. We'll be out of here, then, but I want to thank your cook for her pies and such."

He gestured to the crates and stumps littering the yard. "Gather these up, men, and take them wherever Cale tells you. And get the table indoors."

Every man picked up his makeshift seat, and Cale jerked a thumb toward the barn. "Behind the hitching rail." No sense taking the stumps to the woodpile if folks were coming back. Hugh hefted one end of the table and Jed took the other while Thorson spoke with Helen and set her to blushing with his praise.

Miss Canaday disappeared inside the house and returned with an armload of clothing.

Helen hurried over to him as soon as Thorson walked away.

"We don't get many women folk up here. Shame Ella couldn't stay for a longer visit."

Ella now, was it?

"Be nice if she could stay on until the company returns, don't you think?"

His hat band heated and he rubbed the side of his jaw.

"Well, wouldn't it?" His housekeeper frowned like she did at the boys when they weren't paying attention. "Don't you think she'd enjoy a day of life on a ranch?"

This one-sided conversation was headed in a dangerous direction. Helen's stare cut through him clean as a hot knife through gravy.

"Tarnation, Helen, just say what it is you're trying to say."

She broke out a grin. "Thank you. That's exactly what I thought too, and that director fella said she could stay on. I assured him I'd take good care of her."

Cale's turn to stare. When had he agreed to Miss Canaday staying on?

"I do need a new Sunday dress, you know. And Ella agreed to help." She took out after the gal who was making her slow way to the automobiles.

"Hold on!" Helen gave Thorson a run for his money in arm waving.

Miss Canaday stopped, relieved it seemed, and waited. Then she cast a look in Cale's direction while Helen worked on her.

He couldn't very well stand there gawking like his nephews, so he took to the barn. Tack needed checking and horses needed turning out. And he didn't need that gal underfoot when he had work to do.

Too bad Grace wasn't here.

She'd have Ella Canaday up and trottin' in circles by tomorrow morning. But she was in Denver, last he'd heard. Licking her wounds after that Wild West outfit she'd signed on with went belly up. He snorted. Not one shy bone in his little sister's body. Why, if she were here, she'd show Thorson what a horsewoman could do and knock that Steinway gal down a notch or four.

He slipped through the corral poles and unlatched the north gate, then waved his hat and hollered at the ponies till they lit out. Doc's graceful lope carried him ahead of the others. The gelding had a soft spot for that whip of a woman, the way he ate from her fingers almost dainty like. Doc'd be good to her if Cale could get her on him.

Combing a hand through his hair, he considered the other horses that were brought up. The boys' old mare, Barlow, might be a fair choice. Wouldn't spook if you lit her tail afire. Easygoing.

And why was he wasting his time considering a gentle mount for someone who made it clear she didn't ride?

He scoffed. A lie as plain as snow on Pikes Peak.

He resituated his hat, irritated that she drew his thoughts like a barn cat to cream. He savvied fear and figured she was fightin' her head. But he also knew firsthand that a good spill called for gettin' back in the saddle. His pa had been there for him when he was Ty's age. Tossed him back up on the horse that had tossed him to begin with. There was nothing for it but to ride again, his pa insisted. And he'd been right.

Cale had caught the look in that little gal's eye when she was with Doc, and something deep inside made him want to help her fight whatever held her captive.

He headed back across the corral. Another woman around for a day or so would do Helen good. Lord knew, it was the least she deserved for puttin' up with five Huttons.

Be a heck of a lot easier if he hadn't made that peacock remark.

CHAPTER EIGHT

Was it Helen's offer of the old treadle Singer or the woman's winsome speech that convinced Ella to stay?

Or the opportunity to photograph the ranch and its surroundings?

"A good woman-to-woman gab is just what I need." Helen took half of Ella's load from her arms.

Thorson mumbled something, then faced Ella. "We'll return in two days, Miss Canaday. Don't do anything wild. Mabel doesn't know a needle from a noose, and I can't afford the time to find another seamstress."

He meant no insult, but his off-handed warning stung. Ella rubbed one hand on her skirt and caught Mabel over his shoulder with fire sparking in her eyes. Ella didn't need an enemy, particularly one with the power to influence her employer. Perhaps staying at the ranch wasn't such a good idea. But how could she turn down Helen's hopeful request?

Slim jumped into the open back seat, and Ella touched his arm. "Would you mind putting this basket with the costumes, and I'll see that Clara gets it when I return."

"Sure 'nough."

She grabbed her satchel and left the empty basket in its place.

Thorson shouted for everyone to load up. Engines popped and choked, and the boys ran around in unbridled excitement. Ella pressed her satchel close, imagining a delightful hour to herself photographing the countryside.

Surely she could avoid a cocky cowboy who hadn't even had the courtesy to say pea*hen.*

Hugh leaned against the big pine, watching as she and Helen returned to the house. His face held as much resentment as Mabel's, and he pushed off the tree and stalked to the barn.

Ella's throat tightened. Was there nowhere she could turn that someone was not offended by her?

"We can work on that new Sunday dress I mentioned." Perspiration collected at Helen's temples, and her rosy cheeks shimmered with good will.

Resentment and relief twisted through Ella's mind, an unlikely cord. "Do we have time before supper to look at what you have in mind?"

Helen raised her apron hem to her forehead. "If I don't melt away, we do. I've got beans in the oven, so supper won't take much work other than rolling out biscuits and opening a jar of my canned peaches."

Home-canned peaches. Solace seeped like balm into Ella at talk of meal preparation. The tender comradery chipped another chink in her wall. Simple companionship—she'd missed it more than she cared to admit.

Helen slowed her pace with a show of suffering from the heat, but Ella suspected it was for her own benefit. Half a day on her feet, with more walking that week than she'd done in months, had taken its toll.

The screen door swept a breathy welcome, and Ella fell into the chair at the end of the table the men had carried inside.

Helen ladled a cup of lemonade from the crock on the counter and set it before her.

"You rest a spell there and I'll go get my pattern. Ordered it from McCall's last winter and still haven't got around to cuttin' it. Cost me a whole fifteen cents . . ." Her voice trailed off through the dining room as she hurried to the other end of the long house.

Ella downed the lemonade in an unladylike fashion, then held the cool tin cup to her forehead. At the moment, her bobbed hair was an obvious disadvantage. There was no twisting it up off her neck and face—a dear price to pay this summer for an impulsive decision last spring. She set down the cup and kneaded her shrunken thigh muscle, more weak than sore now that she had her weight off it.

Perhaps a few more days outdoors would build her strength.

A latent longing stirred. Enough strength to ride? If only. She pressed her fingers deeper into the woolen fabric that masked her scar. Cale's brash question cut to the core of the matter. She'd worn a split skirt when she couldn't use it.

Wouldn't use it, she admitted to the white daisies observing from the sideboard. Their cheery faces prodded her. "Yes, yes, give it a try," they shouted with wordless fervor.

Helen returned with an armful of buttery-yellow broadcloth and a pattern that was a fashionable design from McCall after all, but with a slender line. Helen was anything but slender.

"I bought extra goods, seeing as how I'm not exactly a petite thing like you, dear." She chuckled and her ample bosom reinforced the confession.

Ella perused the pattern, noting with relief, that it accommodated a forty-six-inch bust.

"What do you think?" Helen took the opposite chair.

Ella kept her eyes on the print, searching for the kindest way to make her observation. Had she known her seamstress skills would be enlisted, she would have brought along her entire sewing kit and not merely needle and thread. "Have you a measuring tape?"

Helen disappeared into an adjoining pantry and returned a moment later with a folded ribbon. "Now you see why I haven't started on the cutting. Couldn't very well ask Hugh, Cale, or the boys to help me find my girth. They'd have me cinched up with one of their saddle leathers for sure."

Ella swallowed a laugh and stood. "Come over here to the center of the kitchen. I'll take some measurements, and we can spread the fabric on the table."

Helen planted herself in the middle of the room and raised her arms straight out on each side. Ella reached around her to grab the loose end of the measure and jumped at the clap of the screen door.

"What're you doin' to our Miss Helen?"

She turned toward three little faces all wearing the same question. "I'm measuring her for a new dress."

Each boy eyed the folded cloth on the table, then looked around the kitchen with something else on their mind.

"I'm saving what's left over for supper," Helen said, her arms still out like a scarecrow. She brushed the air with her fingers. "Skedaddle, all of you. Shoosh."

They skittered out the door.

Helen *tsked.* "I swear, those boys eat more than their father and uncle put together and the three of them stacked on top of one another wouldn't add up to half a man."

Ella took mental note of Helen's waist, such as it was, and her imagination ventured a guess at the shoulder span of Cale and his brother. Cale seemed broader, more muscled. Perhaps grief had shrunken his twin. It had a way of doing that to a body.

"Cale told me about Hugh and the boys. That their mother died."

The corners of Helen's lips pulled down and she dropped her arms. "A shame. A crying shame, poor thing. She had a hard time with Kip. He came early, and it was just Hugh and her. No midwife or doctor. Hugh blames himself in spite of what I tell him."

Ella held the tape against Helen's shoulder and measured a little past the hem of the dress she was wearing. "You weren't here on the ranch then?"

"Wish I had been. But I didn't come out until after the funeral when I saw those two brothers wouldn't make it with a pair of young'uns and an infant. Liked to killed Hugh, it did. The man didn't speak for nigh on a year, except to scold his boys. He's gettin' some better."

Ella's brows bunched as she looped the tape around Helen's upper arm, remembering a scene beneath the big pine tree.

"Looks like you've had a taste of his tongue-lashing yourself." Kind gray eyes followed Ella's movements.

"I heard him with the boys, thinking he was Cale." Uncomfortable with the familiar first-name reference to the ranch owners, she glanced up to measure the woman's reaction.

Helen tilted her head with a faraway look. "That Cale, now there's a good one if there ever was. Needs a wife, you know."

Ella's ears burned, and she blessed her bob for hiding them.

"'Course, so does Hugh, but he's more likely to catch a porcupine than a good gal the way he lets his harsh words get out there ahead of him." She lowered her voice a notch. "Saw you and Cale visitin' at the corral today. You need a pencil and paper to jot down all your numbers?" Helen uprooted herself and opened a small drawer in the kitchen safe.

"Thank you." Ella took the stub and wrote the measurements.

"You didn't seem too bothered by his attentions."

Warmth bled into her neck and face. Bothered? That wasn't the half of it. She feigned concentration on the figures.

Helen gave a laugh. "Honey, don't you mind me a 'tall. I know a spark in that boy's eye when I see it. And it sure wasn't there when that Steinway woman dragged him off. You got all the numbers you need?"

Ella's mind coughed and clattered like one of Thorson's motorcars. "I—uh—yes. I believe I do. How much yardage did you say you have?"

They each went to one side of the table and unfolded the length until it spilled like melted butter off one end and onto a chair. It was more than enough to make the dress and then some.

"This will be plenty." Relieved, Ella jotted a few more notes. "We can cut it today and start on it this evening if you'd like."

Helen leaned her large hands on the table and regarded Ella with conspiratorial attention. "It's doing me a world of good to have you here, and I appreciate you agreeing to stay."

Her voice lifted on the last word, signaling more to come.

Ella fumbled the paper and dropped the pencil, grateful for an excuse to bend away from the scrutiny. A secret—whatever it was—had Helen's eyes twinkling, and it set Ella's nerves to racing with dread. Or anticipation. Or anger? She could not identify the emotion that flooded her veins. But it undoubtedly had something to do with a certain Hutton brother. One of the tall ones.

~

Ella laid out the pattern and with sturdy shears cut dress pieces while Helen tended the beans. Judging by the rich aroma that filled the kitchen, they were nearly done, and Ella's stomach declared its rumbling approval. Clara would be pleased.

Clara. Oh, what a scolding she might brandish when Ella returned day after tomorrow. She'd want to know all the gossip from the ranch—if she didn't already know it. At the moment, the only thing close to gossip was Helen's mention that the Hutton men needed wives.

And that may be the only thing they had in common, other than their rugged faces and stunning eyes. As Cale had mentioned, he and his brother were as similar as lard and butter.

Vinegar and honey. Lemons and peaches . . .

A hard throat-clearing interrupted her musing.

"As I was saying, my Singer is in the dining room against the back wall with a scarf over the top. It's not one of those fancy 'lectric things you're probably used to, but as you can see, we don't have wires out here yet. You just help yourself. We have a while before supper, and I'll keep those three scamps out of your hair."

Helen wiped her hands on her apron and offered a guilty smile. "I know, I'm pressing you. But I suspect you might be spending some time outside tomorrow if Cale gets his way."

Gets his way? Ella stiffened. What was he going to do, chase her down a canyon like they had the cattle? Throw her over his saddle like he'd already done once. He'd have a fight on his hands at either attempt.

The shears landed hard on the table. She might be weakened physically, but she wasn't feeble-minded. Gathering the sunny cloth and cut pieces with unnecessary vigor, she caught a chuckle on her way out of the kitchen. Helen was as bad as Clara.

No. Worse.

Ella spread the fabric on the dining table and drew a chair to the machine. The white scarf covering it read *1904 World's Fair St. Louis* edged with red-and-blue-painted flags. Imagine that. She, too, had traveled to the Louisiana Purchase Exposition with her father and Nana to see the latest inventions and marvels. Taken her first photographs. Been sorely disappointed that G.W. Yeats's plays were *not* performed at the Irish Village as advertised.

A lifetime ago, those six years.

So much had changed.

She folded the scarf and laid it aside, then raised the machine from its hidden position to sit upright. Before long, she lost herself in her work at the old treadle, just the type of machine she'd learned to sew on at her Nana Elizabeth's side.

A subtle shift in sunlight alerted her to the passing day and approaching suppertime.

The screen door popped, and her head came up with a start. Helen's stern scolding sent a herd of boys stampeding back outside to wash. Ella snipped threads, tied a knot in her stitching, and laid the sack-like beginnings of the yellow dress over the machine, followed by the souvenir scarf.

"I don't know how many times I've told those whippersnappers they have to wash before they eat. At least twice every day going on six years." Helen followed her words into the dining room, shaking her head, and went straight to a sideboard and pulled out a checkered tablecloth. She snapped it open and spread it over the cherry-wood table, smoothing and setting it straight. "You'd think they were all deaf as a post."

No lace or linen as her grandmother insisted upon, but simple blue cotton gingham suitable for three rambunctious boys and their ranching father and uncle. For certain, this easily washed cloth served as a buffer for the fine table.

"How may I help?"

Helen didn't exactly waddle, but she came close. Her feet must hurt. She pointed to a cabinet as they entered the kitchen. "Dishes are in there. Seven of us tonight. Use the china. It's not often we have a guest to put on airs for." She winked at Ella. "Silver's in that sideboard where I got the cloth. Might as well use it as let it tarnish without anyone appreciating its value."

Beans and biscuits with china and silver—a less than worthy meal for such an elegant setting, but apparently not in Helen's eyes.

The woman's words settled in Ella with cold finality. She had tarnished from disuse and would continue to do so if she returned to the Canaday estate. The future stretched before her, as open and empty as the plains that had reached beyond the train's windows on her way to Colorado.

CHAPTER NINE

No storyline. Darndest thing Cale had ever heard, filming before they knew what story they were telling. And painfully reminiscent of shooting in the dark.

He stopped at the back porch and studied the breaks up behind the house, not surprised to find the scene as still as one of Thorson's painted backdrops. His enemy didn't strike by day.

He rolled up his sleeves and splashed the afternoon's dirt from his face and hands. Someday he'd build on a fancy indoor bath house for Helen and the boys, though she didn't complain. Just thanked him for putting a new pump at the kitchen sink and running a pipe outside to drain it so she didn't have to haul water.

Snagging the towel from a nail on the back of the house, he looked for a clean spot. The boys had beat him to it again.

He situated himself for a view through the window, craning his neck to see if Miss Canaday was inside helping Helen. He'd managed to watch the house most of the afternoon and hadn't seen her leave. Likely, Helen had her on that machine of hers sewing up a new dress. That was just fine. He had plans for tomorrow, and he didn't need a city gal underfoot.

His mood soured. A common occurrence since he'd been figuring how to get that bob-haired girl on a horse. He'd also like to know what she thought of their ranching ways with a privy out back and oil lamps and no electric.

Probably not much.

He pushed through the screen door and dropped his hat on a wall peg.

Miss Canaday walked in from the dining room, and her expression froze when she saw him.

That place on his chest pricked, but he'd not be scratching himself in a woman's company. He jerked a nod. "Ma'am."

"Hope you're hungry." Helen shut the oven door with a loud clap, her fresh biscuits reminding his stomach how long it'd been empty. Their guest moved past him with her head down. He couldn't read her eyes.

"See that basket? Put a cloth in it and . . . Land sakes, of course you know what to do." Helen laid a hand on the gal's thin shoulder as she shuffled behind her. "I've been riding herd on those boys for so long I forgot what it's like to have another woman around to help. You waiting for us to feed you on your feet, Cale, or is there something I can do for you?"

Confounded woman changed tracks like a switchman. His nephews stormed in, drawing her query, and lined up like bucket calves, hands held palm up for inspection. He escaped to the dining room.

Sure enough, Helen's sewing machine was sitting upright and covered with a fancy scarf. Probably the makings of a dress in there somewhere. Seven china plates and bowls lined the edges of the table. The "good dishes," as Helen called his mother's service. Rather than pull out a chair, he went to his room to change into a clean shirt and returned to find Jay sitting on the two-chair side with his jaw set and death in his eye. Cale pulled a frown to keep from laughing at the boy's stubborn streak.

The other two were shooting daggers at their brother across the checkered cloth. If Helen sat in her usual place, it'd be between them. He took his seat at the end and put his money on Jay.

Miss Canaday brought the beans and placed a pad under the black kettle. Then she delivered the basket of biscuits and a jar of Helen's berry preserves. Busy about her arrangement, she flicked a glance at the boys. One kicked another and a ruckus erupted that would spook a deaf elephant.

"Enough!" Hugh's harsh command entered the room ahead of him and stilled the boys. Color bleached from their guest's face, but her eyes narrowed as Hugh took the head of the table. Cale slid his jaw sideways. From the looks of it, his elder brother best not tangle with Miss Canaday.

Helen followed with a bowl of peaches and set it in front of Hugh's plate, then tucked her chin back and looked at Jay and his brothers. They all squirmed, as was their habit, but Cale was pulling for the middleman. Little got past Helen, though she was nothing if not fair.

"You will rotate tomorrow," she said with steel in her words. "For now, Miss Ella, would you please take the place next to Jay?"

A smug smile played across the boy's face and his brothers stared at their plates.

The arrangement placed her to Cale's right. He held one hand out and took Kip's with the other. Without hesitation, she placed her slender fingers in his and commenced stitching up his insides right there at the table. He bowed his head with a strong *whoa* in mind and cleared his throat.

"Thank you, Lord, for your bounties and for keeping us all safe today. And for our guest. Amen."

Everyone murmured an *amen* but Hugh, who huffed under his breath. Helen dished up beans. Cale offered the biscuit basket to Miss Canaday, noting that her presence brought an unusual comfort to the table.

"So what was the best part of today, boys?" She broke her biscuit in two and spooned a serving of preserves onto her plate instead of the bread. The basket made its rounds, and Jay copied her every move. His brothers snickered. Helen gave them each an elbow.

"Pie," Ty said, his mouth full of biscuit. "The apple one."

His answer was rewarded. "Thank you. I'm glad you liked it."

Not to be left out, Kip piped up, "They all comin' back tomorrow?"

Hugh huffed again.

"Mr. Thorson will write the story to go with what the cameraman filmed today, and they'll all return the following day."

"You're gonna be here two whole days?" Ty said around his biscuit.

Jay swallowed first before asking, "Can we go to the flicker when it's all done, Pa?"

Hugh grumped an unintelligible remark and Cale considered thrashing him after everyone was in bed—an issue that put a sudden hitch in the idea. Where was Miss Canaday going to sleep?

As usual, Hugh read his mind and glared the length of the table, silently blaming Cale for not thinking things through. Didn't matter it wasn't Cale's doing.

Ella glanced between the two of them. "Who went to the Louisiana Purchase Exposition? I saw the scarf today when I set up the sewing machine."

"I did." Hellen dabbed her mouth and took to the topic like bees to nectar.

"My Ben took me, God rest him. What a time we had. Rode the train from Denver to St. Louis and spent a whole ten days seeing the sights. We went in November and didn't get to see the Olympic Games or Mr. Roosevelt. But the Wild West Show was spectacular, and I had my first Dr. Pepper. Ben saw one of his father's old friends from the Jefferson Guard out on the Pike. Most excitement we'd had in years. Ben bought me that sc—"

"And Grace hasn't been the same since one of those Wild West fiascos came to Cañon City two years ago." Hugh scooped himself a second helping of beans.

Cale did his own glaring. His brother was as rude as a two-bit drunk, and he'd be happy to knock some sense into him. Just not in front of present company.

Ella looked at Cale, her fine brows raised to a peak.

"Grace is our younger sister." He wiped his mouth, afraid bean juice would get the better of him. "You haven't met her yet—"

"—because she's gallivantin' off somewhere trying to be Annie Oakley. Dadblamed fair posters got her all worked up."

Cale counted on his brother not spittin' right there on the carpet, because if he did, Cale wouldn't get to work him over. Helen'd do it.

"And Will Rogers, oh my. That's right, we saw Will Rogers too," Helen said as if she hadn't been interrupted. "Oh, but can he throw a fancy rope!"

"I know."

Everyone's spoon stopped in mid-air and all eyes locked on Miss Canaday in a moment of heavy silence.

She continued eating her beans, spooning them from the bowl's front edge to the back. Jay had a devil of a time copying her.

"My family and I attended too. Like you, Helen, I was quite impressed with Mr. Rogers's performance. I even took some photographs of him. Wasn't he billed as *William* Rogers?" She rested her spoon on the edge of the plate and waited for Helen's reply.

"You got a camera?" Kip's eyes rounded like his bowl.

"Yes, I do." Her smile beamed across the table to the youngster, and something in it warmed Cale's insides.

"Could you take our picture?"

She paused and looked at Ty, then Kip, then Jay to her right. "I think that's a splendid idea. How about tomorrow after you finish your chores?"

"How d'you know we got chores?"

"Have chores," Helen corrected. "You must have been a child six years ago, dear, but you're right about Mr. Rogers. Though it was that riding-and-roping *gal* that stole everyone's attention." Helen stared off over Jay's head, scouring her memory. "Now what was her name . . ."

"Do you mean Lucille Mulhall?"

Again everyone stared at the new woman at the table.

"You run in a highfalutin bunch, don't you?"

Cale jerked to his feet at his brother's snarl, knocking his chair against the wall.

Helen picked up the empty peach bowl and held it out. "Since you're up, Cale, bring some more peaches. I have another jar on the board just next to the stove."

It wasn't a request. Helen's look sawed right through him and he took the bowl with his left hand, his right balled in a fist.

"Tell me, Ella," Helen said, her eyes still on Cale. "What was your favorite spectacle?"

He strode to the kitchen, praying his brother would follow him, but the Lord declined his request and held Hugh in his seat. By the time Cale twisted the lid off a well-sealed jar of yellow peaches, Helen and Miss Canaday were laughing with the boys.

~

"I'm Buster Brown and I live in a shoe."

Ella's poor rendition of the comedic actor did little to prevent hilarity, and the boys nearly burst their skin giggling.

Hugh glowered at the head of the table, and she feared an imminent explosion, but not enough to keep her own delight harnessed. She had laughed more that day than in ages, even in spite of her recent sobering outlook on the future. The children had a way of pulling a medicinal-like humor from her very core.

Helen dabbed her eyes with her napkin. "Yes, yes, Ben and I saw him—that little man with his ugly dog and girl's hat. What a dandy he was."

Jay stuck his chest out. "I ain't never wearin' no sissy shoes." A spoon-full of beans filled his mouth as soon as the words were out.

"You *aren't*," Helen corrected.

"That's what he just said." Kip eyed their cook as if she'd lost her grip which sent Ty into stitches again.

"That's enough." Like a fist to rising bread dough, Hugh's bark deflated his sons. Ella stiffened. She was a guest in the man's home, but she'd had about enough of his surly behavior. And from the look in Helen's eye, between the two of them, they might stand him down.

Cale returned, and electricity sparked between the brothers when he banged the bowl on the table, sloshing peach juice over the edge. Perhaps sibling rivalry was not outgrown.

Helen mopped her temples.

Ella cringed inwardly. Nana would faint at such a display at the table. She pleated her napkin across her lap and calmed herself before continuing.

"The palaces at the Fair were grand, and I adored the Irish Village. But I most enjoyed listening to Mr. Rogers during supper at the Luchow-Faust World's Fair Restaurant."

"In the St. Louis Alps," Helen offered. The young brothers Hutton each wrinkled their brow at her remark. "So beautiful. Ben had himself an authentic Waldorf Astoria Segar when we dined there."

"Dined?" Hugh shoved in a jam-covered biscuit. "That the same as eatin'?"

Helen's barbed look tore through the boys' father but fazed him not one bit. He wadded his napkin and dropped it in his bowl, then scooted back from the table. Helen's throat-clearing gave him pause, and he picked up his dishes and stomped to the kitchen. The boys wiggled and squirmed, and the deep frown on Cale's face spoke of the fabled unspoken communication between twins.

"About tonight, dear." Helen's smile brightened the atmosphere considerably. She did have a way about her. "I think I know of three sprouts who would be more than happy to turn over their room to you. If you don't mind, that is."

Ella minded not in the least, and suddenly her hostess's habit of dabbing at her brow seemed quite reasonable.

"We get to sleep in the barn!"

"Yea!"

"In the loft!"

"In a stall," Cale countered. "There will be no tumbling out of the hay loft tonight."

Six little hands grabbed plates and bowls as three chairs combed across the carpet.

"Not so fast." Helen held them with a twinkle-guarding look, unlike what she'd given their father. "I'll let you off kitchen chores tonight, but you must strip your bed and take the clothes out back to the washtub."

"Yes, ma'am." An angelic trio.

"And pick up off the floor anything in your room that doesn't belong."

Ella harnessed another smile—a frequent occurrence since her arrival that morning. The boys clambered to the kitchen, then back through to the opposite end of the house, and soon scurried past again with the littlest one carrying an armload of wash bigger than he. The screen door slapped behind them, and Helen shook her head.

"That'll be more pie for us." Cale's brow smoothed to the clear expression Ella recognized from his visit to the studio. "They clean forgot about it in their eagerness to bury themselves in a straw fortress."

Ella plated her silver and made to stand, but Helen brushed a hand her way. "You pour Cale another cup of coffee and I'll bring in the pie. We best hurry before those youngsters discover their mistake."

Surprised that Helen would ask a guest to serve, Ella still welcomed the task, preferring activity to simply sitting at the table in awkward silence. She filled Cale's cup, impressed that he had managed the delicate china with his large hands.

As she set down the coffee pot, he leaned toward her with a daring light in his eye that made her heart sputter.

"She'll save a slice for each of them. Hugh too, though he doesn't deserve it." At that, his countenance darkened and he looked away.

"It's all right. I understand the loss of a loved one."

He glanced back at her rash comment, and she bit the inside of her lip. Too easily she shared information here on the ranch.

Helen returned with a ravaged pie tin and served the two remaining slices. "You visit while I see about your room. No telling what's under the bed in there."

Ella stilled and blinked.

Cale chuckled. "Don't worry. Helen's across the hall from you and I'm in the next room. We'll save you if you holler good and loud."

She must have looked aghast, for he laughed at her outright, which stiffened her resolve. "I'll have you know I can deal with whatever it is they have hidden in their room."

"Can you, now?" His eyes continued to spark above the coffee cup as he raised it to his lips. "We'll soon see."

CHAPTER TEN

Ella tugged the quilt against her chin, listening as something scurried along the edge of the wall. She'd made it all night without anything running over her legs, and she'd rather die than call for help. Especially after Cale Hutton's veiled challenge at supper.

The scurrying went still at the corner of the room.

Dim gray light peered in the bare window. Of course. Why would three rambunctious boys have a length of lace for modesty's sake? She raised her head from the feather pillow and stared into the unlighted corner. Nothing. No sight, no sound. Dare she rise before dawn?

Helen's borrowed nightdress tangled about her legs, but she managed to disengage herself from its cottony folds and slip her feet to the floor. A braided rug met her toes and she shuddered with relief. No fur, no scales.

She sat for a few moments, massaging her leg, surprised that it pained her less this morning than in recent weeks. After quickly dressing, she smoothed the quilt, ran her fingers through her hair, and then went to the window.

The sky lightened by degree, revealing an outline of mountains and trees fronted by a great rocky escarpment. A bird twittered, then another, and the smell of coffee slipped beneath the door and teased her nose. Helen started as early as Clara.

She finger-combed her bob again and opened the door to peek into the hall. Cale's door was closed, as was another at the opposite end of the hallway. Helen's was opened and revealed a neatly made bed. Ella slipped out, went into the dining room, and then into the kitchen, where Helen stood at the stove with her back to the doorway.

"Sleep well?" she said without turning. Either she had the hearing of an owl or Ella possessed the grace of an elephant. No doubt the latter.

"Yes, thank you." Only a partial fib. The hours she did sleep had refreshed her enough to lie awake this morning waiting for daylight to reveal what she'd shared the room with. Dousing a longing for strong Irish tea, she took a mug from the cupboard and filled it with rich, unburnt coffee. The aroma soothed her before the brew reached her lips. "You're at work as early as Clara."

Helen glanced up. "You mentioned the Denton yesterday. Fanciest place I know of around here with that hand-carved stair railing and imported carpets and such. Last I knew, Clara Washington was cooking there. Is that who you mean? Fetch me a serving dish for these potatoes, please. In the cupboard where you found that mug. We'll eat here." She tipped her head toward the big worktable they'd used outside yesterday.

An odd sensation strummed through Ella's midsection. "Will there be seven again?"

"No, just you and me and the boys. Cale and Hugh are checking the herd and doing whatever it is they do all day long with those cows."

Her heart shrank a little at the news, though she was not at the ranch for any other reason than to keep Helen company. And work on the woman's dress. She could have it completed by this evening, with an hour off this morning to take the boys' picture. Trial and error had taught her that a shady spot on a clear, bright day would be best, and she decided to try the rough boards of the barn as a contrasting background.

At a customary clatter outside, Helen went to the opened door and stood peering out, hands at her hips. "Soap."

"Yes, ma'am," chorused through the screen with shoving and sloshing from three little Huttons competing for first place at the pump. They had more energy than the entire Selig Polyscope company troupe and then some.

Ella scooped fried potatoes from the large iron skillet into a serving bowl, and her nose twitched at what smelled like fresh biscuits. Grabbing a towel to protect her hands, she opened the oven and removed another skillet puffed up with golden rounds of goodness. Her stomach cried out for butter and honey. She'd eaten like a field hand since she'd been at the ranch.

"You can set that right on this pad." Helen tossed a doubled quilt square on the table and returned to stir gravy in a third large skillet. Ella might die of longing before they sat down to the meal. Wouldn't Clara be thrilled if she came back to town with a little more "meat on her bones"?

"I don't know Clara's last name, but she makes biscuits like you and is determined to fatten me like a prized hog."

Helen paused in her stirring to give Ella a once-over. "I don't mean any offense, mind you, but I agree with Clara. You could use a few more home-cooked meals."

The boys bounded through the door, slowing mere moments before landing in their chairs with hair slicked back, faces damp and shiny. She couldn't help but laugh. "Are you hungry *again*?"

"Again?" Jay said.

"Well, you ate last night, didn't you?"

Ty elbowed the middle brother. "She's joshin' you."

Helen set her gravy skillet on the table and took a seat nearest the window. Ella sat across from the boys.

"Kip, say grace for us."

Ella bowed her head but peeked beneath her fringe to watch the youngest muster his courage. "Thank you, Lord, for this here food and everything. Amen."

"Amen." Helen reached for the gravy spoon. "Get yourself a biscuit, Kip. You're first for saying such a good prayer."

His brothers started in on how they pray good too and how it should be their turn next and "he got more gravy than me." Ella broke a thick biscuit in two, laid each half on her plate, and waited.

"Miss Ella, you can have my turn." Jay paid for his chivalry with Ty's sharp elbow and Kip's giggle, but he bore up like a little man.

"Thank you, Jay. You are quite the gentleman."

"Not more than me, I hope." The deep voice rolled off Ella's shoulders and down her back. Cale Hutton hung his hat on a peg and joined them at the head of the table, smelling like hay and leather and horsehair.

She breathed deeply, drawing the heady mix into her soul. The smell of life she'd once loved.

~

Cale helped himself to a biscuit and winked at the boys. "I thought you'd all be outside by now. What are you doing hidin' in here behind the women's skirts all morning?"

Jay flushed crimson and Ty scowled—his father's son. Kip-the-innocent sopped his biscuit. "We ain't hidin', Uncle Cale. We're eatin'." Full of Helen's biscuits and gravy, his cheeks bulged beneath his somber eyes.

"Didn't expect you, Cale," Helen said. "I'll get you a plate."

"No need. I just came in to check on what your plans were for the day."

Helen stopped and stared, her mouth open but nothing coming out. Ella lowered her gaze, intent on sawing her biscuit into tiny pieces.

He stuffed his biscuit in his mouth.

Helen gave him a hot cup of coffee and what sounded like an ultimatum. "Ella's helping me with my dress. It's not every day I have a full-fledged seamstress to consult with." She glanced at her guest and her expression softened. "And she might want to walk around, stretch her legs a bi— " Flustered, she groused under her breath and returned to the stove where she beat the gravy into paste.

Unmoved by Helen's flub, Ella looked across the table and tapped her fingers, drawing the boys' attention. "I'd like to take that picture of you three this morning. Out by the barn. What do you think?"

"Could you take one of me doin' my rope tricks?"

Jay snorted at his older brother. "You ain't got no rope tricks. Least ways not like Aunt Grace."

"Do so."

"Do not."

"You *don't have*," Helen inserted.

"Told ya!"

"Boys." The command jerked three heads his way, expressions ready for a tirade that wouldn't happen. He wasn't their father. "Finish your breakfast, comb your hair, and tuck in your shirts, then wait for Miss Canaday at the barn."

"I'd prefer they look like they always do. Natural. Like now, just themselves." Ella held his look, daring him to argue with her. "No preening peacocks."

Her barb hit dead center. Was that a grudge she held or just her pointed little chin? "You're the photographer."

She retreated to her coffee, and her dark eyes peeked over the rim. "True, but only a hobbyist."

He bolstered himself with a hot mouthful, careful not to meet her gaze. "If you'd like to see the place, I can show you when you're finished with the boys. That is if Helen lets you out of her sight."

"Humph." A cooking spoon whacked the edge of a pot. "You calling me a slave driver, Caleb Higgins Hutton?"

He could have gone all day without that. Jay and Ty nearly choked. Kip was too busy eating to notice. He flicked a glance at their guest, whose eyes snapped like hot corn kernels.

He stood and grabbed his hat. "I'll be at the barn."

She hadn't exactly accepted his invitation, but she was having a good laugh at his expense. Her voice lilted above the boys and out the open door like a spring-fed creek. But he had chores to tend to, tack to ready for Thorson's crew tomorrow. He had plenty to keep him busy. More than enough, in fact, without giving a tour. What had he been thinking?

Tug lay snoozing under the porch.

Cale slapped his thigh. "Come on, boy."

It wasn't long before a six-legged stampede drew him to the barn door, pitchfork in hand. Ty threw a loop at Jay's feet. Too quick for his brother's yank on the rope, Jay jumped and tucked his knees.

Cale'd had a few calves pull that same trick. "Don't be ropin' your brother." Feeling like a hypocrite, he added what his pa had always told him and Hugh and Grace. "You yank him down and knock his teeth out, you'll be payin' the bill."

Ty coiled his rope and waited on Miss Canaday, who soon caught up, a satchel strap on her shoulder and a lightness in her step. Only a half-hitch this morning.

She was different. More relaxed. Not tied up in a knot like she'd been in town. Almost looked like she was enjoying herself. He leaned the pitchfork against a stall, sleeved his forehead, and reset his hat.

"This way, boys." She squeezed through the corral railing on the north side of the barn and lined the boys up with Jay in the middle.

Cale took a seat on the top pole railing as she reached in her satchel and pulled out a fold-up camera. He'd seen 'em before in a catalogue and marveled that something so small could take a picture.

With a flick of her finger, she opened it and extended a red bellows. Taking a few steps to her right, she peered down into the viewer, adjusting something as she did so.

"All right, boys. I'm going to take several photographs, but I'll let you know and will count to three each time. On *three* you must be perfectly still. Can you do that?"

"Yes, ma'am." Their heads bobbed.

"Stand straight and tall and don't smile. Good. One, two . . ."

Ty crossed his eyes just as she said *three*, and Cale laughed. They all looked at him, ruining the picture. Miss Canaday straightened and fired a glare his way.

"You are not helping."

She was awful pretty.

He dragged his hand down his face, taking a grin with it, and sobered himself for the next picture.

"Let's try that again."

The ruffians complied, and she took several poses, finally letting them choose their own, including one of Ty holding his rope like Will Rogers with his famous big loop.

Cale got so caught up in the picture-taking that he timed his breathing with her counting, and on each *three* stilled himself. When the boys busted up laughing and pointing, he looked at Miss Canaday to find her camera aimed right at him. Her chin tucked but her eyes held a gentle smile.

He gripped the railing.

"We're finished here." She collapsed the bellows and snapped the camera shut. "You can tell Miss Helen that I want to take a few pictures of the scenery and then I'll be in to help with her dress."

Kip looked out across the pasture and back to the house. "What scenery?"

She laughed again, and Cale decided he could stand to hear it more. He jumped down and ruffled the boy's hair. "Maybe she doesn't have mountains and pine trees where she's from." He leaned close. "Tell Helen I've got a job for Miss Canaday and she'll be in after a while. Go on now."

Doc had ambled up to the corral and hung his head over the top pole. Probably huntin' apples, Cale figured, after watching the gal in action yesterday. She made her way to the gelding and, sure enough, pulled an apple from her satchel. Then she rubbed Doc's head and neck and murmured something.

"Doc doesn't take to most folks." Some less than others, like Mabel Steinway. "You want to help me with something before I show you the *scenery*?"

"That depends."

Guarded. He could accept that. "I've got a mare that needs her mane untangled. That suit you while I finish up with the tack?"

"So that's it. You've stolen me away from Helen's dress to groom your horses for you."

Laughter came easy. "You could look at it like that—" Like she'd rather be outdoors than stuck inside with Helen's sewing machine.

He brought a halter, lead, and a bucket of oats from the tack room, then unlatched the gate to the pasture and shook the bucket. Doc's ear perked, and Barlow, always attentive to the gelding's mood, trotted over, head high and tail swishing. Cale rewarded them each with a handful, then slipped the lead across Barlow's neck. He eased the halter over her muzzle, led her inside the corral, and looped the lead around the top pole.

Doc stayed where he was while the seamstress rubbed beneath his forelock saying things beyond Cale's earshot.

"Easy there. Don't be turning my horse's head. He'll start following you around like a pup and forget all about me."

Her laughter rippled over him, all smooth and easy. "I doubt that."

He pulled a heavy comb from his back pocket and started in on Barlow's knotted mane. Ella left Doc and stepped in close. He could see clean over the top of her head.

"Are you trying to show me what to do?" She took the comb from him, her fingers grazing his hand. Starting with short strokes at the tangled bottom, she worked her way up through the knots to the mare's neck.

He returned to the tack room for a saddle that didn't need one blamed thing done to it and set it on the top rail. "Seems you've got it figured out."

Her head tipped to the side. "Appearances can be deceiving."

He cut her a side glance, puzzled by her words.

"You probably thought I wouldn't know what to do with this mess since I have hardly any hair of my own."

He hooked the near stirrup over the horn and set to rubbing the apron leather with a rag for no good reason. "No deception there. Fact is, tells me a lot about you."

Her mouth pulled back at the corners as her fingers fanned wide into the knotted mane. "And what do you think it tells you?"

He dropped the stirrup, picked up the saddle, and turned it around. It told him there was more to her than a dark-eyed, sharp-tongued city gal. "You're willing to try something different."

She nodded slowly, as if measuring his words.

He waited a beat for her story, but she didn't give it. He might as well talk to his horse.

The gelding stood with a back leg cocked and his eyes half closed, listening to every word.

"So is it like I told the boys where you're from? No mountains or pine?" He slanted a look beneath his hat brim.

Her slender fingers combed through Barlow's mane. "Chicago is a big, crowded city with lovely parks, harsh winters, and dirty sky." She looked up at the blue dome above them. "Hills and some forests, but no mountains like you have here."

No wonder she wanted pictures. He couldn't imagine living anywhere else but the Rafter-H, especially a city like Chicago. "I can show you some pretty places if you'll ride with me."

Her skin paled and she tucked her elbows close to her body.

Fear. His gut tightened and he felt again her frailty against his chest that morning in town. Her hammering heart and shallow breaths. "I'll keep you safe."

Her lips parted but no sound came out. Just a glance of her dark, wary eyes before she whispered, "I can't ride."

Same answer as last night. The ground thinned out beneath him like early spring ice, but he pressed on. "Can't or won't?"

A muscle in her jaw tensed.

Coax her, don't run her off again. "Or we could walk out in the pasture a ways, see where the riders came down from the draw yesterday."

She turned away from him, smoothed her hand over the mare's back and rump, and reached for the tail. Every move confirmed familiarity. So what kept her ground-tied?

"All right."

If he hadn't been listening, he'd have missed it. A small step, but he'd take it over nothing. He hefted the saddle back to the tack room and rummaged around for a long lead to a short idea. Finding a soft cotton rope, he coiled it and hooked it over his shoulder.

When he returned, Barlow was lipping the leftover grain from Ella's flattened palm, ears twitching to her soft, low tones. Maybe she'd say more to him if he hadn't called her a peacock.

He opened the gate, and Ella led the mare through and reached for the halter buckle.

"Leave it on her. Just take off the lead."

She cocked an eyebrow at him but did as he asked.

He hung the short lead over the rail and started for the open pasture. "This way."

He shortened his stride.

She walked easily beside him, head up, one arm resting on her satchel as she took in her surroundings.

"It's beautiful here. So clean."

"Unless it comes a storm and you get caught in it without your slicker."

She looked up at him, concern pinching her face. "Really? That fast? Can't you see it coming in time?"

"Oh, you can see it coming. Same way you can see a cougar leaping at you from a high rock."

She shuddered and gripped her elbows but kept walking, a slight limp working into her steps.

"'Course that'd be a rare occurrence in these parts." Though bears weren't, it seemed, but he didn't want to spook her, and lately he hadn't done such a fine job of stringing words together. "See that patch of bright green under the hill there?"

She slowed and looked where he pointed.

"Aspen. They turn yellow in the fall. The only gold you'll find in these mountains this side of Cripple Creek."

She stopped and took in the view. "I've read about the Independence Lode and the fires."

He reached behind her, took her by the shoulders, and gently turned her north where higher, pine-covered slopes rolled up toward the backside of Pikes Peak. "We could see the smoke from here. Worried pa some. Hugh and Grace and I would sneak out at night and climb up the bluff to watch the sky glow red." From behind her, he pointed over her shoulder. "Right over the ridge there. As the crow flies, about fifteen miles."

She turned her head and her breath brushed his chin. "That close?"

Too close. "But not an easy trip unless you're that crow." He stepped around her and continued on, his pulse galloping with her so near. "A little farther, and you'll see the break where the stampede came down yesterday."

Sensing she wasn't following, he looked over his shoulder and caught her rubbing her leg. "You all right?"

She straightened. "Why, yes. I'm right as rain." She ran her hands down her riding skirt and looked around. "Though I don't see any headed our way." Her smile, a bit forced, still brightened the morning.

"Come on then, Rain Woman." He held out his hand and she took it. He'd carry her if she'd let him. Doc and Barlow meandered a ways behind them, grazing. He chuckled.

"What?"

"We've got a couple of tag-alongs."

She glanced back. "Oh, the dears."

"Don't let on. You'll hurt Doc's pride."

"Pride? You're serious, aren't you?"

"As an undertaker. He thinks he's sneaking up on us."

With her hand in his, her soft laugh fanned a spark. He lifted his hat and sleeved his brow before setting it down again. Things were warming up a might quick. If he wasn't careful, he'd set the whole pasture ablaze.

CHAPTER ELEVEN

Ella set her sights on the fence a hundred yards away. Or a hundred miles. What had she been thinking to accept Cale's offer?

Clearly, she'd been thinking of photographic opportunity. Of one chance in her lifetime to capture the sweeping vista that stretched around her, no matter where she turned. She'd promised Nana photographs from her travels, and these would not only thrill her grandmother, but also serve as vivid reminders of her daring days of freedom. Daring, in that she'd broken from expectations.

The meadow cushioned her steps, and the quiet beauty almost made her forget she was crippled. As fatigue crept into her leg, she split her attention between the ground just ahead and the distant fencing, anchored every so many feet by poles set up in a giant X. A man could easily step through the odd configuration, but apparently not horses.

The farther they walked from the barn, the more she doubted her ability to return, yet the sweeter the piney perfume. She drank in the scent, and with it, a flutelike bird's call from her left, answered in a moment with a matching song from her right.

Cale noticed her noticing and answered her silent question. "Meadow larks."

The mountain rose ahead, darkly cloaked on either side of a deep gash where yesterday, horses and cattle had charged through. This close to the steep opening she marveled that the riders hadn't all tumbled out end over end.

She'd once been horsewoman enough for a ride like that.

Pain sliced through her leg, yanking her breath and her fingers from Cale's hand. She stopped and leaned forward, pressing the heel of her hand against her thigh. He moved in, watching silently, his concern nearly tangible. In so many words, he'd called her bold earlier. If only he knew how wrong he was.

His strong hand cupped her shoulder, tempting her to trust him, and it took all her concentration to guard her words. He was much too easy to talk to. Listen to. If she wasn't careful, she'd tell him everything and expose her soul—as scarred as the mountain before them.

She pulled upright and tramped to the fence where she fell onto the bottom pole and braced a hand on each side. Cale watched her without watching, making a show of searching the horizon with his face turned slightly away. But she caught the flick of his blue eyes upon her, and struggled to keep her own from locking with them. Bold indeed.

"This is one of my favorite spots." He tipped his hat back and scoured the azure sky. "This and up on the ridge."

The ranch house and barn were toys in the distance. Doc and Barlow grazed drowsily a few paces away, ears turned toward their master. She took his bait. "Can you see the ridge from here?"

He pointed south, she judged. "See the long low spine that snakes against this side of a darker mountain?"

Squinting, she searched for his spine and snake images, but without success. At her silence, he took a knee beside her and leaned in with his head at her level, one hand braced near hers on the cross pole. Then he aimed with the other, drawing her eyes to follow his two fingers until she discerned the brown line cutting across a green mountain face. If he hadn't pointed it out, she wouldn't have noticed.

"I see it!" Unexpected excitement propelled her words, and they each turned toward the other. His breath smelled of coffee

101

and biscuits. Hunger nibbled at her insides, but not for food. She pushed herself upright, forcing him to back away.

"I can see why Mr. Thorson chose your ranch for the film." She drew in a deep breath and moved along the fence, trailing her hand on the rough poles. "He could fill a dozen reels out here."

One long stride brought Cale even with her. "I meant to ask you about that. Doesn't he have the cart before the horse, taking pictures without a story?"

She pulled out her camera and turned away from him, toward the scarred mountain. "He knows the main idea, the premise, but often what he captures on film generates new ideas, so he writes to fit what shows up. It's easier that way."

She framed the view before her, wishing she could capture the startling blue of the sky and the varying shades of green. "Then again, sometimes he and the cameraman spend all night long at it, arguing and writing and rewriting. At least that's what Pete tells me."

"So you don't help with the script?"

She swallowed a snide remark. "I just mend the tears in the clothing."

"How 'bout acting. You ever been in front of the camera? In the action?"

She *acted* all right. As if she were whole and not brittle. As if she didn't care what others thought of her damaged state. But not exactly in the action. The idea of stepping in front of the camera provoked an unladylike chortle, and she covered her mouth and dropped her head, the bob hiding her face.

"Wouldn't you like to?"

His question drew her glance.

"I dare say, there's very little room for any other woman in Thorson's films when Mabel Steinway is the leading lady."

He tugged his hat down with a blue flash. "Now there's a mouthful."

Laughter escaped too easily with this Westerner and his plain talk. She forced herself still so she could take a photograph.

From the corner of her eye, she caught him fiddling with the end of the coiled rope he carried. She sat on a lower fence pole as he eased toward the horses with a soft whistle. The mare tossed her head and trotted straight to him. Doc ignored the call.

"Good girl, Barlow." He snapped the long cotton rope to the halter and backed away, feeding it out a coil at a time until he and the horse stood a good distance apart. The horse's ears swiveled between her companion and her owner.

Ella's hands tingled. She knew what was coming.

Cale flicked the rope and clicked his tongue, and the mare tossed her head again. Another flick, and she trotted forward, circling him as if she were the rim of a single-spoke wheel and he the hub.

There was only one reason he'd do such a thing, and Ella had already told him twice that she could not ride. *Would* not ride. Her muscles tightened, shooting tension through her leg with a searing pang. She focused her camera and waited for Barlow to trot into the frame with her owner. *Click.*

"Come show me what you can do."

Her fingers twitched, and she exerted special care in returning her camera to the satchel. "What makes you think I know anything about lunging a horse?"

He laughed, and immediately she resented it.

"How'd you know it's called lunging?"

No wonder he'd lured her all the way to the edge of the wilderness with his easy camaraderie. She could neither refuse nor feign ignorance. And if she stalked away like a petulant child, she'd have to drag herself to the house and hide away in the boys' room for the rest of the day.

Very well. She pushed to her feet, testing her weight on her right leg, and pulled the satchel strap over her head so it lay across her chest. She'd show him a thing or two.

Chin high, she waited until the horse trotted past, then strode as best she could to his side and took the lead without waiting for him to hand it to her. How poorly he hid his humor with that flashing dimple. If she had a riding crop, she'd give him what for.

With a quick snap of her wrist, she set the mare into a canter, pivoting on her left heel as the horse wore a flattened circle into the grass. The long easy strides set the mare's mane to waving, smooth and tangle-free. Pleasure pulled at Ella's mouth and lifted her spirit.

Another signal, and the mare slowed to a trot and then a walk until she stopped and waited for Ella's approval. Rather than berate the horse's master for manipulating her into participation, she lavished affection and praise on the animal.

He thought he was so smart. If only she had a hunt seat and a few hedges. Better yet, she could easily clear that zigzagging fence line—

The cotton rope fell from her hand and she backed away, heart pounding. How had this cowboy stirred such fantasy? Made her long to ride again. To lift her face to the wind and fly on the back of a trustworthy mount.

Tears pricked like nettle and she turned toward the fence. Her soul ached as much as her leg, and the struggle to hide both wounds was nearly more than she could manage. She was trapped, surrounded by the beauty of this vast land of forest and ridge and unearthly blue sky—imprisoned by her failure to cope with her loss.

"Nice work." The snap clicked and he came up beside her, coiling the lead as the mare's hooves beat a muffled retreat. "What other secrets are you hiding beneath that shiny bobbed hair?"

She had no breath for words and shook her head, praying he'd let the conversation die.

He looped the coil over his shoulder again and pushed his hat off his brow. He smelled like horses, and her yearning grew. She'd been a fool to come West, into the heart of a country dependent upon the magnificent animals she'd once treasured and the men who rode them. Even more of a fool to accept Helen's invitation.

"Like I said before, you've got a way with horses. You're at ease with both Doc and Barlow." His voiced dropped. "But not with yourself."

She jerked her head around. "How dare you presume. You know nothing about me."

He studied the scarred mountain beyond her shoulder, a similar mark forming between his brows, then slowly met her glare. "You were white as new canvas that morning in town. My guess is, you once rode but you're afraid to now. Is it because you think you can't?"

Her breath stuck in her throat when he hit the mark, and his words reverberated through her like a clanging triangle. The man had no facade whatsoever. He was as open and uncomplicated as the country in which he lived.

Unwilling to expose her soul, her pain, her longing, she crossed her arms with a shudder. What would it be like to live as openly and bare-faced as he?

Again the clanging, only this time it was real, and he shoved his hat down and held out his hand. "Dinner's on. We best be getting back."

She couldn't move. Her right leg anchored her to the pasture. Once more she stood frozen in place, turned to stone by what raced toward her. "Go ahead. I'll catch up to you. Just let me stand here a while and . . . and take in the view."

His scrutiny unsettled her even more. Without taking his eyes from her, he turned his head slightly and whistled. Both horses trotted over, and the gelding nudged her shoulder, knocking her off balance and into his arms.

She caught herself against his chest, ready to berate him for such an underhanded tactic. But one hard hand splayed across her back, and the other gripped her upper arm. The heat of him unsettled her more than Doc's shove, and his raspy words shot fire from the places he touched and into her very toes.

"I thought we'd ride back, but if you'd rather I carry you . . ." A wicked grin deepened the dimple.

She pushed away. "I think not. And I told you, I cannot ride."

"I heard you." He reached for her waist and without effort, lifted her to the mare's back. She clutched her satchel and instinctively swung her leg over.

He clipped the long rope to the mare's halter, and grabbing a handful of Doc's mane, hauled himself atop the gelding. With a dare in his eye and a tug on his hat brim, he presented her with the rope and his challenge.

"Ladies first."

~

Cale's heart missed two full beats waiting for her to either slide off or ride off. When she dragged her fiery eyes from him, found her center, and heeled the mare, he could almost hear the wind rattle his ribs. She'd seared a hole clean through him.

Ella Canaday might have a hitch in her get-along, but like she said, appearances were deceiving. There was more to her than met the eye, especially where horseflesh was concerned.

He'd taken a mighty big chance, but after watching her lunge Barlow, the way she pivoted at first but eventually stepped into the effort and moved out of her rut, he knew she had what it took physically. But on the inside, there was no telling. Something held her back more than her weak leg, yet his gut had said she'd rise to the challenge.

She did.

She sat the mare as easy as a swing at a Sunday picnic, though her knuckles whitened on the rope and her jaw might crack if she didn't ease up some. He was itching to ask her what happened, but he'd already pushed through where he wasn't invited, and he wanted her short time at the ranch to be . . . well— good.

He wanted to be good. For her.

He rubbed at the irritation under his vest. It was a heady thing to gamble with a woman and win, though it wasn't a complete win. She wasn't in a saddle riding up the mountain skirting recalcitrant cows or sloshing through a thin stream. But she was horseback, and that was a solid first step. He let her set the pace.

Barlow worked up to a trot, and she plowed the rope enough to slow yet not turn the mare. He smiled to himself, proud of her grit as much as his ability to read her so well.

The boys and Hugh were not at the barn. Probably hugging the dinner table, waiting like one hog waited on another.

When they got to the corral, he slid off Doc and reached for the mare's halter.

Miss Canaday laid low over Barlow and wrapped her arms around the mare's neck, face turned away with those whispery words again. He'd give his best saddle to hear what she was saying.

When she straightened, she nailed him with a look he couldn't cipher, and it didn't bode well. So much for reading her.

Lord 'a mercy, a woman's eyes could rake through a man's soul and leave nothin' but dirt behind.

She made to slide off, but he didn't trust her leg to hold her more than he didn't trust himself. He reached for her narrow waist. If she slapped him, she slapped him, but he'd not let her fall.

Grounded, she took him in with a dark look until Jay spooked 'em both, the little sneak.

"You comin' or not?"

The boy's query jerked her off balance.

Cale grabbed her arm to steady her.

She drew back and ran her hands down her skirt, glaring at him. "You had no right."

The tight whisper sank in his belly like a stone.

"Well?" Irritation pitched Jay's voice higher.

"Take Miss Canaday."

She moved away.

"I'll see to the horses." He slipped off Barlow's halter and coiled the rope, and the mare trotted off to roll in the pasture.

"You better hurry." Jay held the gate, scowling at him as if he'd stolen his best girl. "You know how it is."

Miss Canaday laid a hand on Jay's thin shoulder and the boy wrapped an arm around her waist as they walked to the house. Her slight limp was no more than it had been this morning. Was she that good at hiding pain? Or was it a different sort of pain that made her fight her head?

At that moment, she slid a look over her shoulder. No scowl, but not exactly a thank you, either.

His nephew was wrong. Cale didn't know how it was.

CHAPTER TWELVE

Crawling under the boys' bed with a skittering creature appealed to Ella immeasurably more than sharing dinner with Cale Hutton. Maybe he wouldn't come inside. Maybe he was ashamed of forcing her to ride when she had plainly told him no.

And maybe she should thank him.

Never!

Waiting while Jay washed, she clenched her fists and blinked her stinging eyes, staving off tears of anger and humiliation. The idea of thanking him was unconscionable. He'd forced his hand with her, clearly against her wishes.

Glancing down at her split skirt and boots, she rued the fact that she had dressed herself into his assumption that she knew what to do. He would never have set her on that horse had she been wearing her low tops and a suit.

And yet . . .

She flexed her fingers open. *She'd done it.* Hope rushed through her in a thrilling torrent. She'd actually ridden again, and the realization tingled through her arms and into her swirling thoughts.

The back screen door snapped her out of her musing, and she pumped chilled water into one hand, then splashed her face, hoping to quell the conflict heating her neck. A questionable-looking towel hung sadly from a nail. She let it be and shook her hands and palmed her cheeks as she stepped inside.

"Just in time." Missing nothing, Helen handed her a napkin. "You've got a bit of water hanging from your fringe there."

Further mortified, Ella patted her hair and face with the clean cloth, then laid it aside and carried hot biscuits to the dining room. Drawing herself up, she marched as best she could to the table anchored by four men of varying sizes and shapes. If she could ride under her own strength, she could bear the remarks of these brothers, whether children in age or in deed. A tiny *humph* pressed against her pursed lips, and she held her eyes to the tabletop where a pot of savory stew assaulted her nose. Crocks of butter and jam waited to be rushed upon, as well as fresh coffee.

Helen took her seat and Ella followed, with Ty at her side and Jay across the table scowling. Cale clomped through the back door and joined them. Again he led in grace, but this time soberness clouded his features, a discovery that pleased her immensely. It served him right, taking advantage of her like he had, setting her up to either accept his preposterous plan or limp all the way back to the house.

Even as she roasted him over the flames of her ire, joy bubbled up, threatening to spill into her cheeks and out her mouth, forcing her to admit her exhilaration at riding again. Even such a short distance. Even at such a humiliating price.

How could anger and exuberance coexist within her? She darted another look his way and found him staring into his stew. Hugh, at the opposite end of the table, scowled as usual. Helen ignored them both and kept her attention on the youngsters and their manners.

Tension charged the air around them, and she suspected it had nothing to do with a brief jaunt through the pasture. Tableware clanked against dishes, stitching the stillness until Hugh snapped it. "Harper lost another one last night."

She glanced up to find him clearly agitated as he mauled the biscuit he was trying to butter. He cut her a scathing look on his way to his brother, as if she were to blame for whatever had been lost.

"While you were strayed off this morning, he rode over to see if we'd been hit."

Strayed off? The heat she'd tried to abate with cold well-water resurged. Did he think she had lured Cale away from his responsibilities?

The boys silenced themselves, and their eyes jumped from their father to Cale as if waiting to see who would strike first.

"You tell him?" Cale spooned in a bite she didn't expect would pass his tight jaw.

Hugh nodded.

"It's that devil bear, ain't it?" Kip's eyes rounded above his whisper.

"Isn't," Helen chided. "And don't be saying such things at the table. All creatures are the good Lord's."

"'Cepting that one."

Helen's gaze turned toward Jay, and he ducked and shoveled his stew.

Ella dabbed her mouth, sought boldness in her coffee cup, and carefully returned it to the table near her plate. "May I ask what was lost? Perhaps we can look for it."

Hugh snorted and shook his head, assuring her that she'd misspoken.

Cale's quick grab of his knife drew her eyes to his face, hard and cold as stone. He sliced off a slab of butter before speaking but did not return her regard.

"Ranchers are losing their stock. Either to rustlers or a marauding bear. Maybe both."

Hugh grumbled into his coffee. "Rustlers don't take 'em one at a time and leave 'em half eaten in the brush."

Cold shivers skittered across her back and she dropped her hands to her lap, staring hard at Helen, willing the woman to disperse the tension with one of her cheerful deflections.

She said nothing.

Hugh soon left the table, and his dishes clattered into the kitchen sink. The screen door banged open and shut, and young shoulders relaxed beneath a collective sigh.

Cale closed his eyes and rubbed his forehead. He'd aged since their stroll in the pasture. "You boys stay close to home till this clears up." His voice was somber, fraught with warning. "I mean it."

"Yes, sir." Jay kicked Ty under the table.

"Yes, sir."

Helen nudged Kip.

"Yes, sir, Uncle Cale."

Weary eyes found hers, apology swimming in their blue sea. "You too, Miss Canaday."

For as mad as she'd been, his formality pained her. It was more than likely for the boys' benefit, she supposed. But he'd not yet addressed her by her given name, though he'd insisted she call him Cale.

She nodded. Voiceless with unexplained disappointment and a new and quickening fear, she was unable to look away from the deep concern cutting across his rugged features.

Suddenly, she felt as welcome at the table as a hungry bear at the corrals.

~

Ella spent the remainder of the day working on Helen's dress, safely indoors away from wild animals and angry ranchers. And completely flummoxed by her conflicting emotions.

Riding Barlow without benefit of a saddle had terrified her—and taken her back to her childhood. Once she found her center on the old mare's broad back, a sense of control overpowered her fear of falling. How quickly old memories overwhelmed her—cantering bareback across the paddocks, loose hair flying, and her father's groom grinning at the rail, faithfully keeping her secret. Her family would have been horrified to learn she rode like a "plains Indian" from one of the Wild West shows.

But she could not bring herself to thank Cale Hutton for his heavy-handed ways. She could have fallen. She could have broken her neck. She could have re-injured her leg.

But she hadn't. And she'd enjoyed a brief reprise of her life-long love of riding. If she gained nothing else from this time at the ranch, she'd gained that. And for that she *was* grateful.

Someday you will love again. Nana's words worked to the surface. Why hadn't she said Ella would ride again? Had she viewed that as more of an impossibility than marriage? But to be fair, Nana hadn't said marriage either. She'd said love.

Only her father insisted that she marry, and within six months of the accident had invited suitors to their home on a regular basis. Even now Ella shuddered at the array of interested and eligible men. Interested not in her, but in her father's fortune.

If only he approved of her choices and used a lighter hand on the bit he'd placed in her mouth at birth.

Her last memory of him wavered, then focused. Standing in Grand Central Station's cavernous waiting hall, he resembled the marble pillars with his unrelenting countenance. He'd gone so far as to blame her behavior on the gaseous tail of Haley's comet and threatened to have her detained for examination.

Nana had intervened.

Dear woman. Unshed tears had sparkled in her eyes at their hushed parting.

"Be careful, dear." Nana's trembling voice gave Ella pause, but she'd gripped her ticket and answered with her own fragile smile. That ticket had cost nearly every cent of her savings after she had "shamed" Patrick Canaday III by taking up with "the rabble and rubbish of a moving-picture company."

She'd thrown her arms around the grandmother for whom she'd been named, the woman whose loving kindness had made life bearable for a motherless child. In a way, Ella pitied her grandmother, for she could not leave the confines of proper society and estate life. "I will, Nana. And I will have wonderful photographs to share with you when I return."

Her father's dismissive huff sealed her resolve, and she waved good-bye as she followed the Selig Polyscope troupe to the train platform.

Later that evening after a light supper, she pushed the memories away and the dining chairs against the wall and helped the boys lay their bedrolls beneath the table. Cale's mirthless order to sleep indoors left them all down in the mouth. And it left her shouldering guilt for putting them out of their beds in the first place.

"You boys are spread out in here like a week's wash." Helen's tone belied her frown.

Kip's lower lip sagged. "I don't like squash."

"Whatever brought that on?" Helen planted her hands at her hips.

"And I ain't weak."

"Land sakes, boy, I didn't say you were weak." She ruffled his hair. "A week's wash. A week's worth of washing. Not a weak squash."

Ty snickered, but Jay patted the bedroll beside him. "Come on, Kip. This is almost like camping out."

Helen wrapped a warning in a bribe on her way to the kitchen. "Quiet down and I'll bring you each a cookie before I put out the lights."

Ella knelt and fluffed the boys' pillows, then scooted over to the sewing machine and settled against its scrolled iron legs. "Would you like me to tell you a story?" She had nothing else to offer that might settle three rambunctious brothers.

"Yeah!"

"About robbers!"

"No, grizzlies!"

She shuddered. Blood and bluster. Not exactly the type of tale she had in mind. "If I am to do the telling, I shall choose the story. But only if you are quiet as a church mouse."

She tucked her stockinged feet beneath her, mentally thumbing through her favorite Bible stories.

Helen brought each bedded boy a cookie, gave one to Ella with a wink and a pat on her shoulder, then ambled down the hall.

Cale and Hugh were nowhere to be seen, probably at the barn securing the animals and doing whatever ranchers did when bears were about. The gun cabinet facing her across the room bore two empty notches where rifles had rested. Evidently, the men were prepared.

A shudder rippled through her. She'd not bargained on wild animal attacks when she'd agreed to stay.

She finished her cookie and dusted her hands, settling upon a story that might entertain three adventurous little urchins. Readjusting her feet, she rested her hands in her lap. "Once there were three boys named Shad, Mesha, and Abe."

"Those are mighty strange names." Ty raised up on an elbow and gave her a doubtful look.

"Except Abe," Jay said. "We go to school with Abe Hutchins."

"Stuff it." Kip suffered for his rebuke but refused to bear his brothers' jabbing fingers in silence. "Stop or I'm telling Pa!"

"I can't continue until you are quiet." She folded her arms and waited for the squirming to still.

Heavy sighs and grunts faded until the mantel clock's ticking filled the room, and her audience returned to staring at the underside of the cherry-wood dining table.

"Shad, Mesha, and Abe lived in a land far, far away, across the Atlantic Ocean. One day, a very wealthy king from another land rode into their town and . . . *snatched* them up as prisoners." She reached out as she stressed the word, and each boy flinched beneath his covers.

"He hauled them away to his kingdom and made them his slaves."

Ty huffed like his father.

"However, these three boys were very, very smart. They learned their lessons and did everything the king told them." She held her breath for several ticks of the clock before continuing. "Except for one thing."

Three little heads turned toward her in unison, expressions expectant.

She feigned a yawn and covered her mouth. "Oh, I'm getting so sleepy. Shall I continue tomorrow?"

"No."

Swallowing a chuckle stirred by the choral refusal, she cleared her throat. "Very well, then."

She adjusted her feet once more and traced a nearby floral pattern in the carpet. "Where was I?"

"They did everything they were told 'ceptin' one."

"Oh, that's right. They did everything the king told them to do. But when he told them they had to bow before him as if he were God, they stood straight and tall."

"Why would he say that?" Jay said.

"Because he was a very arrogant king."

"What's air-gunt mean?" Kip asked.

"It means he thought he was better than everyone else, and he wanted everyone to bow down to him. And everyone did, except the boys."

Three little Huttons lay silent, mulling over the situation.

"What'd the king do?" Ty ventured.

Saddened that he and his brothers did not recognize the story of the three Hebrew children, she wondered if they knew any Bible stories at all. No doubt their father did not read to them or tuck them in at night. A memory slipped in of Nana's gentle teaching and storytelling. How dearly these boys needed such care.

She looked each one in the eye and leaned close to whisper. "He threw them in the fire."

They lay as still as death.

"They died?" Kips eyes rounded with horror.

"No, they lived. Since they knew the king was not God, they were brave and did the right thing—even risking the king's anger that meant they *could* have died. But God saved them from the fire. In fact, their clothes weren't even burned."

She could hear wheels turning beneath the cherry-wood table as Helen came in from the hall and turned down the lamps.

"I figure you three are as smart as those boys, so you already know there's no rough housing tonight."

Surprised that Helen had been listening, Ella gripped the side of the sewing machine and pulled herself upright, hoping she hadn't stepped over an invisible line. Perhaps the story would chase bears from the boys' dreams and fill them instead with images of faraway lands and the courage to make right choices.

She could use a dose of courage herself, though she believed the courage it had taken to defy her father and come West certainly proved something.

But had she done the right thing?

That question remained to be answered, and she tucked it back in the pocket of her heart where she kept perplexing queries.

One unexpected adventure had come from her bold step onto the train. Perhaps riding again was truly within her reach, but next time it would be on her terms, not someone else's.

Next time? The idea rushed through her, so unfamiliar she shuddered in anticipation. Such a thought had not occurred to her since the accident, and after only two days on an isolated ranch in Colorado, it had found its way back to her soul.

An hour later, she lay stone still in bed, listening for the scurry of little feet, when heavy boot steps entered the hallway. They ended at the room next to hers before the door softly closed.

Cale.

A shiver coursed through her at the bold blue of his challenge earlier that day, prodding her into doing the unthinkable. Shifting beneath the covers, she dug through Helen's tent-like nightgown and fingered the long, ugly scar. Her leg hadn't pained her all evening. Perhaps the walk today had been good for it.

And the ride? Muscles long dormant had wakened in response to sitting astride Barlow, maintaining her balance. Demand had required response that she had not believed she could produce. Yet she had.

Harsh steps pounded into her thoughts, scattering her musings. They faded to the opposite end of the hallway and a slamming door cut them off completely.

Hugh.

He wore his anger like she wore her scar.

Closing her eyes, she saw again Cale's worried expression at the dinner table. Was it the bear that troubled him so? Or was it her?

CHAPTER THIRTEEN

The gunshot cracked close and clear.

Brutally awakened, Ella crawled to the window near the end of the bed and flinched again at a second shot. It sparked in the night, revealing the shooter's location mere yards away.

Scuffling noises from the dining room traveled to her door, and it creaked open on an urgent whisper. "Miss Ella?"

"Come in, boys."

She hurriedly wrapped the quilt around her shoulders as the boys pounced onto the bed and shoved their way past each other to the window.

"You think it's the devil grizzly?"

"Maybe rustlers."

"I can't see anything."

A glow at her door announced Helen with an oil lamp. "You all right in here, Ella?"

"Yes, we're fine." She scooted to the head of the bed. "Please, join us."

"Us?" The soft light warmed the room and glinted off three dark heads pressed against the glass. "What are you boys doing in here? Sakes alive, intruding on our guest!"

"It's all right, Helen. I don't mind. It is their room, after all."

The tsking woman joined her on the edge of the bed, and it complained beneath the weight of yet another person on its frame. Moments later, the back door blew open and booted feet entered the kitchen. The boys scrambled off the bed and out the door.

"I'd best put on a pot of coffee." Helen rose. "The mantel clock said four thirty when I checked, so I might as well stay up and get an early start on the pies and cookies for your moving-picture folks." At the door, she looked back. "Not you, of course. Rest in a bit if you can sleep through all the racket."

She bustled into the dining room and on to the kitchen.

Ella gripped her quilted cape and went to the doorway to listen.

A man strode through the dining room toward the gun cabinet, saw her across the hall, and stopped. Rifle in hand, hair mussed, and tall boots bunching his trousers at the knee, he stood before her, bare chest rising and falling with exertion. Every visible muscle stretched tight in defense of his home and property.

Frozen in place, she tugged the quilt tighter and swallowed. Who was he? *Which* was he? Hugh or Cale? Sharp blue eyes and a stormy brow spoke of his frustration over a fight he wasn't winning.

No dimple came to her aid.

She stepped back and closed her door.

~

Cale stared at the door, the image of Ella Canaday burned on his brain, her eyes as big as dollars, as if she'd seen Old Mose himself. He skimmed a hand over his chest, sweaty from chasing after he didn't know what. But if the crashing through brush and cedar were any indication, it sure enough could have been a grizzly.

He reloaded the rifle and shelved it, then grabbed a shirt from his room and went outside to wash. Cold water was just what he needed to douse the emotions churning in his gut. He'd not meant for Ella to see him without his shirt, but her gasp left no doubt that she'd gotten an eye full. He dragged both hands down his face and back through his hair. Of all the confounded lousy timing. He'd definitely made an impression on her. Twice. And neither were for the better.

The scent of freshly ground coffee beans hooked him by the nose and drew him inside. The boys all craned at the window, looking for their father.

Kip could barely see over the sill. "Did you get the devil grizzly, Uncle Cale?"

Helen's dish towel snapped the youngster's backside before Cale could answer. "I told you not to say that. Off with you all. Roll up your beds and wash your hands. We'll have breakfast soon."

The three trailed to the dining room, but Kip stalled at the doorway and looked back.

Cale gave his head a quick shake. No, they hadn't gotten the bear.

But neither had the bear robbed them this night. The tin cans he and Hugh had strung around the holding pen had alerted Tug whose urgent barking dragged Cale from his room.

Again he'd shot into the dark, aiming for the snuffling, ambling sounds. A blamed fool thing to do.

Crammed around the kitchen table a half hour later, the boys finished off most of Helen's hotcakes and sausage. His gut was in such a knot, he had no room for her fine cooking. Floating in coffee, he kept an eye on the doorway to the dining room, but Ella didn't fill it. When a ruckus outside set off Tug again, he shot from the table, grabbed the gun from the rack, and rushed out through the front door with the boys on his heels.

They were earlier than he expected.

Two motorcars rattled up the ranch road and pulled into the picketed area they'd used three days ago. Thank the Lord for small favors.

Thorson, the cameraman, and several others climbed out. So did Mabel Steinway. He turned for the barn, passing his red-faced brother on the way. On second thought, Hugh might send 'em all off in a cloud of blue thunder.

Cale reversed himself and joined the bunch as Hugh began to unload. The ranch needed the money.

121

"Thorson." Cale threw the word over his brother's shoulder with as much goodwill as possible. "Glad to see you again. What are your plans for today?"

He pulled Ty close and ducked down. "Ask Helen to make more coffee and tell her the film folks are back. Eight of 'em."

Thorson's brow dipped, and he nodded at Cale's rifle. "Have you got trouble up here, or are you just unhappy to see us?"

Cale slid it through his hand, butt end to the ground. "Nothing we can't handle. Come on up to the house. Helen's got a fresh pot of coffee cooking."

The director made a show of thumbing his belt, leaning back, and drawing in a deep breath. "What air you have up here. Why, I could bottle this and sell it in Chicago."

Hugh spit.

Cale forced a laugh. "I imagine you could. It'll cure what ails you."

Mabel pushed away from the car where she'd been leaning and batted smoky eyes as she sashayed by.

Jed wasn't in the group. Shame.

Hugh stomped off to the barn.

Cale indicated the house with his free hand, and Thorson took the bait, telling everyone to stay outside and get ready. Mabel slipped ahead and beat them through the screen door.

"What a quaint kitchen you have." She trailed her fingers along the smooth surface of the old table. "And something smells divine."

Helen gave her a quick once-over with a muffled remark and poured her and Thorson each a cup of coffee.

"Why, thank you. Helen, is it? I seem to recall that name from the other day. However do you stand living out here so far from town?" Black eyes peered over the rim of the tin mug as she sipped.

Ella entered from the dining room and lightning hit.

Mabel raised her nose and sniffed, tossing her bushy curls.

"Ella. I'd completely forgotten about you." A smirk pulled her lips as her gaze swept from boots to bobbed hair. "Have fun?" A cutting laugh. "Surely you didn't try *riding*."

Standing so near, Cale felt the electricity fire between them. "Surely she did."

Ella's face reddened. Mabel's nose increased in altitude.

It wouldn't be gentlemanly to hogtie a leading lady, especially in front of the director. "And a fine job of it she did."

Mabel sashayed closer and rubbed her hand up his arm.

"Well, I'm sure you had something to do with that, Cale darling. A strong cowboy like yourself wouldn't let a crippled girl fall off her horse."

Helen slammed a pot on the stove so hard that Mabel yanked her hand back and sloshed the coffee in her mug.

Cale's hands clenched.

Thorson finished his cup with a swig. "Well, let's get at it, Hutton. We've got a runaway scene to shoot. Let me have a look at that horse you mentioned." He jerked his head toward the door. "Mabel. Get your makeup on."

With a swing of her hip, Mabel followed him out the door.

Too late, Cale realized his defense of Ella might be misconstrued. As if he also saw her as a cripple. He saw her as anything but.

Ella smoothed her hands down the front of her riding skirt. Spine stiff and shoulders square, she joined Helen at the stove without a glance his way.

His throat jammed with words. He might not get another chance to speak with her before she left, but he couldn't sort his thoughts. He reached for her shoulder, thought better of it, and turned for his hat.

On his way out the door, he looked back. She stood with her head down, the bob swinging against her jaw like a curtain, hiding her face.

Ella had known Cale and Helen for only two days, yet both had stood up to Mabel on her behalf. What did a person say to that kind of friendship?

Still, she didn't need people coming to her rescue. She could handle Mabel. Though maybe not as forthrightly as Helen with her pots and skillets. A giggle escaped.

"Did you see the look on that painted face?" Helen shook her head. "I never saw such a flauntin' fluff, not even when Ben and I were at the World's Fair, bless his soul."

Without her marcel iron, Ella's fringe hung in her eyes. She brushed it away, considering Helen's surprise if she saw a truly painted face, ready for the camera. "She's an actress—accustomed to people admiring her."

"I'd like to see that floozy ride a horse herself."

Envy darted through Ella, tearing a tiny hole on its way. "She rides quite well, really. In fact, she does most of her own stunts, other than when Mr. Thorson wants a runaway scene. Then he dresses Slim in her clothes and a wig."

A sudden realization darkened her mood. Jed hadn't joined them in the kitchen. Was he even here?

Helen slammed a lid on her roasting pan and slid it in the oven. She'd made three pies the day before, anticipating the crew. Another delectable meal would cover the table tonight, but Ella would not be there to enjoy it. A part of her regretted that fact.

"Excuse me, but I'm going to see if Mr. Thorson needs my help with the costumes."

"You go on and take care of what it is you do. And shoo those boys off if they get under foot."

Ella didn't feel as fresh as she'd like, three days in the same clothes. But she felt stronger. No doubt the activity and fresh air contributed to that.

With fewer halting steps than before, she made her way to the corral where Cale was saddling a dark horse she didn't recognize. Jed was nowhere to be seen, and suspicion wedged its way into her thoughts. It would be just like Mabel to deliberately sabotage his appearance today so Cale or Hugh would be forced to fill in.

Slim stood by, already dressed in Mabel's costume—identical to the one she was wearing. He'd dusted his face with powder and pinned a wig on his head.

Hanging over a corral post were Jed's shirt and scarf and his signature Stetson. Everything had been taken care of without Ella's help. As if she were unnecessary. Suspicion grew.

Pete waited in position with his camera, several hundred yards down the ranch road. From the looks of the setup, Slim would begin the ride here at the corrals, then race toward Pete.

Thorson approached as Slim mounted. "Can this horse run?" He appeared doubtful, circling the placid animal as if checking for signs of life.

Hugh and Cale exchanged a look, and again she sensed their unspoken communication. Hugh's eyes sparked, dangerously cold.

Cale merely tugged his hat down. "He'll run."

"Well, I certainly hope so." Mabel sniffed and planted her hands at her waist. "It won't be much of a runaway if the horse doesn't run. And quite honestly, this animal is half asleep."

Ella agreed, as distasteful as that agreement was. The bay stood with its eyes half closed, ears splayed, and one back leg cocked. But the look on Cale's face sent a tingling sensation up her back. She'd seen that same light in his eye the day before when he challenged her to ride back to the house.

The show was about to begin.

Cale called an old dog out of the barn. He and Hugh separated to either side of the bay's hind quarters and removed their hats. A quick nod. A sharp whistle.

The dog took to the bay's heels and the brothers slapped their hats on its rump and hollered.

"Y'ha!"

125

The horse reared and bolted. Poor Slim's head snapped back like a whip, and she feared the wig would fly off and they'd have to start over. But Slim had the good sense to reach up and grab it before he went to flailing his arm and acting like he was scared to death.

At least she thought he was acting.

Mabel stared after the horse, her jaw slack.

Ella stifled a remark.

All the brothers—young and older alike—doubled over with laughter. It was the first time she'd seen Cale and Hugh on the same side of an issue.

Mr. Thorson and his assistant took off after Slim, careful to stay out of the camera's view frame. She couldn't imagine what the director thought he was going to do, but halfway to the cameraman, he stopped, evidently out of breath, and leaned against a rock outcropping.

Cale swung up on Doc and took off after the runaway. Hugh mounted and followed at a walk, and the boys and other actors ran along after them, leaving Mabel alone at the corral.

Ella joined her and gathered Jed's clothes. "I see Jed didn't make it today. Is he ill?"

Snapped out of her stupor, Mabel closed her tinted lips and regarded Ella with her usual disdain. The yellowish greasepaint she wore for filming fit her tone. "He wasn't feeling himself this morning."

Ella could imagine. More than likely a night sampling the local liquor and ladies had left him worse for wear. Then chagrinned by such unkind thoughts, Ella bit her tongue on further comment, and determined to be more generous and less judgmental. In spite of Jed's history.

Rather than walk the full length of the road, she chose to wait beneath the pine tree next to the house. With Jed's shirt and neckerchief over one arm, she donned his hat, found a small crate from the first day of filming, and carried it to the yard. Mabel did not join her. Nervous, Ella suspected, about filming the end of the chase scene on that horse.

The animal had certainly substantiated yesterday's remark about deceptive appearances. So did Mabel. Yet, if Mr. Thorson chose Cale for the rescuer, deceptive or not, Mabel was in good hands.

Jealousy reared its hateful head and nearly bolted with her good sense. She knew what the setup entailed. Cale would wrap his arm around Mabel's waist. Snatch her from the running horse. Hold her close against his body in the saddle.

Ella thought she might be sick right there in the yard. She turned the crate on end, seated herself, and took several deep breaths, blowing them out slowly through tight lips.

She knew the strength of those arms. The refuge of his hard chest. Her pulse raced like the bay, but she held to her outward calm. No better than Mabel, she was just as practiced in deception, an art she had perfected over the last fifteen months.

In spite of her earlier anger with Cale for manipulating her into riding Barlow, she wanted to preserve that day as something just between the two of them. She did not want to share his attentions with Mabel Steinway, whether he was chosen for a scene or not.

As if he were hers to share or not.

A sharp pang knifed between her ribs.

The only thing she had to share was her skill as a seamstress. Was it enough?

CHAPTER FOURTEEN

Cale had seen some fancy riding in his day—Grace was always willing to show off for the family and anyone who would watch—but Slim sure enough looked like a female floundering on a runaway horse. Trouble was the fella didn't have much of a whoa.

Cale caught up with him before he made the turnoff to the county road. Ol' Snake had nearly winded himself, but he'd be fine soon enough. Finer still for an easier run with Mabel. But Cale had yet to see hide or hair of Jed Barr, and he was beginning to get a funny feeling in his gut.

Galloping alongside his "sleeper" horse, he reached for its bridle, then slowed Doc to a lope. "Whoa there, Snake. Easy, fella."

Familiar with Cale's voice, the gelding quickly matched Doc's stride and eased down to a trot. Cale took the reins and they circled around and back to Thorson.

Slim was gray as goose down.

Cale almost felt guilty. "That was quite a ride."

"You're telling me." More winded than his mount, the man grabbed the front of his dress, clawing for air. Then he pulled his wig off, flinching visibly as pins snagged in his own hair. "This is some horse you've got. Ever race him?"

The question tugged a grin across Cale's face as he recalled a lap 'n tap race at the county fair. "Some."

"Well, my money's on him if I'm ever around for the race."

"You volunteering to jockey?"

"No, sir. One ride on this Pegasus is enough."

If Cale's memory served him right, Pegasus was a white horse. But he doubted color was what weighed on Slim's mind.

He reined in near Thorson and the cameraman. Slim hunted the ground.

The director slapped the fella on his thin back. "Best you've ever done! And Pete got the whole thing."

Slim stepped out of his dress and rolled it around the wig. "Good thing, 'cause I got only one of those rides in me today."

Thorson guffawed but quickly sobered as he took in the bay standing calm and droopy-eared. He narrowed his eyes at Cale. "You got any more unlikely surprises around here?"

"Not if Jed Barr is half the horseman I hear he is."

Thorson coughed and ran a hand over his mouth and exchanged a glance with his assistant. "About that."

Dadblastit. He turned Doc toward the barn. Snake followed meekly.

"Hold on there, Hutton." Thorson lumbered after him.

He *was* holding on. Holding on to his horses and his temper.

Harsh coughing—more like choking—turned his head to find the heavyset man braced on his knees sucking air. Cale stopped. He didn't need a heart attack on his hands. The hospital was a good twelve miles away.

Pete and Slim joined them but didn't look too worried, as if Thorson's wheezing fits were a common occurrence.

The director wiped his mouth and straightened. "Jed couldn't make it today, so we won't be filming a branding."

Good thing, because no cow-calf pairs had been brought up.

"But I need to film the rescue end of this runaway scene. Pete'll splice the film together and it'll look like the real deal."

Cale nudged Doc on.

"You could stand in for Jed."

"No."

Footsteps scuffled behind. "It's not more than a two-minute shoot."

"No."

Thorson caught up and puffed along beside him.

Cale considered squeezing Doc into a trot, but the man was already red-faced again. He reined in, surprising Thorson into a sudden stop. "What about your actors? You've got several here that would work just fine."

"I'll pay you extra."

That was a low blow. Cale considered himself above being bought, but things had been tight the last couple of years. Too tight. *Two minutes?*

He failed to mask a growl. "Two minutes."

"Wonderful! You won't be sorry." Thorson brightened considerably. "And you'll be famous. Why, when the towns people learn a local rancher pulled off the stunt, they'll be asking for your autograph."

Cale snorted outright. The only thing he wanted to sign was a paid-off bank note. "I'd just as soon they didn't know."

"Fine, fine." Thorson swatted the air. "Anything you say." He sent Pete a few yards down the road. "Slim, take your makeup over to the pine tree and get Mr. Hutton's face and neck powdered for the scene."

Cale bristled. The day he wore face powder would be a cold day in he—

The sight of Miss Canaday hidden by an oversized hat like an imp beneath a toadstool cut his thought in half. He wanted nothing more than to sit and talk with her.

Mabel approached, her face plastered with yellow cream and her eyes rimmed with even more kohl than before. "Can you save me from that wild bronco, cowboy? Like you saved someone else on Main Street?"

How'd she know about that?

Miss Canaday's wide hat brim blocked his view of her face, but her rigid posture said she was as shocked as he was. If Thorson hadn't offered to pay him, he'd take off to the ridge. Leave 'em all to figure it out on their own. Get Hugh to do the ride.

That'd be the day.

Mabel and Thorson must have planned this whole thing and left Jed behind on purpose. He ground his teeth more at being set up than at her ghastly appearance.

"He's no bronc, he just likes to run." With a little encouragement.

He dropped Doc's reins to the ground and headed for the yard.

Miss Canaday busied herself with a gabardine shirt he recognized from that fateful day in town.

Mabel reached out to touch Doc, but the gelding was havin' none of it and tossed his head.

Duly snubbed, Mabel whirled and snatched the hat from Ella's head, then held it up for him. Doc didn't like that move either and side-stepped with his ears pinned flat against his skull.

"See if this fits you. You'll need to wear it when you rescue me from that horse." A little fear joined the kohl around her eyes as she regarded Snake.

"I've got a hat."

"But you need to look like Jed." She dipped her chin and batted her eyes up at him. "Please? For little ol' me?"

Miss Canaday clapped her hand over her mouth, and Cale had a notion to plain ol' clap Mabel Steinway. Tarnation, he was losing his manners.

Slim approached with an apologetic expression and what looked like a powder puff.

"Ella." Thorson wheezed. "Get Mr. Hutton set up with Jed's shirt and hat, and we'll get this scene finished and come back another time for the branding."

The way Cale saw it, Jed Barr was costing his boss a lot of money. Didn't chap Cale's hide none. Another day, another dollar. Tomorrow he'd have those cow-calf pairs corralled and ready to brand.

But at the moment he was taken by the rosy brand on Ella Canaday's face and the way her dark eyes churned his insides. Maybe he'd just sweep her into the saddle with him and leave Thorson, Mabel, and everyone else behind.

And maybe he could fly.

~

Mortified that Mabel knew of her mishap on Main Street, Ella's jaw tightened. As tight as Jed's shirt would be on Cale Hutton. Anyone with eyes in his head could see it wouldn't fit, and there wasn't one thing Ella could do about it. Again, she appeared as if she'd failed at her job. And again, it was all because of Mabel and her manipulations.

Ella shook out the gabardine, praying it would miraculously stretch across Cale's chest and at least reach his wrists.

He watched Slim's powder box like a snake watches a mouse.

"Sorry about this, Mr. Hutton, but the camera sees things differently than we do." Slim nervously cleared his throat. "You need powder on your face to even out your skin tone."

Cale ignored him, Mabel, and everyone else, locking eyes on Ella. In three long strides he stood before her as stalwart as the pine, smelling of horse and man and strength. His expression said he wasn't at all pleased with the turn of events but he didn't hold it against her. Clearly, a double message, but she couldn't quite make out the meaning of the other half.

"You'll need to take your shirt off." Flames shot through her insides and burst out across her face and neck. Such discomfort never occurred at the studio. Or on other locations with the regular actors. They didn't stand before her like a giant child, waiting for her to tell them to disrobe.

She'd already seen him bare-chested. Or maybe it was his brother's physique that had burned onto the inside of her eyelids. But it had been in private—if she could call the dining room private. He'd have no undershirt, not during these warm summer months. Lord, help her. How long could she hold her eyes on the piped yoking and pearl snaps of Jed's shirt?

He tossed his vest and chambray on the crate.

Slim saved her from embarrassment.

"Close your eyes and mouth." He hit Cale with a full puff and quickly worked it across his face, ears, and neck.

Ella rolled her lips and swallowed a laugh at his scrunched-up face. The three little Hutton boys had nothing on their uncle.

He blustered and blinked and reached for the gabardine, brushing her fingers. The act drew her eyes to his. Just as she'd feared, he was reading her as if she were a script in his hand.

"Slim is right." She took a deep breath. "You can get by without the greasepaint because you won't have a close-up shot in the chase. But without the powder, your skin will appear darker than it really is and blotchy."

He stared at her, a muscle flexing in his powdered jaw. The powder flattened his weathered tan to the sickly yellow-white that would film more naturally.

"It washes right off."

He slipped his arms into Jed's shirt, tugged at the collar, and started with the first snap. A two-inch gap guaranteed no connection. Moving on to the next one, he dropped his chin to watch what he was doing. No luck. The next snap connected. Barely. And the next one and the next until he had most of the shirt front fastened.

She matched opposite corners of the brown silk neckerchief and handed it to him, resisting the urge to reach around his neck and join the ends herself.

As he tied it on, his perusal unnerved her. Clearly, his candid regard caused him no concern, and he continued to openly watch her. Inwardly she squirmed, as if caught in the camera's eye. What did he want? He was pressing again. Just like in the pasture two days before. Did he think she understood the silent speech he so often used with Hugh? Did he think her a mind reader? If so, he spoke a language she did not understand. At least not completely.

Her heart pounded against her ribs. She stepped back and crossed her arms to hold the hammering beast inside. He picked up the hat she'd worn moments before and tugged it down.

All wrong. The camera could not be fooled. Jed would tip his hat to a jaunty angle.

She moved closer and reached up for the brim, cocking it to one side for a roguish look. And while she was there holding her breath, she might as well adjust the neckerchief so it covered the open shirtfront. Not that it would stay put in the wind of the ride, but it made her feel somewhat better to have him covered.

She retreated again and filled her lungs, at the same time considering the man before her. His stature. His unsmiling face, stern jaw—and too short sleeves. Oh dear. She took one arm and tugged on the sleeve as if by pure will she could lengthen it to cover his wrists.

And the boots. She looked at Mabel, who sat atop the bay a bit paler than before. "Did you bring Jed's boots?"

The leading lady scoffed. "Don't be ridiculous. They'd never fit Cale." Leaning down, she added in less than a stage whisper, "And just so you know, Miss *Hobble*-skirt, your days here are numbered."

Ella froze. What had Mabel said to Mr. Thorson while Ella's absence? Forcing herself to focus on the scene, she again checked Cale's attire. Pete would simply have to shoot a tight frame and leave the boots out of the picture. If that were even possible.

Mr. Thorson blasted through her worry with a boisterous interjection, laid out his plan for Mabel and Cale, and had them walk out to the road and take up their positions with Mabel in the lead. He waved his hat at Pete who remained at his earlier position and waved in return.

"Roll film!" he yelled.

Ella flinched.

He turned to Mabel. "Action!"

Mabel kicked the bay and shot off with Cale and Doc deliberately in her wake. Not as fast as Slim's ride, but a good pace just the same.

Ella stumped to the road, dreading what she might see. But she could not look away, as if she were watching a burning house—full of wonder and agony at the power of the flames and the overwhelming loss.

Halfway to Pete, Cale came alongside Mabel and pulled her from the bay's saddle and into his own. She flung her arms around his neck, and her full skirt whipped around the both of them. Cale reined Doc in just past Pete, who followed the action.

"Cut!" Thorson waved his hat again, completely ignored by Pete, who continued filming.

Even from this far away, Ella imagined the tension between Mabel and Cale.

The rescuer successfully saving the lady in distress.

Her overwhelming gratitude.

Ella's hands balled into fists. This was the stuff of moving-picture romance, the lure that drew viewers to the theatre.

The moment when every woman's heart stopped.

Ella's eyes closed, yet still she saw the heroine's hands reach for the hero's face. She pulled him closer . . .

Turning on her left foot, Ella hobbled to the crate, where she gathered Slim's costume and came as close to running as she had in more than fifteen months. Again, Mabel got what she wanted. And this time, it was what Ella wanted.

CHAPTER FIFTEEN

Stunned, Cale pulled back from Mabel's garish face, and she slipped through his hands. Doc whinnied and danced away from the woman sprawled beneath him.

Thorson hadn't said one blasted thing about kissing, and it better not be on the film. Doggone it, Cale had never tossed a gal off a horse, but this beat all. He jumped down and helped her up.

Pete ran over. "You all right, Miss Steinway?"

She sliced Cale up one side and down the other, then turned on the cameraman. "Tell me you did not get that on film."

"I-I got the whole thing, ma'am. Just like always."

She stomped her foot. "That last part, you idiot."

His face blanched and he pulled at his collar and shied toward the camera. "Uh, no, ma'am. When you were getting off just now? No. I, uh, didn't film that. No, ma'am."

Ten to one he had, but Cale didn't make a habit of throwing good money after bad. "Sorry, Miss Steinway. I didn't intend to drop—"

"You!" The word shot like a bullet and hit him right between his eyes. She whirled and stomped away to the cars.

Looked like filming was done for the day. That'd save him the trouble of refusing any more of Thorson's harebrained ideas.

Pete folded up his camera contraption and headed down the road toward the house. Thorson, Slim, and a few others stood out front. Ella was gone. Maybe she had seen what happened.

Dear Lord, he hoped his brother hadn't seen it either. He'd never hear the end of it.

Snake had moseyed off the road and into the lower pasture, grazing his way toward the hills. Cale swung up and rode after him, gathered his reins, and turned back for the barn. Yes, he needed the money this filming crew brought with it. But no, he didn't need the aggravation. And yes, he wanted to spend more time with Ella Canaday, but no, he probably wouldn't get to.

As he rode into the yard, past the filming crew, and on to the barn, Hugh leaned against the wall, one boot cocked against it and his hat tipped back. Cale would knock him out if he said a word.

He didn't, for once. Just took Snake's reins, stripped the tack, and led him to the pasture.

On his way to the house, Cale yanked Jed's hat and scarf off, and intended to do the same with the shirt. But that would make more work for Ella if he tore something. Instead he peeled it off and dropped everything in the crate, then took his own clothes around back to the wash tub. He'd prefer a dip in the creek, but Helen's bar soap and towel on the porch made short work of the powder. Just like Ella said.

After he finished, he walked around to the front, where Pete, Thorson, and the rest of the men were laughing and shaking their heads. He was certain he knew the topic of discussion.

"Thorson." He joined them with a change of subject. "What time you comin' back tomorrow for the branding?"

"Day after. And the earlier, the better, if that works for you. With a good take, we'll be out of your hair." He offered his hand. "Fine job today. Fine job."

"Just make sure those *two minutes* are in the check." A hard glare and harder grip underscored his point.

The back screen door slapped, and Kip ran around the end of the house. "Miss Helen needs help with the table and then everyone can have pie and cookies."

Two of Thorson's men hoofed it inside and returned with the table. The boys and Helen followed, loaded down with her handiwork. While Thorson rubbed his hands together like he was about to sit down to a feast, Cale retreated to the big pine and waited for Ella.

She finally showed up with a stack of tin cups in one arm, the coffee pot in her hand, and a hitch in her walk. She started with Thorson and made the rounds, giving each man a cup and then filling it. He palmed his jaw, reminding himself he hadn't shaved that morning. No wonder Slim had thrown powder on him.

By the time Ella made it to him, the pie was gone. He'd get the bottom of the pot too, more than likely on purpose, but he wasn't sure why. Could be she was still mad about yesterday's ride home.

He straightened as she approached and thumbed his hat back for a clear view. Her hair teased her eyes, and his hand itched to push it aside before he thought better of it. Instead he accepted her last cup and the thick brew that only half-filled it. She turned away before he could think of what to say, and limped back to the house.

Confounded woman.

After every last crumb was cleaned up, Thorson signaled two men to take the table in. Everyone else headed for the automobiles, and Cale planted a foot on the lone crate, determined to catch Ella before she left.

And then he saw her making her way across the road with Jay beside her. She'd gone out the front door, favoring her right leg like she had her first day at the ranch. He couldn't figure. Yesterday she'd had hardly a catch in her gait, and now she limped like a saddle-sore cowpoke.

He started after her, but doubt hobbled him. Only a fool would miss that she'd intentionally avoided him. If he stopped her, what would he say?

Mainly, he just wanted to know if she was coming back for the branding. And if she'd ever forgive him for tricking her into riding Barlow.

He pulled his hat off, ran his hand through his hair, and re-set it. This was not how he'd hoped things would go.

The motorcars cranked and sputtered and rattled off down the road with the boys and Tug chasing after them nearly to the turn off. He headed for the barn, where he adjusted Doc's saddle and swung up.

The rest of the day he spent doing what he knew best—cowboyin' in the quiet of the mountain parks. Green and sprouting fiery Indian paintbrush and yellow buffalo bur, the parks opened around him like welcoming arms, giving up a dozen cow-calf pairs and a couple of maverick steers that he and Hugh trailed back to the corrals. The familiar thud of hooves on dirt, grit on his teeth, and an occasional bawl raised a reassuring barrier that insulated him from the crazy world of automobiles and crowds and clamor. He had more than enough to fill his days without worrying after some gal who avoided him. Who'd soon enough be going back home to the city.

Early that evening, the corral gate squawked shut behind the last cow and dust hung still and thick, no breeze to send it off. He rode around the barn and cut across open country for the south ridge and a clear perspective.

Some things a man could count on. Like spring calving and summer thunderstorms and the narrow valley before him, cut in two by the road to town. It lay clear and quiet with no sign of wagon or motorcars, as empty as he felt.

A troublesome ache throbbed behind his ribs. Something was missing, and he feared he knew exactly what it was.

A jay flagged by and Doc swiveled an ear, either dislodging a fly or detecting a scurry in a nearby thicket. Cale stood in the stirrups, stretching his legs, then settled and turned for home. From what he'd seen of Thorson's filming in the last week, the cameraman wouldn't need more than a few minutes of action from the branding. Shouldn't take more than a couple hours and then, as Thorson had put it, the whole bunch would be out of his hair.

And Cale'd be right back where he was before the whole moving-picture brigade stormed Cañon City. Right where he should be. Giving more time and thought to the Rafter-H.

A spot on his chest twitched, and he dug in a knuckle. Focus was what he needed. Focus on building the herd, finding the rustlers or bear or whatever was steeling cattle. He needed to meet with the sheriff and other ranchers and come up with a unified plan of attack.

And enter the upcoming rodeo. With the sheriff, that made two reasons to ride into town.

Three, if he counted a wisp of a woman who'd crossed his track and left spur-marks on his hide.

~

Ella gripped the polished railing with her left hand, and with her right, lifted her leg to the next stair. At this rate, she'd be exhausted by the time she got to her room, but she refused to take the elevator. Thankfully, Thorson had called it a day and taken everyone to the café, not noticing as she slipped out the side door of the studio and hobbled to the hotel.

More than ever before, she needed to soak in the bathing tub. Every part of her ached, particularly her soul, and she deeply resented it. She had no business reacting as she had to Cale Hutton and his stunning blue eyes. None whatsoever, particularly since she and the troupe would be leaving as soon as filming was complete.

At the landing turn, she paused to catch what little breath she had left. Eight more steps before she reached her floor. Closing her eyes momentarily, she tightened her grip and saw again the predictable ending to the rescue scene. At least she hadn't photographed it.

With a start, her eyes flew open and she reached for her satchel strap, craning her neck for a view of the hotel lobby. Had she left it at the foot of the stairs? Think. She must think. She had not photographed the scene for several reasons: it was not a still shot and she couldn't bear to see Cale and Mabel in the same frame. All right, two reasons.

The last time she remembered handling her satchel, she'd set it on the bureau in the boys' room. All the glorious relief at finally arriving at the hotel whooshed out on a groan. How could she have left her camera behind? And her needles and thread. What had she been thinking?

Pain darted through her leg, reminding her quite clearly of what she'd been thinking. Or rather, about whom she'd been thinking. And with no telephone at the ranch, she had no way of contacting anyone there short of making another trip.

She could not afford to buy a second camera on her meager salary. Besides, the one in her satchel held all the photographs she'd taken since leaving Chicago—everything she'd promised to share with her grandmother upon her return. She'd simply have to wait until the day after tomorrow and pray the boys' curiosity didn't override good manners.

Oh dear.

Fatigue and disappointment weighed against her upward movement, but at finding her door ajar, worry dropped the proverbial back-breaking straw, and she sank beneath the blow.

Bedding lay on the floor. Chairs lay on their sides. Drawers had been emptied and clothing strewn from corner to corner. With her throat tight and hands trembling, she dropped beside the bed and reached underneath for her main sewing kit.

Gone.

Oh, Lord, no.

Despair pummeled her defenses with gale force, ripping into her very soul. She wept into the discarded coverlet, twisting it in her hands until anger supplanted angst. Who had done such a

141

spiteful thing? No hotel employee would create extra work for themselves or risk an ill report of a guest's privacy invaded and possessions stolen.

She had no jewels or money or wealth of any kind with her, other than the sentimental value of the kit, a necessary tool of her trade.

Only someone who hated her could be to blame. Someone who wanted to see her fail.

One name came to mind.

Gripping the posted footboard, she pulled herself upright, then gathered what she needed for a bath and locked her room, wondering why she bothered. But the Singer sewing machine remained unscathed, thankfully. If it were damaged, Mr. Thorson might hold it against her, deducting its cost from her wages. She'd have no recourse but to stumble home as a failure.

At the bathing room, another lock clicked—her jaw against the defeatist thought. Failure was not an option. She jammed the single chair beneath the doorknob as a precaution, and turned on the spigots for the soaking she craved.

"Lord, please show me what to do." Her words mixed with the splashing flow of running water and swirled into the rising steam, reminding her that her prayers did indeed rise to His ear.

The water received her like loving arms, enfolding her in an unconditional embrace. No judgment. No criticism, simply pure acceptance. Leaning her head on the copper lip, she closed her eyes against the longing of her heart—to be loved in such a way not only by her Lord, but by another.

Of course her Nana cared for her, perhaps her father in his own way, but their love was limiting. It squelched her independence, and their guardedness was especially stifling since the accident.

Peers? Yes, she wanted to be accepted, but she never felt quite like she belonged. She had not fit in with younger single women at home, and she did not fit in with the troupe. Not really. And Mabel reminded her over and over that she was an outsider.

A man? The water's warmth bled into her neck and face. Yes, again. She longed to be loved once more as Charles had loved her, in spite of her age, in spite of her father's fortune. For herself. But that was before her disfigurement and weakening. How foolish to think she would ever appeal to another man in her less-than-whole condition.

Without invitation, Cale Hutton's bold challenge in the pasture rose up, his daring grin and overwhelming presence that assured her he would have carried her back to the ranch house had she refused to ride the mare.

She sank lower and puffed out an irritated breath, rippling the water's surface. He had crossed the line of propriety. Pushed her in spite of her insistence. And done exactly the opposite of everyone else. Perhaps it was his rancher's wisdom that looked past her shortcomings and into her soul.

Dipping her head beneath the water, she rubbed her scalp, ridding her hair of the last reminder of ranch life—a life entirely different from hers. Cale lived here and she did not. He would stay behind when she left. Their lives were as different as . . .

Lard and butter. She rose from the water, his phrase pulling a smile from her lips. His acceptance of her, in spite of their differences, was like sweet butter on one of Clara's perfect biscuits. If only she could look forward to such a life with such a man.

Stepping carefully from the tub, she toweled her hair and tied on her wrapper, acknowledging God's full acceptance of her, His perfect care in spite of any turn of events. He was the one constant in her life, and that realization loosed her tears again. But this time they were not tears of despair, but of gratitude.

~

The next morning, Ella woke with resolve in her heart and strength coursing through her leg. The pain had lessened considerably. She credited all the walking she'd done at the ranch, as well as last night's long, hot soaking.

And that ride in the pasture?

"Let's not jump to unlikely conclusions." The woman in the dressing-table mirror quickly squelched the fanciful idea, and Ella noted the set of her jaw. Just the determination necessary for addressing Mr. Thorson about the theft of her sewing kit.

Dressed, marcelled, and armed with courage resulting from a good night's sleep, she managed the stairs with considerable ease and made her way to the hotel's mouth-watering kitchen. Her empty stomach cried out for Clara's hot biscuits.

When the woman learned what had happened, she added a hearty side of indignation to the generous serving she set before Ella.

"Someone's up to no good, and if I get my hands on 'em before the sheriff, they'll be wishin' they was already in jail." She smacked her wooden spoon against a skillet's edge and sent a blob of its contents flying against the wall.

Ella had never felt so hardily supported. Seated at the small table against the kitchen wall, she bit into a fluffy biscuit and sighed audibly at the blend of honey and butter slathered on it and melting against her tongue. *Butter* would never again hold quite the same connotation.

Clara smiled with satisfaction.

Fearing the woman could read her mulling over butter and lard, Ella voiced a decoy. "I'll be thinking about these all day and not getting one thing done."

The sudden drop in Ella's tone turned Clara with a fist at her hip and a scowl between her dark eyes. Ella's intended compliment had degenerated into a confession that Clara *did* read.

"Was that rancher anything less than a perfect gentleman?"

Ella choked on biscuit crumbs and reached for the glass of orange juice set out with the baked goods. "Oh, yes—I mean no!" Swallowing the freshly squeezed goodness, she untangled her emotions and started with the most recent thread. "I'm referring to my work. I'll be hard-pressed to complete any mending today, and it's my own fault for not taking the whole kit with me to the ranch." But if she had, it would still be there in her satchel. With her camera.

Like the plot of a dramatic storyline, her insides twisted. She dabbed her mouth on a napkin. "It belonged to my grandmother, at whose knee I learned to ply a needle. It is nothing fancy or ingenious, but it helps keep her near." And aside from the company's Singer sewing machine set up in her room, it was all she had to make a living.

With another delectable bite, she considered confiding in Clara, telling her every evil thing Mabel Steinway had ever said and her suspicion that the leading lady was behind the theft. But her upbringing to not speak ill of others behind their backs prevailed. Gossip was still gossip, even if it were true.

Clara slid a roast into one oven compartment and two pies into another. Then she wiped her hands on her starched apron and disappeared into the pantry.

Oh, to be a bug on the wall, catching the Hotel Denton cook at work, photographing her skillful hands dusted with flour or pricking a pie for doneness or testing her thick sausage gravy.

If Ella got her camera back—and she must—she would do just that.

The idea straightened her back, and she studied the kitchen as if through the camera's lens. Morning light was best here, and she envisioned a collection of studies.

Clara's return and proffered gift snapped the shutter on her musing.

"Take this until you find yours." Large, capable hands dwarfed a small leather-bound packet.

"Oh, Clara, I couldn't possibly—"

"But you will. We can't have you losin' your job because some no-good, sticky-fingered thief took your stitchin' tools. What d'you suppose I'd do if some low-down scoundrel made off with my pots and spoons?"

A heavy *humph* punctuated the declaration as Clara returned to her work. Argument was obviously pointless.

The kit was even smaller than Ella's. Plainer, with no embossed covering. But such tenderness accompanied it that it warmed in her hands, softening the edges of her resentment.

"Thank you, Clara. You're a dear."

"Pshaw." The wooden spoon waved.

Ella slid the modest bundle into her skirt pocket and wrapped three biscuits in a napkin for later. "I'll ask Mr. Thorson today if he'd like to place an order for a pan or two of your biscuits. How much would you charge him?"

Another *humph* flopped bread dough out of a bowl and onto a floured board. "A dollar a pan and not a penny less."

A smile slid across Ella's mouth. Clara knew the value of her work and didn't mind asking a good sum for it. "A dollar it is."

She moved toward the door.

Clara stopped her with a sound just short of a cough.

"That trip to the ranch must have done you good. You're not limpin' like you was before."

Clara had never asked, and Ella had never mentioned the accident or her injury. She glanced over her shoulder to find the cook watching her closely. "It did, Clara." She raised the napkin-wrapped bundle. "Thank you again for the biscuits."

A clear yet unspoken invitation hung between them to do exactly what Ella had wanted to do a half dozen times. But not now. She must concentrate on the task at hand and any other surprises that might await her at the studio. If she could just focus on her reinvigoration rather than a certain rancher's blue gaze, she would surely accomplish a great deal this day.

~

"Uncle Cale! Uncle Cale!" Kip galloped toward him with a lopsided gait, dragging a leather bag Cale recognized with a pang of panic.

146

"Hold up there." He met Kip at the end of the corral and lifted the satchel from the boy's shoulder. The weight of it and the permanently molded bulge in the side suggested Ella's camera was inside. "Where'd you find this?"

"In our room." The youngster drew himself up to his highest point, proud of his discovery. "It's Miss Ella's. She left it behind."

A look inside confirmed his hunch and Kip's conclusion. "You're right." He squatted for an eye to eye discussion. "I think Miss Ella would be mighty pleased you found this for her."

Another inch worked into the short stature.

"What do you suppose we should do about it?"

"You need to take it to her. There's pictures of us inside that black box."

"You don't say." He straightened and ruffled the boy's hair that sorely needed to be cut. Frankly, he was surprised that Helen hadn't already corralled him on a stool in the kitchen with a bowl on his head for a good clipping.

He ran his hand through the mane at his own neck. Come to think of it, he could do with a visit to the barber. If he left now, he'd have time to stop at the sheriff's as well and make it back before supper.

"Seein' as how I got a couple errands to run in town, I'll get it to her and tell her you found it."

An ear-to-ear grin cut across the dirt-smudged face.

"But we'll keep this to ourselves here at home. Just you and me. Deal?" He didn't need Hugh chapping his hide about runnin' off on a fool's errand.

Jumping to a sense of importance rather than inquisition, Kip nodded soberly. "Just between us." He pinched his thumb and forefinger together and twisted as though turning a key to his mouth. "My lips are sealed."

"Good man." Cale wrapped the long strap around the bag for stowing in his saddle bags, but a shy question halted his turn for the barn.

"Might you be goin' to Ott's Candy Store while you're in town?"

An enterprising youngster if ever there was. Ty and Jay better keep an eye out. He rubbed his jaw in a thoughtful way. "Now that you mention it, I think I might. You got a preference?"

Another grin lit the boy's face. "Peppermint."

A wink and a nod sent him off in a dusty cloud. If only his father was as easy to please.

Cale continued to the barn to stow his parcel and prevent Hugh's questions from riling him into an ill humor.

But his brother was already gone. Riding for sign and weak fences, he guessed, after this morning's discussion over hotcakes and bacon.

He wasn't convinced that their raiding culprit was only a bear. His gut told him opportunistic rustlers were using the so-called Old Mose descendant as a cover.

Hugh had dismissed his opinion with a huff around a mouthful of berry-syrup-drenched hotcakes.

"There's too many raids," Cale argued. "Not to mention multiple hits on a single night. After what I found up the draw, I agree that a bear's involved. But it's not the lone culprit. And last time I checked, bears didn't hunt in packs."

Hugh shot him a goading look that said he might agree but he wasn't about to out loud.

The one thing they'd seen eye to eye on was driving the youngest pairs to the pastures closer to the house, and they'd already done that. So a trip to town made sense, especially when it came to checking in with the sheriff and getting word about other ranchers. He might even pick up some news at the barber shop. Hank knew everything.

And there was the rodeo to think about. He'd heard talk among the filming crew that Jed was planning to sweep the championship.

Cale let out a sharp snort. He'd be givin' the actor a run for his money where roping was concerned.

Doc took to the trail like they were on a mission. Probably had something to do with the rifle and scabbard Cale had strapped on before heading out. The horse had a second sense about these things.

So did Tug, and it took some stern shouting to get the old dog back to the house. Either it was deaf as a post or gettin' as stubborn as Hugh.

An hour later, Cale rode past the penitentiary and counted three motorcars in front of the Selig Polyscope studio storefront. At least they hadn't pulled up the picket line and moved on without coming back to the ranch for a branding.

Fighting the urge to ride up to the door, he skirted around to the alley behind Hank's barber shop, flipped Doc's reins on a hitching rail, and walked through the back door.

Jed Barr himself lay cocked back in a chair with his fancy boots aimed at the ceiling and his face full of lather.

CHAPTER SIXTEEN

Ella had spent entirely too much time enjoying Clara's cooking and company this morning and paid dearly for it. She stole in through the open front door of the studio, her entry covered by the vitriolic ranting of an uncharacteristically early leading lady.

"Have you seen her work? Have you really taken a close look at it? It's shoddy. Why, I could do as well myself. You're wasting money on her salary."

Mr. Thorson met Ella's eyes in a glance over Mabel's shoulder. The actress whirled and pointed, her outstretched arm stiff and judgmental. "See? She sneaks around and eavesdrops on people's conversations too."

Ella's fingers crushed into the biscuits, and she strode to the costume area where she dropped the flattened bundle and Clara's kit on the table before facing her accuser.

"She didn't have to sneak, Mabel." Thorson's gaze rolled to the ceiling. "I'm sure everyone on this end of town heard you through the open door."

The actress's face reddened and her arms locked across her waist as she glared at Ella. "Well, what do you have to say for yourself?"

Much more calmly than she felt, Ella took a step forward and addressed Mr. Thorson. "Someone ransacked my room at the hotel while I was gone and stole my sewing kit." Meeting Mabel's dark stare, she continued. "I have borrowed one until mine can be found, so I'll be able to carry on with my duties."

"And you think I took it? How dare you!"

The director's arm shot out to prevent Mabel's advance and he stepped between the two of them. "She didn't say that, Mabel. Calm down."

Ella stiffened her back and held her tongue. She would not be cowed by theatrics. But neither would she make accusations based purely on suspicion, in spite of the fact that Mabel's leap to a conclusion shed even clearer light on the matter.

"If you don't fire her, I'm quitting. *Quitting,* I tell you."

Thorson rubbed his forehead, darting a look at Ella. "We've got work to do. A saloon scene and other indoor shots. Can you get by with what you have?"

"Yes, sir. Undoubtedly."

Mabel sniffed and tossed her curls.

"You need to get your mind on your work, Mabel. I expect the two of you to hash this out between yourselves and be ready in ten minutes for the job at hand." He made for the back of the studio as if fiends were on his heels.

Ella stood her ground.

Mabel raised her chin with a dramatic flair before following Thorson. "You're finished here."

So much for hashing things out.

A replaceable costume designer and seamstress had much less pull with the studio than the leading lady, but Ella would not go down without a fight. Crippled or not.

A familiar pain pulsed through her thigh but with less of a razor's edge. She draped her suit jacket over a hanger and sorted the men's shirts. A bar-room scene meant a brawl, but likely only Jed and one or two others would be damaging their clothing. She gathered a half-dozen shirts as Thorson and others came in from the back.

It took mere minutes to arrange furniture and a backdrop into a change of scenery. The large open area was suddenly a saloon with round tables and curved-back chairs, poker chips and card decks, shot glasses and bottles full of tea. Pete set up his screens to reflect daylight from the windows directly onto the set.

"Where is Jed?" Thorson's voice rang through the building.

"At the barber." Jed's unwitting friend tried ducking Thorson's bullet glare, an unexpected recompense for his information.

They could not film the scene without the leading man, but the director's ill mood said otherwise.

"You." He jabbed a finger at the unfortunate cowboy. "Stand in for him. Over there."

Rising rather cheerfully to the occasion, the man moved into position.

"Ella. Woolies for this man here."

From her collection she produced three pair of chaps: angora goat, haired cowhide, and tanned leather. All were claimed.

Locals began arriving to fill in the background. She showed them where to sit and traded out hats and coats with some of the more well-dressed individuals who appeared to be prominent businessmen in the community.

Thorson and his assistant walked the actors through the fight scene, reminding them to throw broad, round-house punches, respond with exaggerated facial expressions, and fall with overstated force.

Everyone took their places, Pete signaled his readiness, and Thorson's hand rose like a spire. "Roll cam—"

Jed Barr strode through the front door and everyone turned to look.

"Cut!"

Jed's friend took on a sheepish look, accentuated by the wooly chaps he immediately stripped off and handed over. Thorson swore under his breath, Pete shook his head, and Mabel examined her fingernails.

Several locals nodded to Jed as he passed. "Mr. Barr."

Remarkably, he called them each by name, cementing his popularity with the town's people. At least the men. Ella suspected a few members of certain female social circles did not utter his name with such deference.

A half hour later, the brawl was completed with only a handful of punches connecting with actual chins. Jed, a master at deflecting a flying fist, appeared unscathed other than a tear in the seam of his right shirt sleeve.

She collected it from him, halting as he spoke to her under his breath. "Saw the rancher at the barber shop."

His low-voiced comment sent her heartbeat into a flurry for no reason she could justify. The news stunted her movements as she gathered chaps, hats, and a pointed glare from Mabel, who left the room on Jed's arm, unaware of a wink over his shoulder to Ella.

Her pulse thrummed.

Rancher? Which rancher? Hugh didn't seem the type to ride into town just to visit the barber. But was Cale? Did he have business here? And if he were here, would he stop by the studio? Seek her out?

Ridiculous.

She puffed out a disgusted breath and piled the clothing on her table before stopping two gentlemen who attempted to leave the building in studio vests and coats.

Purely forgetful, they apologetically assured her. A matter of habit.

With a tight smile, she offered her thanks. Indeed. She'd heard it all before.

The crew dispersed for lunch. She dispersed the clothing and took her mauled biscuits to one of the gambling tables, where she claimed a chair facing the door. Just in case.

Finger indentations clearly marred the golden-topped mounds that resembled pancakes more than they did Clara's delectable biscuits. With a heavy sigh, she tore one in half and shoved it in her mouth. How good it would be with Helen's sliced beef and coffee.

A shadow dimmed the light pouring through the door, and she looked up in mid-chew.

The hat and vest said Cale, but the newly shaved jaw and trimmed hairline stirred doubts. Her half a biscuit enlarged, filling her mouth, throat, and mind with wordlessness.

"May I come in?" He sounded like Cale.

Choking, she covered her mouth with the napkin, and with her free hand waved him in. Nana would have a stroke at such manners.

He doffed his hat and his dark hair shone. *Shone.* She tried to remember what Hugh's had looked like at the dinner table but could dredge up only the man's scowl.

"Mind if I sit down?"

Where was a good hole in the floor when she needed one?

Cale nearly gouged his cheek clamping down a laugh at Ella's shock. Laughter would add nails to his already lidded coffin, not help him resurrect a conversational tone with her. Pretty as ever, her cheeks got all pink as she swallowed. A couple of pitiful-looking biscuits lay on the table, and she brushed at the crumbs.

"Pardon me. You caught me with my mouth full." She swept a look his way and his insides tumbled.

Smelling too much of Bay Rum No. 4, he palmed his jaw. "Thought I'd get a shave while I was in town visiting the sheriff."

Her brow wrinkled. "The sheriff? Is there trouble at the ranch?"

His decoy worked. "Same as we've had. But I want to know what other ranchers besides Harper are reporting. Maybe offer a reward for a successful bear hunt, or rustlers caught red-handed."

She shuddered, sinking his hopes. Due recompense for starting out with violence rather than what he'd intended.

He cleared his throat and fiddled with his hat. "You left something at the ranch, and I have it in my saddle bags."

Her face brightened like an electric light. "My camera satchel! You found it?"

"Kip did. Told him you'd be proud of him for bringin' it to me."

Relief softened her features, and she fingered the collar of her blouse. Her eyes flitted between him and the biscuits.

He screwed up his courage. "Thought you might enjoy a soda at the drug store, then I could return it to you." Out loud, his carefully planned words sounded more like a ransom than an invitation.

Fortunately, she took them at face value.

"That would be lovely."

Lovely? Did that mean she'd forgiven him?

She folded the biscuits into her napkin, left them on a table by the costume rack, and gathered a jacket that matched her green skirt.

Scrambling to not miss his opportunity, he took the jacket from her and held it as she slid one arm into it and then the other. Somewhere he'd heard ladies liked that sort of thing.

"It's not far from here. Just a few blocks."

She smiled up at him, and he doubted he could make it the whole way there without tripping over his spurs.

Outside, he offered his arm—something he'd seen his father do for his mother on Sunday mornings when they made it in for church. To his great surprise, Ella tucked her fingers in the crook of his elbow. His throat got tight. Maybe he'd been right to stop at Hank's before he came calling. Not that this was calling. Not exactly.

Shortening his stride, he matched her pace, which was nearly smooth. He'd like to think he'd played a part in helping her get stronger, though he was pretty sure she'd argue that point.

Palace Drug held down the corner of Sixth Street and Main, where he opened the door for her and followed her inside. A line of stools fronted the soda counter on their left, and a couple of tables huddled in front of the window. When she hesitated, he nodded toward a table and pulled out an iron-work chair for her, feeling just about as gentlemanly as he ever had. His shirt buttons pulled a little tighter.

"Thank you."

He sat facing the window, and she studied the store over his shoulder, looking everywhere but at him. He sure would like to hear her story if he could just figure how to get it out of her without prying. Unlike every other woman he'd been around, she was less than eager to talk about herself.

But he didn't do chit-chat. Just like he didn't run Helen's sewing machine. Probably stitch his fingers together, which was how he felt sittin' in a flimsy parlor chair with the need to make conversation. They'd come flying past here last week in his race against the buggy horse, but he highly doubted she'd want to talk about that.

It'd be a short soda if he didn't come up with something quick.

A girl in a striped apron took their order and asked if they'd like a pastry. Ella declined. He eyed the display case across from them and saw a couple things he'd like to try. Maybe next time.

The idea notched a bur under his skin. *Next time* meant she'd still be around, which she wouldn't be. And he sure enough didn't plan to sit in Palace Drug by himself any time soon.

He leaned back. "Been busy sewing and such since you got back to the studio?" Now there was a stirring bit of conversation if he'd ever heard it.

She frowned and considered the table before raising dark worried eyes. "Someone broke into my room at the hotel."

He leaned forward, his shoulders tightening, ready to find the culprit and work him over. "Did you report it?"

She ran a hand under the back of her bobbed hair. "I told a few people."

"The hotel manager? The sheriff?"

156

She puffed out a breath with a nervous glance. "I think I know who did it."

Their sodas arrived, and he cooled his temper with a long sip through the straw sticking out of his glass. His free hand clenched in his lap. He'd like to catch the scoundrel. "That much more reason to report it."

She twirled her straw between her thumb and forefinger, first one way and then the other, twisting his gut into a knot.

"Who do you think it was?"

Leaning in, she measured him with a look before lowering her voice to a whisper. "I shouldn't say because I have no proof."

Intuition. Helen ruled by it. "You just know, don't you." Like he just knew when the herd was in trouble.

Her glance confirmed his suspicion.

He took a shot in the dark. "Mabel."

Quick as lightning, her fingers clamped around his sleeve. "Shhh."

His arm flexed of its own accord.

She pulled away, but not without a warning glare. "I said I can't prove it. I just sense it."

If she sensed it as well as she sensed a good horse and how to handle it, she was right on the money. "Anything in particular that leads to the . . . *sense?*"

She picked up her glass and pulled the cold liquid through the straw, puckering her lips and spurring his thoughts off in the wrong direction. A flick of her pink tongue across those lips nearly unseated him.

He pulled his straw from the glass, crushed it in his fist, and gulped a mouthful. She didn't seem to notice.

"Whoever it was, they took my sewing kit. It's what I use on the set for repairs. But rather than take it with me the other day, I grabbed some needles and thread and hid the kit under the bed before leaving for the ranch."

Another dainty sip.

He looked away from her. Stared at a horse and buggy tied outside next to an automobile. Reviewed the number of cattle gone missing at the ranch.

"It wasn't a very good hiding place because the kit was the only thing missing."

He frowned, pushed his hat up, and rubbed his forehead. "Was it valuable? I mean, was it worth a lot of money?"

"No." She shook her head, and her hair swayed against her face in that way that made him want to run his hands through it.

"That's the thing. It's valuable only to me. It was my grand-mother's."

None of his business, but he had a hunch why she suspected Mabel.

She met his gaze and lowered her voice again. "Only some-one who wanted to see me fail would steal it."

"Favorite Dry Goods is a block away. I'm sure they've got one. I'll buy it for you."

His statement startled him as much as it did her.

She stared, then blinked. Twice. "No." She tugged on her jacket. "I mean, thank you, but that won't be necessary. Besides, I could never let you do something like that."

She lowered her gaze, and her face went all pink again. "I should be getting back."

He rose as she did, kicking himself for making her uncom-fortable. Much more of that, and she wouldn't give him the time of day much less tell him anything about herself. Like why she limped and why she took a job with Selig Polyscope. And why she wasn't married with a passel of kids.

He moved ahead of her to open the door.

She stopped with a glance his way.

"Thank goodness I didn't leave my camera in the room."

Camera. Right. His excuse for seeing her again. "Doc's wait-ing behind the barber shop. Just up the street."

He offered his arm, and once more she took it. If he could line his words out as easy as he bent his elbow, he'd make some progress. "I saw Jed there this morning."

Her fingers tightened and she took a moment before she said anything. "One of his friends almost got to play the lead in a bar brawl because he was late."

Figured. A no-show one day and late the next. He ground his teeth. If Barr worked for him, he'd fire his sorry hide. "Why does Thorson keep him around if he isn't dependable?"

"He has the looks."

He gave her a look of his own but caught only the top of her dark head.

"And he can ride. Trick ride, even. He has a good way in front of the camera."

Cale let go an opinionated grunt. Evidently, he did too, but only for two minutes.

"He's entering the rodeo, if we're still in town by then."

His turn to flinch. They couldn't leave already. He wanted to talk to her more and take her riding up on the ridge and . . .

Ott's Candy Store reared up on his right and he slowed. "I need to stop in here for Kip and his brothers. Sort of a reward for finding the camera."

She smiled, and he decided he'd buy her the whole store if she wanted it. If she'd let him.

Which she wouldn't. "After you."

She preceded him through the doorway and into a wall of irresistible aroma. Peppermint. Chocolate. Coconut. Caramel.

"Oh, but it smells delicious in here." Her shoulders scrunched and she stopped at the glass-topped counter.

"What strikes your fancy?"

Her bob began to sway. "No—"

"Can't very well buy for the boys and leave you out, now can I?" A weak argument, but doggone it, he wanted to get her *something*.

A smile teased her lips. She eased along the case, halting briefly in front of a tray of chocolate balls. *Bonbons*, a small card read.

He caught the eye of the man behind the counter and held up four fingers. "In two bags. Two in a bag." Helen deserved as much, and a lot more, but this would do for now. "And four peppermint sticks."

"Four?" Ella quirked a half-smile. "One for Hugh?"

He snorted. "Not likely."

A small laugh escaped her lips. He paid the man, gave her one bag, and rolled the tops down on the other two.

At the next block, he made a right turn. "Doc's in the alley behind the barber shop. If you don't want to walk down there, you can wait here and I'll bring your satchel."

"I can walk."

He stopped and faced her. Her chin had tightened, her shoulders were stiff.

"That's not what I meant." His neck itched. "I know you can walk. And a fine job you do of it too."

She raised her head to look him in the eye and crossed her arms into a barricade.

"I mean, you're hardly limping at all today."

Her head tipped to the side, but her eyes never left his.

His collar band tightened. "Not that you limp, mind you."

One small foot began to tap.

"You do real well for someone who . . . who . . ."

The paper sack crinkled in her hand. "For someone who's a cripple?"

Tarnation, he was digging himself deep. "No. That's not what I was going to say." He pulled his hat off and ran his sleeve across his brow. "You know I don't see you like that. I mean . . . what I'm trying to say is—"

"Yes?"

"Well, if you were a horse, I wouldn't put you down."

CHAPTER SEVENTEEN

What did a lady say to a man who compared her to a horse? A lame horse, at that.

If he didn't have her camera, she would leave him there at the alley's entrance and march straight back to the studio. After pushing him off the curb.

"On second thought, I'll wait here."

He moved toward her. She moved back. A perfect dance step if they were dancing. But the only fancy footwork at the moment was Cale Hutton attempting to remove his boot from his mouth.

"Ella, please."

He'd used her given name. "Do you have my camera or don't you, Mr. Hutton?"

His jaw locked and his eyes dulled.

She straightened her spine and held his gaze. She might be maimed, but she refused to be pathetic.

He finally turned and strode down the alley.

Tears threatened. She pressed her fists into her eyes, crumpling the bag in the process, and drew a deep breath. He hadn't actually called her a cripple. That was Mabel's line, so oft repeated that no one could forget it. Especially Ella.

Why had she planted the insidious barb into their conversation when he was simply attempting to be . . . what? Generous? Kind? Sympathetic? She didn't want his sympathy.

She stomped her foot—something she hadn't done in ages—and the act jarred up through her lower leg and into her thigh. Who was she kidding?

Yes, she'd grown stronger and was improving each day. But that didn't mean Cale Hutton would see her as anything other than what she was—someone deficient who didn't belong in this town or his life. The less time she spent around him, the easier it would be to leave when the filming was finished.

Besides, he'd never apologized for that day at the ranch. That should say something about his character.

Clopping hooves announced his approach, and he rode around the back of the building and into the street. He dismounted, opened his saddle bag, and pulled out her satchel.

She moved into Doc, wrapping her arms around his neck and breathing deeply, drinking in his familiar scent, willing it to soak into her clothing, her hair, her soul. She rubbed beneath his forelock, keenly aware that she might never see him again aside from his mad chase scene in the film.

Cale stepped up on the sidewalk and handed her the satchel. As she took it, he captured her hand and held on until she looked at him.

"I'm not good with words, Ella. I'm better at herding cows than saying what I mean. But I was hoping we could spend more time together before you leave. Whenever that is."

Something in his eyes matched what trembled in her breast. A hunger, a yearning to know more. Experience more. Was he trying to say what she had foolishly hoped to hear?

Impossible. He was merely speaking from guilt. Trying to make up for that rash horse remark.

She pulled her hand from beneath his strong fingers and stepped back. "Thank you for returning my camera." She considered giving back the candy, but that would be a hateful thing to do. Purely an emotional retort, repaying wound for wound. "And for the soda and chocolate."

His broad shoulders drooped almost imperceptibly, and defeat swept his face.

"Please thank Kip for me, as well."

She spun on the ball of her left foot and walked to Main Street and around the corner toward the studio. The weight of her satchel on her shoulder offered familiar solace, the smooth, well-worn leather beneath her hand a reminder of who she was and where she didn't belong.

The weight of regret nearly pulled her to the ground. She'd give the chocolate to Clara.

The heels of her low-tops clipped clean and smart on the sidewalk, no hint of a limp. Only a lingering, burning pain that had risen from her leg and worked its way up and into her heart.

~

Cale stared at the corner where Ella disappeared—waiting, praying she'd return. Forgive him. But he hadn't asked her to.

Her footsteps still pinged in his ears.

When his vision darkened around the edges, he realized he was holding his breath and pulled in a searing draught. Doc blew against his back and gave him a shove. Cale stumbled forward. Even his horse knew he was an idiot.

He swung into the saddle and reined toward the opposite end of town and the sheriff's office. Whatever he learned there couldn't make the day any worse than it already was.

Crossett's buckskin dosed at the hitching post, alongside Harper's buckboard and nag. And Herb Rupley's Studebaker huddled off to itself. Something was going on.

He flipped Doc's reins around the rail and walked inside to a bunch of sour-faced men.

"Cale." Sheriff Payton jerked a nod. "Good timing."

Not exactly, but he'd take what he could get. He acknowledged the two ranchers—neighbors, both of them. "Crossett. Harper." The fruit grower lived across the valley. "Rupley."

Hooking the toe of his boot on an empty chair leg, he flipped it around and straddled it. "You all here about what I think you're here about?"

Sober nods confirmed his hunch, and then the others focused on Sheriff Payton.

He leaned back in his desk chair.

"With the four of you, we've about got the makings of a posse. Trouble is, we don't know what we're after."

Everyone started talking at once. Arms waved, voices raised, tempers tore loose.

"Hold on, hold on." Payton stood and leaned forward, hands propped on his desk. "If we're not unified, we won't get anywhere."

Cale thumbed his hat up a notch. "How many of you lose livestock to a bear?"

Three hands went up.

"Trees," said Rupley. "They're climbing my apple trees and busting them. I won't have any fruit come fall if all my trees are broke down."

Cale doubted Rupley's trouble was anything other than a black bear or two along the Arkansas. If they had a cow-killing grizzly on their hands, it wouldn't wander so far off from its mountain territory for an apple.

The sheriff straightened. "How many of you have lost cattle to rustlers?"

Sharp glances cut around the room and two hands rose.

"Cale, what about you?"

"A bear for certain. At least twice. But I'm wondering if there are men working along with this Old Mose rumor. Taking advantage of a situation."

"You see tracks?" Crossett asked.

"Just a drag trail. A busted corral pole. And a thousand-pound steer that no man dragged off and left half eaten."

Mumbled comments circled the room like buzzards over the kill.

"But one of my other neighbors has lost more than one animal at a time, which is what makes me think we've got more than one enemy working against us." He took his hat off and shoved a hand through his hair, startled to find it short. "I want to call the Cattleman's Association together and raise reward money." He looked at Rupley. "And anyone else who's interested."

Harper scoffed. "Reward for what?"

"For a successful bear kill or rustlers caught red-handed."

"That last one'll be like pulling money out of thin air," the sheriff said.

"I agree," Crossett added. "But we have to do something, and the more eyes we have out there, the quicker we'll find what's raiding our livestock."

"And fruit trees." Rupley chewed on an unlit cigar, making it bob up and down like a crow's head.

Harper stood. "When do you want to meet? I'll spread the word at the bank. I'm headed over their right now."

Cale tugged his hat down. "This Saturday at the rodeo grounds. Most folks come to town for it. Let's meet at noon north of the holding pens. That gives us a few days to get the word out."

"My wife'll tell her sewing circle tomorrow morning," Rupley said around his cigar. "That for sure will get the word out in a hurry."

The others chuckled, but Cale failed to see the humor since females weren't high on his list of things to comprehend at the moment.

He was last to the door, but the sheriff stopped him. "I hear you've got a scene in that flicker."

The man's snapping eyes made Cale's skin twitch. "A good horse race, that's all."

"Like the one on Main Street?" A poker face stared back, earned from years of interrogation.

Of course he knew. So had the barber. Cale jerked a quick nod and left before Payton got into details.

Doc seemed eager to leave town as well, and Cale rode him up Main Street at a determined walk, steering clear of more than a few coughing rattletraps. More of 'em every time he came in. Everybody was in a hurry these days. Had to have the latest contraption to get where they were going faster than four hooves could carry them. He leaned forward and patted Doc's neck. He'd take four hooves and a big heart over four wheels any day.

At the 300 block, Cale sat taller and stared straighter. No sense ogling the studio, hoping Ella might be looking out the window as he passed. Main Street's tree-lined roadway took him past the penitentiary and on to the Soda Springs.

His tension bled into Doc, and the gelding quivered under the saddle, aching to break into a hard run. Once past the springs, Cale gave him his head at the turn out of town, needing to run off steam as well. He'd accomplished what he'd come to do—see the sheriff and return Ella's satchel. What he hadn't planned to do was dig the hole deeper between them.

He leaned over the saddle horn and pushed the reins, urging Doc on, leaving his foul-ups and what-ifs behind. The gelding's mane whipped his face, and pounding hooves matched the pounding in his head.

At the rock overhang that marked a quarter mile, he straightened and reined Doc in to an easy lope, tension spent. Muscles hot and bulging, lungs straining. By the turnoff, they slowed to a cooling walk, and Cale took stock of the next four days.

He had a rodeo to get ready for, which didn't mean much more than checking his ropes, cleaning his tack, and pulling out his best shirt. And figuring what he'd say to people who asked about that chase scene in Thorson's moving picture or the buggy incident in town. If the sheriff and barber knew about them, everybody knew, which meant Hugh would soon enough. If that dadblamed kiss from Mabel made it into the flicker, he'd never live it down.

That evening, he and Hugh strung more tin cans around the corral and portioned off the night for hay-loft duty.

Hugh called first watch. No surprise there. He hadn't slept well in about six years.

"I'll spell you at midnight." Cale didn't expect to sleep much either.

But he must have dozed off because a shotgun blast ripped him from a dead sleep. Boots still on, he grabbed his double-barrel 12-gauge beside the bed and charged out his side door.

Tug sang lead in a tin-can chorus, and another shot flashed from the loft. He ducked instinctively and hugged the shadows, staying close to the house. Gun smoke tainted the air, and his skin crawled with an unseen presence. In the stark silence that followed, a heavy whiffling sent chills up his neck. No human made sounds like that. A branch snapped. He raised the gun and fired. The old side-by-side tore the night open with its cannon roar. Another blast, and whatever it was crashed through the brush.

He and Hugh had deliberately chosen scatter guns hoping they'd hit something this time.

They missed again.

~

Clara's fresh biscuits appealed not one bit to Ella this morning, though two slightly dented bon-bons from Ott's Candy Store were gladly accepted without comment other than an unquestioning thank-you. Given the woman's capacity to know every stitch of news in town, Ella was certain she'd already heard about the fray at the alley.

Her stomach knotted like a hanky in an old maid's bodice. The irony stung, but she pulled a polite smile across her face before leaving for the studio. No time to chat today. She had an early call for the branding.

Returning to the ranch enticed her as much as a foot race with Mabel down Main Street. Seeing Cale again would only dredge up still-fresh memories of their time together—pleasant until she put cruel words into his mouth. What could she possibly say to him now? The less she saw of him, the better. But short of feigning sickness, she had no escape. Staying in town was not an option. Thorson had ordered everyone into the cars, which ensured a less-than-comfortable ride as she crammed in with three cowboys on a seat intended for two people. Boxed lunches from the café took up every nook and cranny.

The borrowed sewing kit, a few extra spools of thread purchased at Favorite Dry Goods, and her camera nestled snugly in her satchel atop her lap. Thanks to Cale. Guilt pricked her conscience, insisting she owed him an apology.

Whether she used her camera or any of the sewing notions mattered not. She'd take no more chances leaving personal valuables in her room. In spite of the fact that Mabel was with the troupe, Ella intended to keep an eye on what mattered.

Which had her scanning the horizon for a tall cowboy as soon as they turned off onto the ranch road. Disgusted with herself, she dug through her satchel and acquired a headache from burying her face in its recesses while bouncing along the rough road.

No little boys ran to meet the motorcars as they sputtered into the pasture. In fact, the Hutton youngsters stayed uncharacteristically close by the house, lingering around the large table and upturned crates, dour-faced and brooding. But her thoughts raced at sight of their father and Cale atop their mounts, soberly watching Mr. Thorson and the rest of the crew approach the horses tethered at the corral. Both brothers rode with scabbards and rifles.

The hair on her neck rose.

She crossed to the yard, encouraged by a reserved but gentlemanly welcome from Jay, and climbed the back-porch steps with a furtive glance toward the nearby ridge. The bear must have returned. And today the crew would be branding calves. *Oh Lord, protect them all.*

Not surprising, berry pies sat cooling on a smaller table beneath the kitchen window. The aroma warmed and pierced her in the same breath, flooding her with memories of her two days beneath this roof.

She reached deep for a cheerful tone. "You've been busy, Helen."

Two sturdy arms embraced her with a hearty welcome and nearly squeezed the tears right out of her. She blinked rapidly, suppressing the urge to let them fall undeterred.

"Almost as busy as Cale and Hugh." Helen gave her a meaningful look before handing her a table knife. "Would you mind?"

Happy to be occupied but anxious over what she suspected, Ella laid her satchel aside, rinsed her hands at the sink, and set to slicing pies into eight servings each. Taking hold of a blackberry pie tin, she inserted the knife at the far edge and cut through its sugar-encrusted topping. Berry filling oozed.

"Did the bear return?"

A scoff-like sound affirmed her fears.

"I saw both Cale and Hugh with rifle scabbards on their saddles. And the boys were moping in the yard. Do they expect trouble in broad daylight?"

"Hugh said they're not taking any chances." Helen set a cup of hot coffee on the table near Ella. "The boys can't go off playing or riding and chasing one another, and I tell you, they are fit to be tied. We had enough shotgun fire last night to wake the dead, and my nerves are stretched as tight as a new fiddle string. Haven't seen the like in all the years I've been here."

Ella shivered, remembering an earlier attack and the resulting glimpse of a disgruntled, shirtless rancher. "Did they get anything? The men. Did they hit the bear?"

"Drew blood, according to Cale. He went out at sunup and found a trail. Looks like they stopped the varmint from making off with another animal, but now it's wounded. At least grazed, which could make things worse."

Dark berry filling dripped from the knife, and Ella scraped it on the edge of the pan and picked up her cup. "Sounds like I'll be needing this coffee."

"The day's full of all kinds of upheaval." Helen scrutinized her attire with a raised eyebrow. "Why, look at you, all gussied up in your city shoes and a skirt and jacket. You don't plan to take part in the branding?"

Ella drew in a deep breath. "Not today. I would have stayed in town had Mr. Thorson not insisted that every last company member attend." She was counting on her low-tops and pale green suit to keep her quarantined in the kitchen.

Helen took a chair at the end of the table, her own coffee in hand. "I've worked some on detailing the dress you finished for me. Since you're not joining the excitement, maybe you can look at what I've done." She carefully sipped the steaming brew, then hissed and rolled her lips. "And we can discuss why you're running scared from something you already conquered."

Ella nearly splashed coffee onto the berry pie she'd just sliced. Helen was nothing if not blunt. Honestly, *more than meets the eye* took on new meaning when Helen's eye was involved.

She propped the knife on the edge of an unsliced pie and took the chair at the opposite end of the table. She'd be leaving soon. Leaving the whole painful business with Cale behind, as well as this beautiful setting and Helen's friendship. What did she have to lose with a full disclosure other than another piece of dignity?

"Cale came to town and we had words."

Helen's expression remained neutral, at least as much as could be seen above her coffee cup. She nodded slowly, inviting Ella to fill the silence with the rest of the story.

"He brought my satchel. I forgot it the other day when we left after Mabel's rescue scene on the runaway horse." The image of Mabel throwing herself at Cale still burned. She held her coffee in both hands and flicked a look at Helen, whose casual posture belied her eagle-eyed attentiveness.

"Before he returned it to me, we had sodas at Palace Drug and then stopped by the candy store so he could buy peppermints for the boys."

Helen's eyes brightened. "And bon-bons. My, but it's been too long since I enjoyed such a wasteful pleasure. My Ben used to treat me to them on occasion, God bless him."

Perhaps it was Helen's familiarity with love lost that encouraged Ella to share her sorrows. An affinity between them. A common ground.

She held the cup close to her lips to catch the words. "He bought some for me too."

Helen nodded. "I thought so. He had more than his hair trimmed that morning. Something pained him deeply, based on the way he resembled his brother when he walked in the door, cut close to the quick."

"He always resembles his brother." The words spilled out before she could stop them, sharp and not at all what she intended. Guilt stabbed again, puncturing her breath. She knew what Helen meant, but bolstered herself with another swallow of unsweetened coffee. "Our conversation worked around to my . . . my weakness. My tendency to limp."

"Does he know about the accident?" So matter-of-fact and unpretentious.

Ella stared into her half-full cup, looking for a reasonable answer.

"Why haven't you told him?"

"Why would he care?"

A low chuckle raised Ella's head.

A smile teased the woman's soft wrinkles.

"My dear, he cares a great deal for you."

Ella's pulse jumped to her neck, and the earlier headache sharpened to a pinpoint. "But I don't belong here. I'm leaving soon, and I'm . . . I'm so much less than he needs or wants."

Helen set her cup on the table with purpose, and her kind eyes pressed into Ella like salve on an open wound. "Less than? Less than what, dear? Intelligent? Attractive? Accomplished? Generous?"

Ella's stomach turned upside down and threatened to bend her in half. She wasn't any of those things, and she'd certainly been anything but generous with Cale that day after his insulting remark.

She met Helen's gray gaze and took a chance. "He said he wouldn't put me down if I were a horse."

The older woman clapped her hand over her mouth and guffawed in a most unladylike fashion. Her hilarity infected Ella in spite of her embarrassment, and she allowed a small laugh.

Helen fanned herself with her apron hem, then dabbed her forehead. "You're just not accustomed to the way our menfolk around here talk. Honey, Cale paid you a fine compliment."

Ella sniffed and smoothed her tea-green skirt. Compliment, indeed.

"*Less than*, as you put it, to a rancher is cause to put an animal out of its misery, particularly one that is unable to pull its weight or get around without pain." A quiet chuckle slipped out. "Mercy me, I'll admit he could have said it a bit gentler, but in his rough-edged, cowboy way, he was telling you that he values you."

Shame prickled Ella's brow, and she set down her coffee. Valued her? Highly unlikely now. "I'm afraid I made a mess of things." She unfastened the top button of her jacket, suddenly wishing for a cool breeze to waft through the oven-warmed kitchen.

"It all started when I put words in his mouth. Words that are Mabel's, not his." She turned the cup in circles on the table.

"What words might those be, if you don't mind me asking?"

Oh, she minded, but refusing was pointless. "Actually, just one word." She flicked a glance at her hostess. "Cripple." Even now, here in the safety of the cozy kitchen, the word cut deeply. "I accused him of thinking of me as a cripple. That's when he said what he did."

No laughter followed her confession, but neither did judgment. Helen reached across the circular patchwork of pies, freed the coffee cup, and wrapped her work-worn hand around Ella's with a soothing squeeze. "We all have a wound that makes us limp, dear. Some more than others, like Hugh who is crippled in spirit. That's a much more difficult injury to deal with than a hitch in your gait."

Something shifted inside. Helen's words seeped through the woman's fingers and into Ella's core, dissipating a heavy shadow that had lingered there for the past year and a half. A thin and gauzy hope settled in its place.

Helen pushed to her feet and took her cup to the sink. "I dare say, Cale doesn't see you as *less than* anything at all. Why, you've filled him up in a way no one ever has. As if you're an answer to half my prayers."

She sniffed and pressed her eyes, then busied herself at the sink for a moment.

Ella wondered what the other half of her prayers concerned and decided they had to be for the boys or Hugh.

Helen dried her hands on her apron and turned to face Ella. "If you don't have your mind set on going back to Chicago with the movie people so soon, it'd sure be nice to have you around for a spell. I know I could keep you busy with sewing projects and pie-baking and putting up preserves." Her face brightened as she voiced her ideas.

"Give it some thought. You could stay here at the ranch for a while. And we could see what develops."

CHAPTER EIGHTEEN

She'd floated out of the third car like a spring leaf from a cottonwood tree, carrying her satchel and wearing those black strapped shoes she wore in town. Cale had clamped his jaw and tried not to stare. As successful a venture as shooting the marauder last night, though he'd nicked it.

Daylight had revealed a scant blood trail among other things.

He fingered a red-rimmed circle in his vest pocket, one he'd found near the corrals this morning when he and Hugh were taking down the tin-can wire. Whether it was dropped last night or earlier didn't matter. It cemented his hunch about a double-prong attack.

Not too many bears he knew of carried poker chips from a gambling parlor on Cripple Creek's Bennett Avenue.

He reined Doc toward the corral as Barr's cowboys mounted up and gathered around.

"You're loaded for bear." Barr jutted his chin at Cale's Winchester '95, sure to bring down what he aimed at if it wasn't the middle of the night and dark as the inside of his boot.

"If necessary."

The powder-faced actor moved in closer and lowered his voice. "You boys weren't packing last time. You expecting trouble?"

Just what Cale needed—a word-of-mouth wildfire lit by a moving-picture crew. He tugged his hat down. "Can't hurt to be ready."

The only person he wanted to talk to was Ella Canaday, and she'd made it clear as day that she didn't want to talk to him. Didn't even wear her riding skirt and scurried into the house as if the rogue bear was after her instead of his calves.

Hugh took the lead toward the branding area they'd staged away from the house at the lower holding pens, and the men—Mabel included—followed. Cale rode drag with Tug, eyes on the scrub oak and thickets around them. If they were lucky, last night's episode had scared the creature off for a while.

Smoke fingered into the morning sky from Hugh's branding fire, an ancient signal denoting a gathering place. Two steers and eight cow-calf pairs huddled in the opposite corner. Hugh lifted the irons he'd laid in the fire earlier, and the double H's with an inverted V above them glowed hot and orange.

Cale untethered his rope, built a loop, and snagged a little bull calf. Barr was paying attention and caught its back feet. Mama wasn't too happy about it, but a couple of other cowboys cut her off and forced her out through the gate.

A half dozen people lined the fence, and three more crowded the pen on horseback. Mabel perched on the top pole, paying little attention to what was going on. Pete set his camera up in the far corner, the sun at his back. Thorson pushed his hat up, raised his arm, and hollered, "Roll film!"

By noon, all ten head were branded without incident, and Thorson had several minutes' worth of struggling calves, smoking hides, and Jed Barr's mug in the mix. He wasn't half bad, Cale grudgingly admitted to himself. Seemed to know his way around a rope and iron.

Surprised that everything went as smoothly as it did, he let the last calf out to find its mother and circled the bawling animals clustered at the near end of the meadow. Nothing like announcing fresh meat on the hoof to whatever lurked out in the cedars, be it man or beast. Tug trotted beside him, ears up but unalarmed. The dog was so old, Cale couldn't count on its nose or ears for anything at a distance. Maybe it was time to get a pup.

Leaning on his saddle horn, he waited for the others to mount and head back. Hugh stomped out the fire and cooled the irons in the small creek nearby, sending a hissing through the air that made a couple of fellas take quick notice. Cale approved of their alarm. It paid to pay attention in snake country.

By the time he made it back to the house, most everyone was scattered under the big pine, eating their way through boxed lunches and Helen's pies. Jay, Ty, and Kip manned the table, sneaking a skinny sliver when they thought no one was looking. Mabel shared a crate with some unfortunate dude, but Ella wasn't in the bunch.

He decided he didn't care.

At the corral he looped Doc's reins around the hitching rail and loosened his cinch a notch. What Ella Canaday did was no concern of his. Nor was where she ate or how she was getting on after that fiasco yesterday in town. He slapped his hat on his chaps so hard, Tug skittered away, tail tucked between his legs.

Dadblastit. "Come here, boy." He bent down and rubbed the old dog's scruff. "You've done nothin' wrong, fella. Go on and see if you can mooch a piece of meat off one of those city slickers."

The mottled dog took off as if he understood English. Probably did.

Cale screwed his hat down, blocking his view of anyone trying to catch his eye as he strode to the back porch and the wash tub. With absolutely no intention of looking through the kitchen window to see if Ella was inside.

He hung his hat on a peg, kept his head down, and rolled his sleeves up. Cold water had a way of clearing a fella's brain, especially when splashed in his face over and over again. Eyes closed, he braced his hands on the edge of the tub for a minute, then reached for the towel. Log wall met his fingers, and he jabbed a splinter beneath a nail. *Dadbla—*

"Looking for this?"

His eyes popped open to the towel dangling from the fingers of one Miss Ella Canaday. Everything he could, should, or ought to say stampeded through his mind, but not one single word lined up proper behind another. He took the towel, pulled out the splinter, then wiped his neck and jaw.

Two words clicked into place. "Thank you."

"You're welcome."

"When did you—"

"Just now. I held the screen quiet."

He rubbed the towel over his head. He was worse off than he thought if she could walk right out on the porch without him hearing her.

"I wanted to apologize." Not a meek bone in her body, she stood there squared up and rifle straight. But her eyes were soft around the edges.

He raked his hair back. "All right." A born conversationalist, he was.

Her shoulders relaxed, and her mouth pulled in a straight line. Not exactly a smile. But not daggers like she'd shot at him the day before.

"I saved a piece of pie for you inside."

His nose dragged his eyes to the screen door, where he detected leftovers from Helen's early morning baking. "Thank you."

He followed her inside to a cup of coffee and a quarter pie at the end of the small table. Ella claimed a cup from the counter and stood off to one side. Helen was elsewhere.

He wasn't about to sit and eat alone with Ella watching him like a heifer at an auction. He pulled out the near chair and indicated the other one at the opposite end. "You havin' any?" If the Good Lord required a speech for passage through the pearly gates, he'd sure enough be left outside with the bankers, bandits, and other varmints.

"Here." He forked his pie in half and scooted the plate toward her.

Her gaze flitted between him and the offering.

It wasn't that hard of a decision—yes or no. Suited him either way. If she didn't want to eat with him, fine. He reached for the plate.

She grabbed it quick-like and scraped a portion onto a saucer from the counter. Then she sat down and returned his plate to him. "Thank you."

If either of them said *thank you* one more time, he'd start spittin' like Hugh.

He raked in a bite to keep himself from saying something stupid.

"Helen said the bear returned last night." Her hand paused with her fork midway between the saucer and her lips.

Her perfect lips, the color of summer chokecherries before they ripen in the fall. He focused on his plate and filled his mouth again, nodding.

She sighed. Resigned.

Swallowing, he looked up. "I winged it."

Interest brightened her face and she leaned forward, brows raised. "You did? What happened?"

Her reaction set pride to bouncing off his ribs, competing with berry pie for room in his belly. "I didn't bring it down, or slow it down, as far as I can figure. But I found a blood trail this morning at daybreak. We may have scared it off for a while, at least until this filming business is over."

Not that he really wanted it to be over, because then she'd go back to Chicago.

She took another bite and tilted her chin. "Well, now it knows you're serious."

Her hair curled around her face like a bower, and he wanted to touch it, see if it was as soft as it looked. Press his lips against it and tell her that he was serious about a whole lot more than just bringing down a rogue bear.

~

The tightness between them eased a bit, allowing Ella to finally taste the sweet berries inside Helen's flaky crust rather than dried crow. Apologizing had never come easy for her, a trait she'd inherited from her father. But if she couldn't admit when she was wrong with this kind and thoughtful man, when could she?

She pinched off another bite with her fork. "How did the branding go?"

Not raising his head, he gave her an under-the-brows look that gave her pause.

"No problems." He flattened his fork against crumbs and purple juice and licked it clean before pushing the empty plate aside. "When do you leave?"

Her heart plummeted to her toes, and she struggled to keep her expression from falling with it. Things were not as Helen had suggested. The boys would miss her when she left, but evidently not Cale. Was he eager to see her gone?

She took his plate and her unfinished pie to the sink, where she scraped her remaining bites into the chicken-scrap can. "I'm not sure. We have enough film for at least two one-reelers, maybe three. It depends on what else Mr. Thorson wants or if he already has what he needs."

Chair legs scratched the wooden floor, and a sudden warmth at her back sent her rational thoughts scurrying like squirrels. He'd trapped her between the table and sink.

"You ever been to a rodeo?"

His low tones sent her imagination bucking out of control, and she hung on for dear life. She stacked the plates and turned to meet the second button of his shirt. The button that wouldn't fasten when it was Jed's costume he wore. His chest expanded with a breath and she looked up, past his unshaven jawline and into the blue of his eyes.

"At the World's Fair." She swallowed, ordering her heart back into place.

"Heard about that coliseum from Helen. Here we just circle the wagons."

Her puzzlement must have shown, for his mouth pulled up on one side, pinching the dimple. "Our Wild West Days are this weekend. I'll be entering."

His voice dropped to a near whisper, low and deep like distant thunder. "Thought maybe if you were still around, you might come watch." He didn't move or offer her a way of escape, but stood solid and sound, presenting a most inviting refuge.

She dashed the thought and sidled along the counter, squeezing around the opposite end of the table, exhaling once safely on the other side. Perhaps she'd misjudged his question about her departure date. Smoothing her wrinkle-free skirt and looking out the window, she kept his towering presence in the corner of her eye and carefully chose her words. "I could take photographs. If we're still in town, that is."

He rubbed his right arm, flexing the elbow several times as if loosening a muscle. "Will you be photographing Jed Barr? I hear he's entered in the bronc busting."

Only if Thorson paid for her prints, which he would not. She was an amateur. A hobbyist. Risking a glance at Cale's face, she found it guarded, void of emotion.

"I don't plan on it." There were always plenty of photographers capturing his image. "I prefer more unusual subjects."

"Am I unusual enough?" The dimple flashed, then disappeared.

Her breath caught at his slip, but she schooled her features and forced her hands to relax their nervous fumbling. "Depends on whether you fall off or not."

"I don't plan on it."

His re-use of her words left her wondering if he mocked her.

"Not in the roping, anyway." He folded his arms, enlarging the idea of a safe haven. "Your money on me winning or losing?"

"I do not gamble." Suddenly sensing she'd opened herself up for a counter argument, she crossed her own arms, fending off the impression.

His chin dipped and he gave her a look that stripped away every last shred of her defenses, leaving hidden thoughts exposed and easily read. If she didn't evade his penetrating gaze, he'd have her admitting she gambled repeatedly—cutting her hair, taking a job with Selig Polyscope, coming to Colorado. Riding Barlow. Yes, that little jaunt had been her biggest gamble of all.

The screen door swung open and Jay strode through, importance stretching him to his fullest height. "Mr. Thorson says they're leaving, Miss Ella. Says to hurry up if you don't want to get left behind again."

"I have never been left behind, Jay." Her ire rankled, though not with the boy. "But that's of no matter. Thank you for bringing me the message."

He hesitated, shoved his hands in his front pockets, and addressed the toes of his scuffed boots with a quiet voice. "Be all right by Kip'n Ty and me if you did get left behind."

Her gaze flicked to Cale of its own accord, and she snatched it back, stooping to meet Jay eye to eye. "Thank you very much. I appreciate your offer, but I have a job to do. Maybe we'll come back to Cañon City another time, and I can see you again."

Without warning, he flung his arms around her and she dropped to her knees to keep from toppling. He smelled of sweaty little boy and broken heart, and all her longings for a husband and family rushed to the surface.

Just as suddenly, he broke away and dashed out the door.

Cale offered his hand, and she took it simply as a matter of balance in a shaky situation. But when she attempted to withdraw her fingers, he tightened his hold until she met his gaze.

His brow lay smooth above darkening blue, no worry creasing the ridge. No dimple stitching his rough cheek. He stepped closer. She might touch his face were he not holding her fingers so fiercely.

"Saturday." The single word vibrated into her hand and up her arm. "I'll see you Saturday."

He smelled of grown-up man and hopeful heart, and she reminded herself that nothing awaited the two of them together. They came from opposite worlds, and she'd be returning to hers as soon as Mr. Thorson gave the word.

Cale's world waited outside the screen door. But she faced a long train ride back to an unknown future.

She freed her fingers and her voice. "If we're still here."

He opened his mouth to say more, but clamped it shut, cutting off his berry pie-scented breath. Then he, too, scrambled out the door, pausing on the porch to grab his hat.

From the window, she watched his long strides devour the distance to the corrals, where he tightened Doc's cinch, swung into the saddle, and headed away from the barn. Without a glance to his right or his left, he angled toward the distant ridge he'd pointed out that day in the pasture. She imagined what it must look like there atop the rocky spine that snaked above the valley. No doubt it offered a good view of the ranch, the road to town, and much more of this beautifully rugged country.

A frown tugged her brows. She was learning things about herself that were not necessarily welcome, a completely unexpected offshoot of this venture. She had not set out to view her internal workings, but, rather, the West. The wide-open, unaffected spaces. The imposing Rocky Mountains that jutted so brutally from the plains.

Instead, she'd just confirmed that she was, in fact, a gambler. Willing to wager, at least where a certain rancher was concerned.

CHAPTER NINETEEN

Saturday morning Cale rode into the rodeo grounds at the north end of Ninth Street, a loose ring of automobiles already forming an arena next to the holding pens. Several slots waited for others to scoot in and plug the gaps. He recognized Rupley's Studebaker and a couple of other ranchers' new motorcars. He couldn't stem the tide, but he'd sure enough give up his spurs before he'd trade his horse for a heap of tin and rubber.

Members of the Cattlemen's Association clustered off to themselves on the west side, and Cale joined them. Dismounting, he held Doc's reins loosely, unwilling to ground tie him with so many clackety cars coming and going. The gelding raised his head and pricked his ears, and Cale followed his notice to a wagon headed their way. Helen's Sunday straw hat set her apart from Hugh on the seat, and the boys bounced in the back. Ty was swinging his loop over his head and everyone else's as well. Grace would be proud.

"What's your plan, Hutton?" Joe Grady from over Black Mountain cut right to it.

Cale turned back to the group. He'd heard Grady had lost more than a dozen head. "I think we've got more than one enemy."

Crockett scoffed. "Yeah. We got ourselves a herd of bear."

A couple of men laughed.

Grady swore under his breath. "Or one big grizzly with Old Mose for a pa." He crossed his arms and spread his stance, ready to take on any who disagreed with his theory.

Cale looked around the group. "How many of you found bear sign on your spread?"

Four men flicked a hand.

"How many of you lost cattle with no sign of anything?"

Five more added to the count.

Herb Rupley joined the group, cigar dangling from his teeth.

"Rupley, we're takin' a tally on our losses. How many trees have you lost?"

"A dozen last I checked."

"Rustlers?" Crockett laughed at his own joke.

Rupley's cigar bobbed.

"It's a bear and a big one. Plain as day. And I've got the claw marks and broken tree trunks to prove it."

The information rippled around the group, sobering them all, but Cale still doubted Rupley's suspicions. Too far out of a grizzly's range.

He looked at each man. Most he knew, had grown up around them and their families. All totaled, they'd lost a lot of money to whatever was stealing their cattle.

He took the chip from his vest pocket, flicked it in the air, and caught it along with every man's attention. "I think we've got more than one culprit. A bear for sure, but rustlers too. I found a half-eaten steer on my place, but some of you have lost animals with no evidence of a fight. I think someone is sneaking in under cover of the Old Mose rumor and makin' a profit on the side."

He opened his hand and silence pulled the small group tighter. From the corner of his eye, he noticed two cowboys hanging off to the side, hats low and facing away.

He lowered his voice. "I gamble, but with beef prices, not poker chips from Cripple Creek."

A couple of swear words and mumbled remarks bounced among the cattlemen.

"Old Mose ain't just whiskey talk, and you know it, Hutton. You saw his carcass laid out six years ago." Grady's dark eyes held decades of memory behind them. "He was big enough to take one of our young bulls, and it's more than possible he sired a cub or two that could end up doing the same. There's nothing to keep one from pickin' off our stock."

Cale pocketed the chip. "I didn't say it wasn't true, Joe. But we've got more than a bear to deal with."

"Do we need a posse?"

Crockett's question fired off a round of argument, and Cale held up his hands.

Hugh ambled over from where he'd left the wagon and stopped just outside the circle. "We can't form a posse. That's the sheriff's job. But we can send a couple fellas up to Cripple Creek to talk to the butchers. See who they're buying their beef from, other than us."

Surprised by Hugh's level-headed suggestion, Cale asked for volunteers. Three of the ranchers with no bear sign raised their hands.

"Good. Sooner you can make it, the better. Let the sheriff know what you find." He looked at the others. "Who's up for a bear hunt?"

A half dozen raised their hands.

Hugh caught his eye with a nod. "I'll take 'em," he said.

"Before you break off to plan the hunt, how many of you are in favor of offering a reward for rustlers?"

Every man agreed, some more heartily than others. Even Rupley.

"All right. Harper, you collect the money and take it to Sheriff Payton to hold for us. Tell him what we're doing. We'll all meet at the café a week from today. Noon."

Dust was kicking up around them from automobiles driving in, and the men went their separate ways. Cale pulled Rupley aside, the man's cigar bobbing like apples in a horse trough.

He thumbed his hat up and scratched his cheek, smooth from a close shave this morning. "I know you've got bear trouble, Rupley. That's clear from what you've said. But I doubt it's a cattle-killing grizzly. They don't wander down this far from their haunt. My guess is, it's probably a family of black bear from along the river satisfying their sweet tooth."

The cigar shot up at a hard angle and stayed there, drawing Cale's eye to Rupley's bowler. The man stared at him for a good half-minute before the cigar drooped.

"I suppose you're right. I was hopin' to kill two birds with one stone."

"Appreciate it, I do. But you don't need to contribute to the reward pot."

Rupley resisted. "I'm a community-minded man, Hutton. The ranchers' problems are my problems. I don't mind pitching in."

Cale offered his hand. "Much obliged."

Rupley strode off to his now-dusty Studebaker, climbed in, and drove away. Cale wouldn't be surprised if Herb Rupley ran for public office in this year's election. Probably win the ticket.

A holler turned his head to a ruckus in the horse pen. He snagged Doc's reins and ambled that way, sizing up the competition that sat around on their cow ponies, ropes coiled neatly against their saddles. He recognized most as working day men from area spreads, a couple from as far away as Pueblo, probably on borrowed horses.

At the pens, a bronc from Tol Witcher's string, Tornado, was breaking in half. The so-called "demon in horseflesh" was no bigger than any other range-raised horse, a thousand pounds tops. But he was an ornery son-of-a-gun. If Jed Barr drew him, it might be good watchin' after all.

The chuck wagon teams had set up their camps a ways off, and wild-horse racers stood next to their readied saddles, waiting for the show to begin.

More automobiles arrived, forming a second ring around the first. He swung into the saddle and looked for the three touring cars the moving-picture folks had driven out to the ranch. More specifically, he was scouting a little bob-haired filly that came up to his chin. And into his mind more often than was convenient.

There was a crowd of people for certain, and if the picture folks hadn't pulled up stakes, she was hiding out somewhere. Unreasonable disappointment dallied his gut and tried to drag away his concentration. He turned from the onlookers, untied his rope, and built a loop. He was there to win the roping and take home some of the purse money. He'd best keep his wits about him and not get his spurs tangled over some city skirt with dark eyes and a mind of her own.

~

Ella climbed from the touring car, grateful for the ease of movement afforded by the split skirt and boots. She hiked her satchel strap and situated the wide-brimmed hat she'd snagged from the costumes, grateful, also, for the opportunity to enjoy the day's events incognito.

Everyone she'd met that week, whether at Gilmore's Laundry or Favorite Dry Goods, or just passersby on her walk to the studio either mentioned Cale's daring Main Street rescue or stared openly and whispered as she passed. Such attention made her uncomfortable. And to think, Mabel lived for it.

Dust rose on the opposite side of the large open lot where several corrals held horses and cattle. Just as many cowboys, it seemed, milled next to them, swinging ropes and laughing. Everyone, spectators and contestants alike, was in high spirits.

She tugged her hat down and angled away, seeking an indirect approach. She did not want any of the Huttons to recognize her. Invisibility was paramount for what she wanted to photograph, and she did not want to distract Cale from his competition.

Their last encounter in the ranch kitchen made it clear that distraction—for her as well—was a distinct possibility.

Sharp voices caught her ear, and she peeked from beneath her wide brim at two cowboys in a heated argument. One wore wooly chaps similar to those in her collection, the other a pair of what she'd heard men call batwings due to their wide, loose leather. This pair was adorned with silver conchos and fringed pockets and trimmed with a double row of silver studs. Easy enough to duplicate with a heavy sewing machine, and she determined to do so.

Appearing as uninterested as possible, she pulled out her camera and eased closer, focusing on the corrals at a right angle to the arguing cowboys, but the same distance away. Peering through her view finder, she caught errant words from the conversation. *Cripple Creek, butcher,* and *brands* were among the terms that fired between the two. Slowly she turned, catching them both in her frame. *Click.*

The man in batwings threw her a dark frown. Her pulse quickened, throbbing against the hat band snugging her temple. She turned slightly and focused on several horses tethered at the corral. He moved her way.

She eased toward another group of cowboys, some holding ropes, all wearing hats, and feigned more photographs while watching the man in conchos. More theatrics in a public setting were exactly what she did not want. She circled the group, careful not to give the impression she was escaping, though her heart raced as surely as Doc had the day Cale swept her off the street.

And there he was, broad-shouldered and confident, in complete control, milling in a loose circle with other riders, a loop tucked under his arm. She stopped and focused, waiting for her nerves to steady and for Cale to ride into the frame in perfect profile.

Doc held his head high, anticipation bouncing his steps. His perked ears swiveled back to his master one at a time, listening, ready for his next command while taking in all the activity around them. Could there be a more noble steed? A grander knight?

When had Cale Hutton evolved from uncouth cowboy to grand knight?

The automobile behind her squawked, shattering the moment and unsettling not only her nerves, but several cowboys' mounts as well. She made her way back to the makeshift arena and squeezed in between two fenders, as close to the pending action as possible.

The two arguing men had vanished.

Though the Cañon City Wild West Days lacked the pageantry of a World's Fair exposition, the community made up for it in enthusiasm. Spectators cheered contestants by name. Family members and friends waved and yelled from the crowd, thrilling over each wild bronc that dumped its rider and each steer that got away.

As she expected, Jed spurred his bronc in grand style, fanning the air with his hat, and making a showy dismount. But breath lodged in her throat as Cale prepared to chase down and rope his fleeing steers faster than his competitors. She knew the action would be ghosted on her film, but she took several photographs anyway, reminders of her days in Colorado.

By late afternoon, she was covered in dust and exhausted from opposing rounds of tension and excitement for some competitors and sympathy over loss and injury for others. People backed their automobiles from the circle, the crowd thinned, and cowboys collected their winnings. Jed's voiced boomed above the crowd, inviting the company for a round of drinks before the big dance downtown, and they all piled into the cars. She held back.

She didn't have the strength to attempt fitting in where she did not. Working with the company members was one thing but socializing with them as they drank and caroused was quite another. Mabel's tongue would no doubt be loosed even further, and with fatigue pressing upon her, Ella didn't trust herself not to do or say something that would remind Mabel of her threat to quit if Ella wasn't fired. It would take every last ounce of her strength, but she preferred to walk back to the hotel.

She took her time crossing the empty lot, strolling rather than marching, keeping her leg muscles as loose and flexible as possible. Images of a copper bathing tub full of steaming water drew her on, providing the motivation she needed for the long trek. Automobiles passed her with horns blaring and arms waving. No one offered her a ride.

Nor would she have taken one from a stranger.

The sun surrendered to the tug of Fremont Peak, inching closer to the rocky point west of town, and the air cooled. A welcome change, this mountain climate, compared to Chicago's swathing summer humidity. A few riders passed her on their way to town, and she hugged the edge of the road as daylight dimmed, unwilling to be trampled by a startled horse or run down by an automobile. One such narrow escape was quite enough.

A steady clopping behind her announced yet another rider headed into town. The trotting slowed to a walk as it drew closer, and she moved farther off the road and into the grass of another field. From the corner of her eye, she saw the horse come alongside her, and the rider slowed to match her pace, backlit by the sinking sun. The silhouette of hat and rider lifted the fine hairs on the back of her neck.

"Looks like you could use a ride."

Cale's deep voice lifted her spirit, and her pulse leapt unexpectedly. She took a moment to harness her emotions, and with a hand, shielded her eyes as she gazed up at his sun-shrouded figure.

"I'm fine," she lied, channeling all her energy into even steps that did not favor her right leg.

He held Doc to a steady walk and looked straight ahead, his hat brim low. Had he heard her? The reins lay loosely in his left hand. He wouldn't be reaching down for her, unless he switched hands. *Please, no. Not again.* She angled a bit farther from the road. Doc shadowed her ploy.

Was he going to dog her the entire way? Surely not.

"I see you have your camera."

Not looking her way, he *assumed* she had her camera, though she always carried it in the satchel. A safe assumption on his part.

"Yes. It was an interesting afternoon."

"As good as the World's Fair?"

She glanced up again to find him still focused ahead, as should she. The uneven ground challenged her fatigue, and at that moment, a hollow opened before her without warning. Stumbling, she quickly straightened, but her ankle had bent sharply, and it throbbed with each step.

She drew in a tight breath. "Yes."

"Yes, what?"

Briefly irritated by such an inane response, she squinted ahead into the growing dark. No more glances his way. She had to watch where she was going, though it became increasingly difficult in the dying light. "Yes, it was good. Entertaining."

Instead of commenting, he kicked Doc into a sudden leap. Two long strides ahead, the horse whirled to a stop before her and he stepped off and waited as she approached.

Unable to see his expression, she tensed at his imposing form. Both man and beast towered above her, blocking her way unless she shied into the road or across the open field. Either option could prove foolish, yet what did he intend? Her fingers tightened around her satchel strap.

She slowed her steps until she stood at Doc's head. The horse whiffled against her shoulder. She rubbed his velvety nose and drank in his scent.

"He'd like to give you a hand." A hushed snort—from the man, not the horse. "Or should I say *hoof.*"

"Thank you, but—"

Hard hands clamped about her waist and hoisted her off the ground. "I'll take that as a yes."

Without warning or asking permission, he swung her up to the saddle.

She gripped the saddle horn, an unfamiliar appendage to one accustomed to riding English. But not as unfamiliar as a man stepping up behind her, seating himself on the saddle's skirt and hemming her in with one arm around her waist, the other hand taking the reins.

If she didn't breathe, she'd faint. Even Charles had never dared such a maneuver.

Cale did not hold her so close that she couldn't breathe, she simply couldn't breathe because he was so close. Her hat brim crimped against his chest, and after a few steps forward, he pulled it off her head and handed it to her.

"Here. Hold this. Please."

She complied, strictly from shock at his abrupt manner, though she couldn't very well toss it aside. It wasn't hers.

The gelding's easy gait soon had her relaxed, her leg muscles loosened, her back not as stiff. Cale's arm pulled gently at her waist until she rested against him, the buttons of his vest pressing into her right shoulder blade. His breath tickled the top of her head. She'd never felt more protected.

A coiled rope lay beneath her right leg, but the heavy fabric of her skirt prevented it from rubbing. Doc seemed unbothered by her boots brushing his ribs, and she could barely make out the swivel of his ears as he listened for his master's voice while taking heed to what lay ahead.

Time slowed to rhythmic plodding. A silent prayer of thanks ascended for Cale coming upon her when he did.

His chest expanded. "If I see Thorson anytime soon, I'll be telling him what I think of him leaving you to walk back to the hotel in the dark."

If such a meeting occurred, she had no doubt that it would not be cordial. She'd heard an edge to Cale's words before, but she'd never had their intensity vibrate up and down her backbone. The sensation compelled her to defend her boss's decision. "I'm sure they would have taken me. I just didn't want to go with them."

His arm tensed ever so slightly. "Why not?"

She pulled a deep breath and let it escape in a sigh. Truth was easier spoken under cover of darkness rather than while looking into the other person's eyes. "They were going out for drinks and then to the dance. I don't enjoy either. Nor do I enjoy pretending to enjoy or forcing myself to fit in where I don't belong."

His wordless response skimmed the top of her head, and she wasn't sure if his derision was aimed at her or her coworkers. She'd never spoken quite so boldly to any man, not even to Charles. Especially not to her father.

Warmth blew close against her hair, as if he'd dipped his head. "You look like a tick under a toadstool in that hat."

Her turn to huff. He chuckled, and she offered silent thanks that he couldn't see the smile spreading on her face.

"Where do you want to eat?"

The question caught her off guard more than the toadstool remark.

"I'm sure Clara will have a biscuit or two set aside for me. You needn't worry that I'll go hungry."

Barely lifting the rein against Doc's neck, Cale turned them to the left and into the electric glow of Main Street after hours. Several establishments were open—the cigar shop, the tea parlor, a billiard hall, the nickelodeon, and a saloon. And the inviting glow of the Hotel Denton beckoned ahead. She sat up, keenly aware of the draft behind her and the absence of Cale's close support.

He stopped before the hotel's hitching post, stepped down, and tethered Doc. She flexed her ankle and each muscle in each leg, predicting the outcome of dismounting under her own strength. Without the benefit of stirrups, it might be tricky. She plopped the hat on, gripped the horn, and leaned forward to swing her right leg over the cantle. From her position with the wide hat brim pulled low, she didn't see Cale reach for her.

"Oh!" She gripped the hands belting her waist as she rose in the air and descended gently to the street. Those hands remained firm, and she had to tip her head back to see beneath her hat brim. The streetlight hooked the dimple in his cheek. "Do you make a habit of acting unannounced?"

The dimple deepened. "Never had need to." He released his hold and stepped back, one arm extended as if he expected her to topple.

She adjusted the satchel, straightened her spine, and moved toward the sidewalk, where she stepped up and turned. He was only slightly taller now, but it was easier to look him in the eye as she spoke. "Thank you for the ride home. You and Doc"— she stroked the horse's handsome head and scratched beneath his forelock—"were a welcome surprise. I must admit, the distance was farther than I remembered from the drive out earlier today."

Keeping his thoughts to himself, Cale stepped up beside her and offered his arm. With only the slightest hesitation, she tucked her fingers inside his elbow and together they approached the gleaming glass and oak-paneled entrance to the Denton. He opened the door and waited for her to enter—a gentleman in chaps and spurs and dusty boots. One who smelled not of cigars, stuffy libraries, and men's cologne, but of horses and cattle and hard work.

What would her father have to say about that?

CHAPTER TWENTY

Ella walked like she had a rock in her fancy stitched-top boot, and Cale suspected she was holding back for his benefit. Danged if he didn't want to know what lamed her, but whatever the cause, it pained her more when she was tired or upset.

The way she'd leaned against him on their ride to town told him she wasn't upset.

But he was. His blood boiled at Thorson leaving her stranded, in spite of what she'd told him, and he'd see to it that he said his piece.

With a nod to the front desk clerk, she hobbled to the stairway, and took hold of the ornate railing that curved to an end like a handle on a pitcher. Then she pulled off her ridiculous hat and gave him a look that made his knees weak. He hooked his thumbs in his belt and spread his stance to keep from buckling right there in front of her.

"Thank you again." She smiled.

His insides turned to mush, and he tugged his brim. "My pleasure, ma'am." The phrase made her cheeks go pink, and he'd say it over and over just to get the same response.

But when she pivoted in that way she had, he closed the gap and covered her hand on the railing. "I'd like to buy you supper."

She turned back, surprise and doubt sparring in her eyes. "Oh, there's no need."

He pulled out his winnings and held the roll between two fingers. "This is burnin' a hole in my pocket. I'm hungry enough to eat my stirrup leathers, and I don't much care to sit in that fancy dining room all by myself."

As he'd hoped, she smiled and her shoulders eased. Her glance slid through the dining room entry and returned to his wad of bills. "Don't you need that money for the ranch?"

Encouraged by her weakened defenses, he offered his arm again. "I doubt you'll eat enough to rob my heifers."

They must have struck a handsome pose as they entered, for every slick-haired head turned their way. Either that, or he smelled like a coyote.

The women gawked too, eyeing him from beneath feathers, plumes, and flounces atop their piled-up hair. Cale thought more kindly of Ella's wide-brimmed *toadstool.*

She tugged his arm toward a swinging door, and in two steps they stood inside a kitchen that would make Helen's mouth water. His was already—just from smelling what the cook was pulling from the oven. When she turned around, her dark eyes locked on him with a once-over that left him doubting his welcome.

He doffed his hat.

Ella's fingers tightened at his elbow. "Clara, this is Cale Hutton of the Rafter-H. He won the roping today at the rodeo and he's buying me supper."

Clara set the roasting pan on a large worktable and shoved her fists against her waist. "Lawd, child, I know who he is. But what is his dirty self doing in my kitchen?"

He backed up, but Ella clamped her hand like a vise and laughed out loud. "Don't be mad at him. I brought him in here to meet you."

Clara shook her head and picked up a carving knife. A very large knife. "Next thing I know, you'll have all them moving-picture folk in here, traipsing through my clean kitchen." She threw him a crusty look. "Well, what you got to say for yourself? Cat got your tongue?"

He coughed. "No, ma'am." He coughed again, as sure of himself as Kip under Helen's glare. "Smells mighty good in here. Ella tells me you're a fine cook."

She picked up a sharpening stone and dragged the knife over it, first one side and then the other, staring at his dirty boots.

Ella's fingers relaxed. "You work too hard, Clara." She loosed him from her grip and brushed the cook's cheek with a kiss.

Jealousy beat a path from his toes to his head, and he bit down on a big knot of envy to keep from saying something stupid.

"Humph." A smile sparked in the woman's eyes but didn't infringe upon her mouth. "Go on, you two. Best get your table 'fore they all fill up."

He dipped his chin and backed away. "Nice to meet you, ma'am."

Another *humph.*

Ella giggled like a girl and set him to wondering what it would have been like to go to school with her, like Hugh and Jane had.

Fewer heads turned when they re-entered the dining room, and he cut a trail for the table in the near corner. The waiter approached with a towel over his bent arm and a thin mustache over his straight lips. Cale assisted Ella with her chair, silently blessing his pa for showing him such things, and took the seat across the small table, his back to the wall.

The waiter held out his hand. "May I take your hat, sir?"

"No, you may not."

Ella's startled look corrected him. "I mean, no, thank you."

A sniff pulled the man's nose higher, and he addressed Ella. "To drink, ma'am?"

"Tea would be lovely."

"Coffee," Cale added.

With a quick bend at the waist, the waiter left them and disappeared through the swinging door.

If his brother could see him now, he'd spit a hole through the carpeted floor.

He turned his hat over, slid it under his chair, and leaned forward. "I've never laid eyes on Clara. How'd she know who I am?"

Ella laughed, and the sound rippled over him like it had the day they walked the pasture, easing his doubts about eating at the Denton.

"I've no idea. All I know for sure is that she knows everything that goes on in this town, who's involved, and their childhood history."

He stared at her.

She laughed again, angling away to hang her hat on her chair and set her satchel on the floor. "That's exactly how I felt at first, but she has a heart as big as her kitchen stove. And just as warm. You've nothing to fear."

That bucked him up and he drew his chin back. "She doesn't scare me."

Ella's eyes twinkled like candles on a Christmas tree, and he suddenly wanted her to spend Christmas with them at the ranch. How in the world was he going to ask her that?

He shoved his hand through his hair, hunting a decent conversation topic, unable to forget how he'd blown things up his last trip to town. He didn't want to ruin the evening that was turning out to be the best part of the day, his winnings included.

"Did you get many good photographs today?"

"I believe so. Before and during the rodeo."

The waiter returned with their tea and coffee, the cups even flimsier than his mother's china. Ella added cream to her tea and lifted the cup to her mouth. Her eyes drifted shut with pleasure, and he had to look away. Into his black coffee. The coffee he might not get to drink if he had to use the silly excuse of a handle. But he'd be hanged if he'd let something like that keep him from enjoying every bit of the meal he was paying for. And gladly. He turned the handle away, wrapped his hand around the cup, careful not to squeeze for fear it'd break, and took a swallow. Wasn't half bad.

Ella chuckled.

"What?"

"You seem surprised that the coffee is any good."

If she could read him that well, he was in a heap of trouble. He carefully returned the cup to its matching saucer. "I suppose I am. And it is."

He pulled the napkin out from under his silverware and wiped his mouth. His ma hadn't raised no heathen. "Tell me about your pictures."

Her eyelashes swept down, and her hands dropped to her lap where she likely smoothed her skirt again, looking for what she wanted to say. She wasn't the only one who could read a person.

"I took pictures of the setting. The way the nearby ridge hung like a backdrop to the rodeo. Also some of the cowboys and the corralled horses." She glanced up, suddenly shy. "I took one of you on your horse riding in a big circle with the other ropers."

He reached for his coffee. "We were just warming up." Exactly like he was at the moment, though warmer than he cared to be.

"That's what I thought. I also took some of you chasing the steer."

"Did you get me catching it?" That was the whole point, wasn't it?

"Of course. And some right before the wild-horse race." Her eyes grew bigger and she leaned in. "Do they always bite down on the horse's ear to make it stand still like that?"

He chuckled. "Pretty much. They *are* wild horses. They're not going to just stand there all polite and let some wooly cowboy climb up on their back."

"Speaking of wooly, that's one of the pictures I took—the cowboy in the wooly chaps. I also snapped a picture of him before the rodeo, arguing with another cowboy. He didn't look too happy when he heard the shutter click."

A vague memory flashed across the back of his mind—

"Your meal, ma'am, sir."

Mr. Mustache set a steaming plate in front of each of them. Creamy mashed potatoes, sliced roast, glazed carrots. Given the present company and the food before him, every memory he'd ever had vanished into thin air.

A moment later the man returned with a cloth-covered basket and a small bowl of honey.

Ella closed her eyes and inhaled. "Biscuits. Clara's *piece de résistance.*"

"Better than Helen's?" He lifted the cloth and offered the basket to Ella.

"That's hard to say. They're both awfully good. But with honey—oh, my."

A hand slapped down on a nearby table, and Cale and everyone else in the place turned toward the racket. The offender guffawed and hit the table again. "That'd be Old Mose. I was here when Pigg and Anthony brought him in. Biggest bear you ever saw."

Cale turned back to his meal but pinned his ear on the fella's conversation.

"Killed three men, they say."

He glanced at Ella to find her pale as the tablecloth, obviously listening as well. He laid his fork down and reached across the table for her hand. It trembled. "Do you want to leave?"

Her dark eyes were big as the biscuits, but she shook her head. "No. I'm fine. I just . . ."

He lowered his voice. "Just what?" Her hand was soft and cool beneath his fingers, and he stroked the back of it with his thumb.

"I worry about you and the boys at the ranch. If it's like you say, and that bear is a descendant of this Old Mose—"

"Don't you worry. We're takin' care." He gave her hand a light squeeze and released it so she could eat. "A lot of it's just talk. Besides, it's not all a bear's doing."

She waited for him to continue, her glance flicking between him and the table off to his left with the big talker.

"We met today, the Cattlemen's Association. Before the rodeo. It's not just a bear, it's rustlers too. A couple of ranchers are going up to Cripple Creek this week to talk to the butchers. A few others are gonna hunt bear."

Her eyes narrowed. "That man with the wooly chaps I mentioned? When he was arguing with the other cowboy, I heard him say Cripple Creek."

Cale froze, his fork of potatoes halfway to his mouth. "You hear anything else?"

She stared at her plate, pulling in her memory, and then looked up at him. "Yes. I thought it was odd at the time, because I know about Cripple Creek, the gambling, and the gold mines. Even a little about the labor wars up there a few years ago."

His stomach cramped around the food already in it. "But?"

She dabbed her mouth with her napkin. "I heard a couple of other words that didn't make sense to me then. I couldn't catch complete sentences, of course, so nothing really fit together."

"And?"

"Brands."

"Brands?"

"Yes. I heard the word *brands*. And *butcher*."

~

The fork hit his plate and Ella flinched. Mashed potatoes had flown off and landed on his saucer, but he didn't seem to notice.

His big hand balled into a fist, the knuckles whitening, and his jaw clenched. The overall image was remarkably like his brother.

A chill shimmied up her back. She'd ruined a lovely evening.

He caught her eye, and his scowl softened. "I'm sorry." He scraped the potatoes from the saucer and wiped the cup clean with his napkin. "Just surprised me is all."

His apology endeared him to her. A rugged man like that, apologizing for his reaction? Her father would never have done such a thing, in spite of all his social graces.

"This picture you got of him. Does it show his face?"

"A profile. And the other man too. I remember him because of his distinctive chaps—covered with conchos, two fringed pockets, and silver studs."

Cale's jaw worked sideways, and he pushed his food around his plate like a little boy who didn't want his supper. "When you gonna develop the film?"

"Usually I send it back East to Kodak and they develop it, then send me prints and a new roll."

"Can you get it developed here in Cañon City?"

"I could ask at the newspaper office."

"Do that." The hard lines of his face softened as he leaned the slightest bit forward and lowered his voice. "Please."

She gave a guarded smile, uncertain of her success at getting the film developed or at managing her feelings.

They finished their meal in near silence, Cale obviously distracted by what he'd learned but doing his best to not let it show. And failing miserably. She wanted to reassure him, wrap her arms around his burly frame and tell him everything would work out.

She was in over her head.

On their way out, she glanced around the room, noting how frighteningly under dressed she was—and not caring a whit. She'd just had dinner with the kindest and most gallant man she'd ever met, aside from Charles. He'd rescued her from a long and painful walk back to the hotel as well as another lonely supper in her room. A few disparaging looks from formally clad diners were well worth his courteous company.

They stopped at the foot of the stairs for the second time that night, and with her hat in one hand, she gripped the finial with the other. "It was a lovely meal. Thank you again."

Without a word, he scooped her into his arms and started up the stairs, his jaw set in a firm line.

"Excuse me—" She bounced as if he were about to drop her, and her arms wrapped around his neck of their own accord.

"That's better." The dimple fought for purchase, but his forced scowl refused to give it room. "I wouldn't want to drop you and have to come all the way back down to pick you up again."

She tilted her head back and laughed, full and free, unlike anything she'd felt in fifteen months. "You are impossible, Mr. Hutton."

His eyes darkened to late-evening blue and the dimple won out. "Tell me you're not on the top floor."

"The second." Holding to him as she was, her face mere inches away, she could make out individual hairs in the forest sprouting across his jaw. She had only to lean in and brush her lips across its rough surface. Closing her eyes, she pushed back from temptation.

At the second-floor landing, he set her to her feet and held her waist until she stood firmly on her own. The sensation of his hands seeped through her blouse and under her skin, remaining even after he let go.

"I couldn't very well let you climb these stairs after a long day, now could I?" His concern-tempered voice warred with the humor in his eyes.

Understanding him better since her visit with Helen, she longed to tell him more. Tell him *why* she limped, why she'd come West. His tenderness moved her deeply, stirring emotions she'd thought dead and buried. She rested her hand on his arm, and he covered it with his own. Words crowded his gaze, seeking escape. His lips parted.

She moved away, out of the reach of his arms, his aura, his strength that somehow stole into her when he was close. "You are most kind. I'm glad you got to meet Clara. And I'm . . . I . . ." Quickly she turned and left him behind before stumbling into a plight that would only end in heartache once she left him behind for good.

CHAPTER TWENTY-ONE

Cale threw himself into haying and fence-mending and anything else that kept his mind off Ella Canaday. But nothing worked for more than an hour or two, then he'd be right back where she left him at the top of the stairs, watching her fancy boots carry her down the hall and out of his life.

Satisfied the new patch in the north fence would hold, he shoved the wire cutters in his back pocket, swung into the saddle, and turned for the house. Was Ella still in Cañon City, or had the company pulled up stakes and left? Did she get those pictures developed? Might she consider staying on for a little longer? Like forever?

He barked out a laugh, and Doc flicked an ear his way.

After three days listening to Hugh chew on the same old bone about how she'd run him off his feed and left him high and dry, Cale did better on his own, away from everyone else and the temptation to snap their heads off. He hadn't started spittin' yet, but he was giving it serious consideration.

The sun beat down clear and bold, no clouds to leverage the heat. But iron-bellied clouds teased over the mountain peaks boding a summer storm. With plans to stake out a calf at a small lake on Crossett's spread, he and the other ranchers might get more than a bear for their trouble tonight.

If only that were all that ate at him. His head and gut churned with more than a cattle-killing bear. He'd waited a long time for the right woman. He just hadn't figured she'd show up with a moving-picture company sporting bobbed hair and city duds.

But Ella Canaday suited him right down to the ground.

Now all he had to do was convince her.

Coming upon the meadow where they'd spent the afternoon, he reined in at the north edge. June-green with sweet grass and wildflowers, it lay like a thick carpet. A family of mule deer fed off at one end, the lead doe's head high, watching Cale. Two younger does, a yearling, and several spotted fawns grazed nearby, their long ears swiveling, catching every sound, whether squirrel or jay or Doc swishing his tail.

He angled toward the barn, flushing quail from a juniper thicket. Their heavy, startled flapping evidenced why they skittered along the ground most of the time. Still, they stuck together. A family.

Late afternoon, he and Tug set out for Crossett's. Grady had offered a bucket calf, and the bear-hunt bunch agreed to stake it out where they'd found bear tracks along a watering hole. Hugh said he'd meet up with him there. From the roll of slate-gray clouds tumbling into the valley, they'd all better hurry.

Once over the ridge that bordered the Rafter-H on the southwest, the high park opened up like a mountain prairie, and Doc took easy to the level, grassy land. Cale's mind opened as well. His thoughts didn't crowd each other but spread out like grazing cattle with room to roam. And the Lord Himself seemed to ride herd on those thoughts, turning one this way and another that.

A heavy sigh rolled out, and Cale's gaze ran along the distant line of jagged peaks. "I could sure use some help, Lord." Doc swiveled his ears at the low prayer. "With Hugh and his hard-edged ways. The cattle and whatever's gettin' after them.

"Ella." Her name slipped out on a whisper with a rope attached and dallied to his heart.

A distinct impression tugged on that rope and left him knowing he had to talk to her. Had to tell her how he felt and find out firsthand if she was willing to share her past with him. Because sharing was what life amounted to out in this high-park country. A man shared his life and his labor, his wins and his losses.

Some tried to go it alone, but they didn't last long.

He and Hugh and the boys all had each other, but it wasn't the same. Their ma had often said two were better than one, teasing them as twins, since they usually fought over who got what. But he'd looked that passage up in the family Bible after Hugh lost Jane, and figured it wasn't talking about twin brothers.

Since Ella Canaday came to town, he was more convinced than ever.

Thunder growled long and low, rolling off a distant range and dragging near-black storm clouds with it.

He heeled Doc into a lope.

Crossett and Hugh sat back on the high ground, holding Grady's reins as he staked the calf. Once the little fella was secure, Grady backed his way off the sandy patch, sweeping a good-sized juniper branch over his tracks, flushing his smell.

Lightning hit across the valley, and the horses flinched. Crossett's buckskin danced in place, but the old rancher held him short and kept him from bolting.

"Heck of a night to lay wait for a bear." Grady tossed the branch aside and swung up. "Won't be sittin' it out in that aspen thicket."

The storm front teased into the valley, and Cale turned his collar up, the smell of rain heavy and fresh. "I rode through a hollow that'll hold us till the storm passes. If you don't mind gettin' wet."

"Better wet than fried." Hugh spit and turned Shorty in the direction Cale had come. "We can cover in the thicket after the storm blows over."

Crossett called his hound to follow, and the men spread out along the depression and dismounted, reins in one hand, rifles in the other. Cale untied his slicker, glad of it, and screwed his hat down, praying they'd not get hail.

Lightning hit a hundred yards ahead, just past the watering hole, and the calf bawled. Another spear of hot, blue light, and Cale doubted any bear would be out on a night like this. A fat raindrop hit the back of his gun hand, followed quickly by another. Within two swishes of the calf's tail, the sky busted open. Doc's ears splayed side to side and a back leg cocked as he settled in for the downpour. Water ran off the brim of Cale's hat, a regular waterfall in his line of sight to the calf. Too late he regretted not tarping his saddle. Slicker or no, a wet seat on the ride home would soak him to the bone.

Lightning danced across the valley, blown by a strong westerly wind, and as suddenly as it had started, the rain stopped. Silence settled over the men and horses, save for the trickle of a quick stream.

No one made to move from their cover. Cale glanced at Grady, his trail-covering a wasted effort. No scent remained after a gully-washer like that, and if there was a grizzly out there, it could lumber up on them without knowing they were there. The back of his neck crawled.

The calf bawled—a hopeless sound on a rain-washed night. Cale could just make out its form in the dusk, thanks to the fast-moving storm. With its back to the water, it stretched to the end of its tether, lonesome and abandoned, a sacrifice for every other bovine in the area.

But for good reason.

Time stood still. Stringy clouds scuttled across the sky, pulling stars in their wake, and Cale rolled his shoulders and stretched his neck. A slivered moon peeked over the eastern ridge that marked the Rafter-H, and the scent of wet grass filled his nostrils. Coyotes yipped in the distance. The calf bawled.

What felt like hours later, Crossett's hound whined, and he hushed it. Tug sat up and cocked his ears, and Cale lamented not leaving him behind. The calf bolted in a half-arc, away from the aspen thicket like the secondhand on a watch.

A breeze still trailed the storm, which left them downwind. Brush crackled.

A hulking shadow lumbered across the open space between thicket and water hole, puffing and snorting. Rifle chambers loaded. He aimed.

The night split open with gun fire, and the calf took off across the meadow, its rope shot through, but not the bear. It loped over a small rise to live another day.

Hugh spit. A couple men swore, but no one offered to chase a mad and possibly wounded bear in the dark of night.

Gunpowder tainted the air, masking the clean smell of rain-washed earth. Cale gathered Doc and swung up to a wet saddle.

"At least we know it's not a phantom." Brady sheathed his rifle and mounted. "I'll come back at daylight for the calf."

"If he wanders our way, we'll gather him for you," Hugh offered.

"Much obliged."

"I'll take the dogs out in the next couple of days," Crossett said. "See if we can find a trail. We can't give up now."

Cale resituated his hat, in complete agreement. They'd have to finish what they started, and they needed to do it before fall. That meant they had a couple months before cold hit the high country.

He joined Hugh for the ride home, Tug trotting along behind.

The whole situation felt like Old Mose all over again.

~

Ella clutched the bedding beneath her chin, eyes squeezed tight against the blinding light. Every muscle clenched. Another hit.

"One thousand," she mouthed, not reaching the second number before thunder rattled the windows of her hotel room.

Unbidden, the scenery changed, dragged from the stage of her sleep-deprived mind as rain lashed Charles's automobile, washing like a river across the windshield.

"I can't see a blasted thing! Oh God, help us. I can't see the road!" His hands gripped the steering wheel, his face ghost-white in the lightning's flash.

The car slid. Charles turned the wheel, but it was no use. A horse screamed, illuminated by blinding blue, up on its back legs and pawing the air.

It crashed through the windshield into Charles. Both car and horse slid off the road and rolled. Fire shot through Ella's leg as it snapped. And then everything stopped—the engine, Charles's frantic prayers. The horse's screams. Everything but the rain.

She bolted upright, gasping for breath, her lungs seared. Knives cut through her thigh, and she gripped it with her right hand, shocked to find it in one piece and dry. Blinking she looked around the room, dimly lit by the streetlamps below. Thunder rolled in the distance. She threw the covers back and sat for a moment on the edge of the bed, mentally groping for her bearings.

With a hand on her nightstand, she stood, and the teardrop beads of the lamp's shade betrayed her trembling. Two halting steps took her to the dressing table, where she bypassed the small drinking glass and tipped the carafe to her mouth. Water escaped to run down her neck and beneath her gown, cooling her feverish skin.

Still shaking, she set down the carafe, pushed it back from the edge, and stumbled to the bed. Curling onto her left side, she hugged her knees. Tears ran across her face and onto the bed linen, but sleep fled with the storm.

It was the first time since coming to Colorado—the first sleepless night, the first return of the nightmare. The first storm. Like the one that took Charles's life and her strength—an early and unexpectedly harsh spring storm.

But this was June, and she was a thousand miles away in Colorado. Cale had warned her about the sudden summer squalls, how they rolled into the high country and could catch a person unaware. She shivered and reached for the blanket.

Aching and tight, she watched the east window of her room until the black square dimmed to gray. Against the will of every muscle in her weary body, she pulled the coverlet around her shoulders and made her way to the window. Buildings blocked the sunrise but for a line of blood-red across the open roadway, seeping beneath low clouds. Time slowed, and crimson crept into the cloudbank, firing it from within.

Thou makest the outgoings of the morning and evening to rejoice. The phrase always came to mind at a glorious sunrise or sunset. And she'd always marveled that such a phrase was found in the poetry of the Psalms. Who but one who had seen the splendor could write such things?

Her chest released its frantic grip, her fingers their stingy hold of the coverlet. A new day rose before her. Never before used and carrying promise.

~

Clara was not to be fooled. Hands on hips and brows pulled as low as dawn's reddening cloud line, she *tsked* Ella into the kitchen's single chair. "Did our thundersome rain-maker scare you last night, or you been pining for that dirty ol' cowboy?"

In spite of herself, Ella lost her hold on a smile and picked up the coffee waiting on the table next to a plate of gravy-covered biscuits. Her stomach moaned with anticipation. "I did think about him, but not in that way."

"Humph." Clara turned back to her stove as if she weren't interested.

The tact worked.

"When I was at the Rafter-H, Cale told me about the sudden storms here, how they could roll across a mountain valley with little to no warning and drench a person caught unawares."

"That's true enough." A glance flew over her shoulder. "You afraid of lightning?"

With puffy eyelids and dark moons circling her eyes, Ella knew denial would be taken as a bald-faced lie. "Not exactly."

Another glance invited her to expound.

The spicy-sausage aroma demanded attention and she cut into a gravy-topped biscuit. "It brings back bad memories." Sensing that Clara was as generous a soul as Helen, she pushed against the second layer of rock wall encasing her heart. "I was in a motorcar accident a year ago last March. During an unseasonably fierce rainstorm in Chicago."

Clara's salt-and-pepper head nodded in rhythm with her stirring spoon.

"I lost the two things most important to me in life: my fiancé, Charles, and the ability to ride." She shoved in a bite, bidding for silence and time.

"And that's why you come all the way out here with them moving-picture folks. Runnin' from your past."

A second forkful stopped halfway to her mouth. Such a remark was not the compassion and understanding she'd expected. How dare Clara tell her she was running away. She laid her fork on the plate and pressed the napkin to her lips, intent on leaving as quickly—but politely—as possible.

Clara had other plans.

She moved to the counter, rolling her hands in her apron as if rubbing off the aroma of her talents. Sadder, truer eyes had never gained a hold on Ella, so full of pain and wisdom and caution all rolled into an unearthly mix.

"We all lose something precious to us some time or other, but it's how we handle it that makes us who we are." She picked up her large coffee pot and filled Ella's cup. Then her voice dropped to a soft timbre, like a mother soothing a wounded child. "You can't undo the past, girl, so there's no use wastin' away for it. It'll cripple you for sure if you spend your heart wishin' for what you can't have. Best leave it in the Lord's hands. They mighty big."

Ella blinked back tears and picked up her hot cup, closing her eyes against the steam that washed her swollen cheeks the way Clara's tender words washed her soul.

"But this old woman could be wrong."

The clear contradiction jerked her eyes open.

"Could be the good Lord brought you all the way out here His own self." With that, Clara ambled back to her stove, set the pot down with a firm hand, and raised a wooden spoon. "You best be gettin' on. Can't have those fancy folks wondering what become of their seamstress."

Clara's words played over and over in Ella's mind as she walked to the studio. Like a one-reel moving picture, they rewound and flooded light into her clouded emotions, opening possibilities beyond what she dared wish for. She had no idea what those possibilities might be, but the very idea that they existed spawned hope where none had lived for fifteen dark and lonely months.

"Just in time."

Thorson's commanding voice broke into her reverie, and she pulled the studio door closed behind her.

"We're filming at the river again. The footage we got earlier was ruined in development. We'll need extra costumes for Jed and Mabel, just in case something goes wrong. We leave in a half hour."

That meant they'd leave as soon as possible. Ella gathered riding skirts, boots, hats, and the shirts Jed preferred. Reaching for extra scarves, she dislodged a wig that tumbled to the floor with a thump.

Wigs didn't thump.

Stooping, she picked up the hair piece, and out tumbled her Nana's sewing kit. A gasp caught in her throat and she clutched the kit to her waist, looking over her shoulder for anyone who might be watching from the wings. Finding no one, at least no one she could see, she tucked the kit in her satchel and continued gathering costumes.

But something else Thorson had said stuck in her mind like a splinter—*development.* She'd completely forgotten to ask at the newspaper office if they could develop her film. Not that it couldn't wait until she returned to Chicago, but Cale wanted to see her photographs of the two arguing cowboys.

A memory spun through her of his gentleness the evening he carried her up the stairs. If only . . .

An automobile backfired, destroying the mood. It was just as well. She had no time for pointless reminiscing, nor time for checking with the newspaper. Her film would simply have to wait until another day—if she had another day plus the time it took to develop her pictures. Mr. Thorson had not yet announced when the company was leaving.

CHAPTER TWENTY-TWO

Cale set out before daybreak. The fiery sunrise threatened another storm later in the day, but his slicker lay dry and tied behind his saddle. His rifle and rope were at the ready as well. No telling which direction the bear might go next. If they'd wounded it last night, could be it was dying out in the scrub somewhere. Or not.

He doubted it would show itself on the road to town, but he wasn't taking any chances.

And neither was he waiting any longer to talk to Ella Canaday. It was the not knowing that rubbed him raw. She might not even be in town, but at least he'd find out. That was something. But if she and the company had already pulled out, she might have left a letter and a photograph for him. The idea soured his stomach. Just thinking about her being gone wore a hole in his gut. He didn't even have an address for her in Chicago.

She'd sure enough worked herself under his skin, and the timing couldn't be worse, what with bears and rustlers. Maybe he'd talk to the sheriff first. Find out what the others learned in Cripple Creek. Stop by the newspaper office and run a piece on the reward. Maybe even find out if Ella had left her film there.

Then, if she was still in town, he'd take her to lunch, or the soda springs, or for a walk along the river.

At the bend into town, he caught sight of three familiar touring cars headed west along the railroad tracks. Could be they were aiming for the Hot Springs Hotel a couple miles upstream.

Two riders trailed after them. The man riding the big white horse looked like Jed Barr from the way he sat the saddle. The sorrel probably carried Mabel Steinway. Wasn't Ella. Even from this far away, he knew that.

His heart hitched a beat. He'd been right about her ability to ride. Saturday night confirmed it, the way she sat on Doc. Until he pulled her against his chest.

The sheriff could wait. He turned upstream.

The Arkansas ran full bore, tumbling down from the great gorge, intent on taking anything with it that got in the way. Not the perfect time to ford it on horseback, though it looked like Thorson was bent on doing just that. Grape Creek would be running heavy after last night's storm, but the river flattened out just below it, with low banks and few boulders. No whitewater. If the horses crossed there, upstream from the hotel, they might make it.

He touched spurs to Doc and caught up to the crew at the hotel. Most were crossing the swinging foot bridge, including Ella with her arms loaded and another over-sized hat that blocked his view of her face. But relief at seeing her nearly made him light-headed. He followed the riders from a distance, cutting a wide circle around Mabel.

Thorson, with Pete hauling his camera, hiked up to the creek on the other side of the river, the director's arms windmilling here and there. A racket drew Cale's attention to a line of motorcars and the hotel's hack coming up the road behind him. A crowd to watch the filming.

Thorson signaled from across the river. Jed and his mount took to the water, the rush of it tucking the white's chin and drawing his ears sharp toward the muted roar. But Jed gave him his head, and they made it across. Onlookers cheered. Jed played to the crowd, reining in and tipping his hat to the crowd. Then he took position at the top of a small embankment, sheer cliffs hanging behind him like a granite curtain.

Mabel heeled her horse to the water's edge. From the look on her made-up face, she wasn't keen on the idea, and her horse danced and flattened its ears, evidently in agreement. She kicked it repeatedly but held the reins short in her panic. The mixed message sent the horse sideways into the water. Halfway across, it slipped, spooked, and tossed Mabel in the drink. Cale unlashed his rope and charged around the crowd toward the bank.

His first throw dropped the loop around the floundering, screaming woman, but she had sense to take hold. He jerked the slack and dallied to keep her from being swept away in the swift current. Backing Doc in slow, easy steps, he drew a waterlogged Mabel from the churning river and onto dry ground. The crowd cheered again.

Cale dismounted, then loosened his rope as Jed splashed across the river and caught the other horse's reins. In spite of the bright summer sun, Mabel shook like leaves in the fall, soaked to the bone and mad as a plucked jaybird.

Thorson had run back across the footbridge and up to the commotion, red-faced from the effort and sucking wind. "You . . . all . . . right . . . Mabel?" He reached for her shoulder, and she jerked away. Someone from the crowd offered her his suit coat.

Thorson rubbed his hatless head and looked at Cale. "I can't thank you enough, Mr. Hutton."

Cale coiled his rope and glanced at Mabel, encircled by sympathizing citizens. "Water's cold this time of year. Still running full of snowmelt. But she looks to be unhurt."

Thorson's shoulders rose with a deep breath that he shoved out hard. "We'll just have to try it again."

"In a pig's eye!"

He whipped around to a fire-spitting Mabel, the coat clenched tight in her trembling hands. "You can get somebody else to ride that fleabag across that death trap, because it's not going to be me."

Jed heeled his horse closer. "But Mabel darlin'—"

"Don't you *darlin'* me!"

Thorson's mouth gaped as his leading lady tromped to the hotel's hack and climbed in, followed by the driver.

Quick to recover, he eyeballed the crowd, much closer now, as well as the crew across the river. "Where's Slim? We'll just have to dress him up. Canaday!"

Cale's hackles rose at the harsh yell, and his hands clenched, reminding him of what he wanted to tell the man about deserting Ella after the rodeo.

She must have crossed on the footbridge shortly after Thorson, because she emerged from the crowd, holding costumes and wearing a smaller hat. But not by much.

Thorson's arms went to work. "Where's Slim? Get him dressed for the ride."

Her chin came up and she flicked her dark eyes at Cale. His knees nearly buckled.

"He won't do it, sir." She stepped closer with hardly a hitch. "He said he's not crossing the river on a horse, no matter what. That's why he stayed on the other side."

"Why, that lazy, no-good little—"

"Maybe a local can do it."

Thorson stopped his tirade, blinked at her a couple of times, and then turned to the long-eared onlookers craning for every word. "Well? Who's up to ford the stream?"

Cale grunted. Wasn't exactly a stream. But he nearly choked when the crowd took a collective step. *Back.*

Ella drew herself up, snagging Cale's scrutiny. He looked deeper. Past the costumes and hat and bobbed hair to what he believed was the core of Ella Canaday. It sparked in her clear eyes, supported by the set of her jaw, reinforced with her square-shouldered stance. His earlier conviction solidified. She could ford the stream. She was horsewoman enough, especially if she rode Doc. But she'd never volunteer.

And she might never speak to him again.

He reset his hat. "I have a suggestion."

Thorson's flushed face and cold-steel eyes swung his way. "What, Hutton?"

"You need a sure-footed horse for the crossing. That little sorrel isn't up to it. You could see it as Mabel urged her toward the bank." He tugged on Doc's reins and the gelding moved closer. "But Doc here can do it. Best horse around." He patted Doc's neck in affirmation.

Thorson gave him a once-over, then planted his hands at his belt and cut Cale a sharp glare. "Maybe so, but you don't look a lick like Mabel Steinway."

The crowd snickered, a few guffawed. Humor rippled over Ella's features, but she rolled her lips and ducked her chin.

"You're absolutely right, I don't. But I know someone who can pass for her and fit into her clothes—and I don't mean Slim. Someone who's more horsewoman than Mabel ever will be." He flashed the costume girl a quick glance. "In fact, she's already ridden Doc and they proved a good match."

Ella's head shot up so fast, her hat fell off.

～

Cale Hutton was out of his ever-loving mind and she told him so.

He smiled. *Smiled!* "Why, thank you, Miss Canaday. I've always considered myself to be an ever-loving soul."

Steam churned just inside her ears, scalding the words piling up on themselves, stuck behind her gritted teeth.

She'd walk away, but her feet had sprouted roots again—three steps from Mr. Thorson's tomato-red face. He glared at her as if he'd never seen her before, as if she were an imposter, stealing the spotlight from his star performer. She *would* be an imposter if she tried such a foolhardy move as riding across the river in Mabel's stead. Ridiculous. *Ridiculous!*

And the spotlight was exactly what she did *not* want, metaphorically or otherwise.

She darted her focus from the director to Cale. *How dare he?* This was the second time he'd forced his hand with her where riding was concerned. And yet . . .

She swallowed around the rock in her throat, admitting to herself that she *had* ridden Doc. For a while, anyway, taking note of his rock-solid build, his trustworthy nature. Until Cale pulled her back against his chest. The memory quickened her pulse.

She'd ridden Barlow too, but that was different. Both times were different. Riding through a pasture or along a roadway was nothing like fording a river. Cale Hutton was the gambler this time, gambling on her horsemanship. And wagering her *life*.

The dimple flashed, but he stuck his tongue in his cheek and peered all the way into her soul. Suddenly exposed, she couldn't hide the pain of dashed hopes, nor the longing for a second chance. His jaw clenched and the slightest dip of his chin betrayed his confidence.

And filled her with . . . what?

Silently she commanded her lungs to participate in her wellbeing before she fainted dead away. *Oh Lord, help me now, please. I can't do this . . . can I?*

"Is he talking about you?" Thorson rubbed his jaw and looked her up and down. Then he tipped his head toward the gelding whose kind eyes took in every nuance. "You've ridden this horse?"

She nodded, unwilling to open her mouth for fear of what might come out.

"Well, we don't have all day. Change clothes. Pete'll get you powdered up. It won't be a close shot, so powder will do. And kohl around your eyes." He turned to a technician. "Go get Pete and tell him to bring makeup and be quick about it."

The young man dashed off, much more spry of foot than anyone there.

She bent for her hat and Thorson zeroed in on her again, his face a paler shade, closer to under-ripe cherries. "Just ride across the river and up the embankment to Jed. Then turn and face the camera, right next to him. It's the big finale."

He hadn't asked if she was willing to try, but trying wasn't an option. Deep down in her walled-up heart she *wanted* to do it, to ride again, free and unencumbered.

Remarkably, she trusted Cale's judgment—for all his bull-headed, independent, know-it-all ways.

Beyond question, she trusted his horse.

All she needed now was to trust God to see her through the challenge.

He'd seen her through a lot worse.

"All right."

A pent-up breath escaped through Thorson's seamed lips. He shot Cale an unreadable look and clomped off toward the bridge, mumbling under his breath.

Ella juggled the costumes, sorting out what she'd need, and gauged the distance to the hotel and back. Surveying the automobiles, she chose them as a closer cover, and singled out two women from the crowd as lookouts. They barely contained their glee.

Moments later, outfitted in Mabel's costume, complete with a wig and hat, Ella passed through the crowd to quiet comments of "We're pulling for you," and "You can do this."

She coveted their confidence.

Pete seated her on the running board of the nearest automobile and came at her with a kohl pencil. She drew back.

"It won't hurt, sit still. Do you want Thorson yelling at us any more than he already has?"

She blinked.

"Don't blink." He gripped her shoulder and pulled her straight. "Tip your head back but don't close your eyes. Stare at something over my shoulder. The sooner you cooperate, the sooner we'll get this over with."

She'd never considered how hard it was to hold one's eyelids open when faced with a pointed object in another person's hand. The oily pencil pulled a line from the inside corner of her eye, over to the outside edge, and lifted. Pete braced the heel of his hand against her chin, and drew a line under her bottom lashes, stopping where the first line had begun.

He lowered his hand and squinted, studying his work. "Good. One more."

She blinked.

He frowned.

"My eyes are drying out." After blinking several more times, she tipped her head back. "All right."

He repeated the process, then smudged the lines with his finger and added a few marks to her brows.

"Close your eyes."

Well aware of what came next, she drew a deep breath and complied just before the powder hit her face.

Pete smoothed it down her neck and under her collar, then stepped back to admire his work, judging by the half-smile on his face. "Not bad. Not bad at all. From a distance, everyone will think you're Mabel."

She shivered at his misguided compliment. Mabel was the last person she wanted to emulate or be mistaken for.

Pete gathered his tools, slapped his makeup box closed, and took off at a run. Stopping suddenly, he whirled around. "Break a leg!"

As soon as the words left his mouth, he blanched. "I mean …" His glance jumped to her right leg and back to her face.

"It's all right, Pete. And thank you."

He bobbed his head and returned to his race against the sun, across the footbridge, along the opposite bank, and several yards up a small rise across Grape Creek near the chosen bluff.

Ella smoothed her split skirt and scrunched her toes in the scrolled, high-top boots. Break a leg indeed. Her moment of triumph—or failure—awaited.

Cale approached with that easygoing, long-legged stride she couldn't afford to appreciate at the moment. Doc stayed "ground-tied," as he called it, but followed with eyes and ears.

He stopped so close, the heat of him radiated against her powdered face. He thumbed his hat brim up, fighting the dimple and losing. Scrubbing one hand over his mouth, he erased the near smile, took her hand with the other, and her breath with his words. "I believe in you."

His deep tones wrapped around her like a warm wind on a cold day, seeping through her skin and into her bones.

"God gave you a natural gift. I don't know why you hide it and fight your head. Maybe it's none of my business, but it's there. A blind dog could see it."

His calloused hand tightened around her fingers, infusing her with strength. The confidence shining in his Colorado-blue eyes fed her own.

Marveling that she was no longer angry about the outlandish position he'd put her in, she allowed his words to penetrate her reserve.

He touched the coiled rope on his shoulder, still wet from rescuing Mabel. "I'll be close by in case anything goes wrong, but it won't. You know Doc is true. He'll get you across."

Releasing her fingers, he trailed his hand up her arm to her shoulder, and his eyes darkened to evening blue. "I won't let anything happen to you. Just ride like you know you can."

A faint rumbling filled her ears, but it wasn't thunder on the mountain, the river, or Cale's throaty laughter. Afraid he might hear it, she turned toward Doc and the rushing water, her steps still uneven but stronger than when she'd arrived in Cañon City. She'd have four strong, healthy legs beneath her, as well as the watchful eye of a man she was willing to trust with her life.

Doc whiffled his greeting, and she buried her face in his neck. "I'm counting on you, boy." A deep-chested answer vibrated beneath her hands, and she reached for a fistful of mane.

Cale linked his hands for her left foot, and she stepped up, shifting forward in the seat so much larger than her customary English saddle.

Sliding her booted feet into the wide stirrups, she glanced at Cale with surprise. "They're the perfect length."

He took Doc's bridle with a half-smile pulling one side of his mouth.

Thorson's holler across the river swept downstream with the water, but his waving arms were loud and clear.

"I'll be right here." Cale stepped back with a tug on his hat brim. She reined Doc toward the riverbank, hearing nothing but the rushing water and the other odd rumble—the tumbling of stones from the heavy wall around her heart.

Jed and his horse, Lucky, entered the river, water quickly rising above the horse's knees and churning close to the stirrups in midstream. Up the opposite bank, he made for the bluff top once more where he turned Lucky with a flourish, waiting for Ella to follow.

She knew the camera rolled.

She knew Thorson held his breath.

She knew the silent crowd behind her waited spellbound to see if she would make the crossing or be thrown into the Arkansas River.

And she knew, as Cale had reminded her, the gift that God had given her.

Like Peter climbing from the boat to walk on the sea, she heeled Doc forward, keeping her eyes on the opposite bank. Leaning forward with a pat on the gelding's neck, she committed to the journey. "Come on, boy. It's just a little water."

Ears perked forward, he stepped soundly into the rush, finding purchase on the slick rocks of the riverbed.

Halfway across, the water's roar thundered around her. Powerful. Unrestrained. Untamed.

Doc didn't flinch or hesitate but crossed confidently until he climbed the opposite bank.

Quickly taking charge, she reined him up the embankment to Jed's side atop the bluff and faced the camera. Thorson would want her looking at Jed as if he'd saved her life—which he was completely incapable of doing—so she gave him her best wide-eyed Mabel imitation.

Surprise rippled across Jed's features, at her riding or her acting she couldn't tell. He leaned from his saddle for the signature kiss.

"Cut!"

Bless Thorson's soul. She slapped her stirrups and Doc lurched forward.

Jed caught himself before he took a spill.

Ever the showman, he covered his blunder with a wave of his hat and winked. "Maybe next time, darlin'."

In a pig's eye.

CHAPTER TWENTY-THREE

Jealousy collided with pride, swamping Cale's judgment before it all rolled into relief. Good thing he wasn't mounted, or he'd be charging through the Arkansas and right over the top of Jed Barr.

The crowd erupted behind him, applauding, cheering, hollering. Even Thorson's crew across the river jumped up and down and waved their hats.

Ella rode down the embankment and across Grape Creek where Thorson met her with an outstretched hand and a pat on the neck for Doc. The lump in Cale's throat was so big he could hardly breathe.

The director talked to her briefly, and Ella shook her head. Doc side-stepped, a sure sign that he'd picked up on her tension. Thorson's arms flailed, but Cale couldn't see Ella's expression for the distance and that danged hat. She reined around Thorson and headed downstream toward the Hot Springs Hotel.

Cale hoofed it for the footbridge.

Running in spurs wasn't the smartest thing he'd ever done, but he couldn't lose her now. He kept Doc in the corner of his eye, praying Ella wouldn't kick into a lope and ride all the way into town. At the bridge, he slowed and screwed his hat down tighter.

He didn't fear heights, but crossing a flimsy, swinging wooden-slatted footpath wasn't his idea of vertical security. His rope in one hand and the other skimming the thin railing, he ran across the bridge, bucking it harder with every stride.

Ella had reached the front of the hotel, and Cale stopped on solid ground to catch his breath as she approached. A smile lit her face like the Fourth of July, in spite of her ghostly makeup. A prayer of thanks shot from his gut—for her safety and her success.

He resituated his hat and stepped up to Doc, cupping the gelding's muzzle in one hand as he looked up at Ella. "Nice job." Confound it, he'd had a mouthful to say earlier, and now could find only two words.

He reached for her.

She reined back.

"I can do it." No snip. Just a bite of confidence he hadn't seen in her before. It made his chest tight.

She swung her right leg over, then leaned into the saddle as she freed her left foot from the stirrup and slid to the ground.

Handing him the reins with one hand, she pulled off the hat and wig with the other. "He was a champ."

Cale stood as close as he could without stepping on her toes, but she didn't shy away. Just pulled a cloth from her pocket and started wiping her face.

"So were you." His voice scratched out rough, but he didn't care. And he didn't care what she looked like. He stilled her hand and pulled her closer.

Stunned, her lips parted, and her eyes grew wide as he looped his other arm around her and did what he'd wanted to do since snatching her off Main Street.

~

Ella's mind spun with contradiction—the soft promise of Cale's mouth and the firm hold of his arm. The weakness in her legs and the strength of her desire.

The smell of him enveloped her in sunshine and leather and earth.

She dropped everything and encircled his waist against all propriety, leaning into the refuge of his very real, very masculine presence. Perhaps she was dreaming.

He lifted his head with a deep moan, and she opened her eyes to his beautiful blue gaze. Emboldened, she fingered his unshaven jaw, and he caught her hand in his own and held her fingers to his lips. The dimple won out and his eyes twinkled.

Her heart danced.

Doc nudged his master, throwing them both off balance, and Cale clutched her to him all the harder. Laughing, he kissed the top of her head, her temples, her cheeks, his breath sending shivers of delight all the way to her booted toes.

"As far as leading ladies go, you leave them all in the dust."

Movement near the hotel caught Ella's eye, and she glanced away to see Mabel watching from a corner of the building, wet and deflated, the hotel's hack driver urging her back to the coach.

Near pity for the woman threatened to steal the moment until Ella remembered what Cale was saying. A smile shot across her face. "Do you say that to all the women who ride your horse?"

"Yes, ma'am."

His words touched a tender place, and she stepped back but not far. He refused to release her, and the flexing of his jaw muscle hinted at more to come.

"Every single one."

She lowered her gaze, unwilling to fall any farther into the blue depths. How silly that she should care if he'd let other women ride Doc. A sudden squeeze of his arms drew her eyes to his sober face. No teasing. No dimple.

"You're that single one."

The prettiest phrase she'd ever heard.

"You two gonna stand here all day, or you gonna help us load?"

She jerked free at the taunting voice to find Pete hauling his camera over his shoulder with the rest of the company in his wake. She dipped her head, counting on her fringe and leftover powder to hide any telltale blush.

"We're just tying up some loose ends here." Cale's deep voice set her to fussing with her hair and searching for the cloth she'd used earlier.

"Yeah." Pete laughed outright. "I can see that."

Mortified, she picked up the wig and hat, straightened her spine, and met Cale's laughing eyes. No real words of affection had followed his kiss, and she accepted it for what it was—a celebratory moment of triumph for both of them.

"I should be getting back to the studio. But . . ."

"Yes?"

If she were not careful with her words, she'd spill her soul onto the grass at his feet. That would never do. "Thank you for your help. Your encouragement. For such a trustworthy horse and . . ."

His expression would be her undoing, for the laughter had faded into the ebb and flow of longing and restraint, an image of what warred in her very own breast.

Her voice diminished to a whisper. "Thank you for believing in me."

"I'm not the only one. From what I could see, Thorson was pretty pleased with your performance."

He'd noticed. She pushed her hand through the sweaty hair at her temple. "Indeed."

"If you don't mind my asking, what did he say?"

Her gaze held on Cale's honest and open face. "He wants to film me in other riding situations."

"Will you do it?"

She shook her head.

A wrinkle formed between his brows. "Why not? You're fully capable."

"I know that now. Because of you." She must be careful. The ground beneath her was thin at best. "But I don't want to be an actress. I'm not here to take Mabel's place, or anyone else's, for that matter. We'll be leaving soon, and I'll be returning to Chicago."

His eyes dimmed. If she'd shoved a knife into him, the pain could not have shown more clearly.

"When do you leave?"

How quickly triumph crumbled into tragedy. She fussed with the wig, turning it over and over inside the hat, like the emotions churning inside her midsection. "I don't know. But I imagine we may hear Thorson's decision today."

Cale scrubbed his hand across his mouth and kicked at a loose rock near his feet. "Come back to the ranch first. One last time. There's something I want to show you."

One last time. A knife opened her own heart and she clutched at her collar.

He took her hand. "I'll meet you at the studio, find out if Thorson will give you a day. Then we'll ride to the ranch on Doc, and I'll bring you back tomorrow." A smile broke through his somberness. "We did that once before, remember? It's only five times farther to the ranch than the rodeo grounds, but I'll let you sit the saddle."

How could sadness roll from her lips in a soft chuckle? No one but this cowboy had ever been able to lighten her spirit like that. Not even Charles.

"All right. I'll meet you there."

With a heated look, he touched the fringe at her cheek, then turned and swung into the saddle—the gallant knight in not-so-shiny spurs who had stolen her heart.

The realization struck her full force as he trotted upstream to a shallow place and crossed the river without incident. She had made a similar crossing—an impossible feat for one so crippled by fear. Yet, in risking the impossible, she'd crossed more than a raging mountain current, and now she found herself on the other side of emotions she'd once thought were gone forever.

Cale and Doc turned for town. She turned for the foot-bridge.

Her lips throbbed with sweet memory, and she clutched the hat as she crossed the wooden slats, water rushing below her like her past—the same, yet somehow changed in the passing. Last to arrive at the touring cars, she climbed into the one with her clothes and other costumes and quickly checked her satchel for the sewing kit. Relieved at finding it still tucked inside, she fell against the seat back, tired, spent, and happier than she'd been in a very long time. A short-lived happiness, with departure pending, but happiness nonetheless.

The engine chugged to life, and the car lurched forward.

"That was quite a ride you made today." Slim hung his hat on his knee and flung his arm across the back of the seat.

Ella turned her head away. Sweaty didn't begin to describe Slim's condition or aroma. She took a long deep breath of fresher air before facing him. "Thank you. But I'm sure you could have done the same."

A snorty huff. "I doubt it. Mr. Hutton wasn't about to let me ride his horse, and I wasn't about to ride Mabel's. It was you or nothing, and I think Thorson would've had a seizure if you hadn't stepped up."

Interesting turn of phrase, in more ways than one, but a topic she didn't care to discuss. "When do you think we'll be leaving?"

Slim lowered his arm, a small but welcome blessing.

"I heard him talking to Pete about going back to the Rafter-H one more time to film a few background shots. Scenery, horizon, that sort of thing."

Hope shot through her veins as the automobile thumped over a rough patch, jarring her teeth and knocking Slim against his side of the car. After what she'd just done for him, surely Mr. Thorson would give her the day, particularly if he was planning to film scenery at the ranch. No costumes required.

She wasn't sure what made her so giddy—the bumpy road or the possibility of a certain cowboy's arms around her one last time.

When they pulled up to the studio, that cowboy was waiting in front, his horse's reins dangling to the street, he himself in the building's shadow. Slim hopped over the side as soon as the car stopped, and Ella gathered the costumes.

Thorson stepped out of his motorcar and approached Cale, no doubt talking about returning to the Rafter-H. She hurried to the sidewalk, careful not to stumble.

"Word in town is there's a killer bear out your way. Do you know anything about that?"

Ella's heart, not her feet, staggered. She'd forgotten about the bear and rustlers and disappearing livestock. And her film. She glanced down the street toward the newspaper office. There might be enough time to get her film developed. But she wanted to hear what Mr. Thorson said, and she couldn't be both places at once.

~

Cale battled his desire to watch every move Ella made while focusing on what Thorson was saying. He yanked his hat off and scrubbed through his hair. "Something's stealing cattle, so we've got our eyes peeled. But whatever it is strikes at night. Bears don't typically try anything in broad daylight, and neither do rustlers. If you stay close around the ranch house, you should be all right. Hugh and I are armed at all times, just in case." *And I aim to marry Ella Canaday, so she won't be leaving with you.*

Worried he'd said that last part out loud without realizing it, he watched Thorson's face for a reaction.

"All right. We'll be out early tomorrow, just a few of us. We should be able to film what I want by noon. That suit you?"

He jerked a nod. So far so good. The man hadn't laughed, cussed, or hollered, so Cale's intentions were safe. He reset his hat and stood taller. "I'd like to take Miss Canaday to the ranch today. She could ride back with you tomorrow. Or I can bring her back in the wagon."

Thorson's eyes narrowed and his chin tipped. "So, you got designs on my seamstress?"

Cale swallowed and gathered the explanation he'd prepared, but Thorson clapped him on the shoulder before he could get the words lined up right.

"Looks to me like you're the one that got her riding. While she's there, maybe you can talk her into doing a little more of it for our moving pictures."

Thorson was wrong on two counts, but Cale bit the inside of his cheek rather than give him the details. He touched his hat brim and stepped back. "Tomorrow, then."

As soon as the director disappeared through the studio door, Ella deserted whatever task had kept her busy at the nearest automobile listening to every word.

Cale smiled in spite of himself. She was as bad as Doc. "How soon can you be ready?"

"I couldn't quite make out that last—" She clapped her pretty little mouth shut and looked away. Her cheeks turned as pink as a summer rose. "I mean . . . I take it he didn't mind."

"He and a couple others are coming out tomorrow. You can ride back with them." He moved a half-step closer and lowered his voice. "Or I could bring you back in the wagon. That way you could stay longer."

A shy smile played at her mouth, and if they weren't standing on Main Street, he'd kiss it right off her lips.

"Well, I need to change clothes—"

"Don't. You're dressed just right if we're riding Doc. And for where I want to take you."

She glanced down at her loaded arms, then into the studio. "I still have to take care of all this. And there's one more thing. Two, actually."

He waited, watching thoughts dart across her face.

"I haven't had the film developed, so I'd like to stop by the newspaper office and see if they can do that. And I need to get a few things from my hotel room."

Her cheeks got all pink again and she avoided his gaze.

He knew better than to press that last issue. "Can I take the film for you while you go to your room?"

"You'd do that?"

He couldn't decide if she was prettier when she smiled or when he caught her off guard. "Absolutely. In fact, I need to stop there anyway and see if the editor will run a notice about a reward for names and information connected to cattle rustlers." He shook his head and ran a hand over his face. "Should have done that by now, but I got distracted."

"By a river crossing?" Her innocent look, completely play-acted, dared him to deny it. If they didn't get on the road, and quick, he'd lose his self-restraint. He pulled at his open collar. "I can take your camera or just the film."

"It's right here in my satchel. But let me unload these costumes."

He followed her into the cluttered studio and waited for his eyes to adjust to the dim interior. No one was around, but voices came from beyond the painted partition. Thorsen's, for one. He itched to leave before the man decided he needed Ella for some chore.

"Here." She handed him a black cylinder. "Ask the editor if he can develop Verichrome film for a Kodak 3 pocket camera, and if not, see if there is anyone else in town who can."

She folded his fingers around the film and gave him a soft smile. "I'll meet you in the Denton lobby."

CHAPTER TWENTY-FOUR

At the hotel, Ella filled her satchel with the necessary items she'd need for an overnight stay, then dropped in her camera, an extra roll of undeveloped film, and her sewing kit. After a quick inventory of her room, she slipped out and locked the door with a satisfying *click*. If Mabel came calling, she could take what she wanted. Everything that meant anything to Ella was in her satchel. And waiting downstairs in the lobby.

She stopped at the landing and leaned over the railing, craning her neck to see if Cale had arrived, but she didn't have a complete view. Gripping the railing in one hand and her satchel strap in the other, she made her way down the stairs. Anticipation had temporarily banished her fatigue, but weariness was creeping back into her leg. The day was taking its toll, and her body ached for a warm water-filled copper tub, not a long horseback ride to the Rafter-H.

Her heart, however, had other ideas.

Especially when she caught him standing before the large window, looking out on the street—a perfect opportunity to drink her fill undetected. Broad-shouldered and solidly built, he reminded her of the lofty pine at his home. Protective, sheltering, and bearing a sweet perfume all his own.

He turned suddenly, as though he'd heard something.

Had she sighed?

Immediately his alerted features shifted into a much-too-masculine smile.

Her stomach flipped over and she hiccupped.

"You all right?" He approached, the question pulling his brow.

"Yes. Fine, thank you." She gripped her satchel strap and drew a deep breath through her nose. Throwing herself into his arms would certainly be a most inappropriate thing to do.

Doc waited for them in front of the hotel, his reins draped through a ring on a granite hitching post. Cale gave her a leg up, handed her the reins, and then stepped in the stirrup and swung up behind her.

With the welcome sensation of his close proximity, she reined Doc toward the edge of town.

She relaxed once they made the bend in the road and turned north away from the river. Here, no curious eyes followed their unusual pairing atop a single horse rather than riding in an automobile. She minded their situation not at all, though Cale would no doubt prefer the saddle seat to its leather skirt.

A gallant knight indeed.

She looked across her shoulder. "What did the newspaper editor say?"

Cale leaned in and bent around her at a most disconcerting angle, his breath dusting her face. "He said he'd have the film ready tomorrow afternoon."

So much for conversation. Any more of that, and she'd have to get off and walk. "Perfect." She straightened her spine, determined to ask no more questions until they were safely to the ranch with more space between them.

Based on her empty stomach and the rumbling of Cale's behind her, it was sometime after noon when they rode into the yard, greeted by the old spotted dog and three young and boisterous boys.

"You came back!" Kip's gap-toothed grin lit his dirt-smudged face.

"Told you." Jay stopped jumping up and down and struck a mature pose. "Welcome back, Miss Ella."

Ty took hold of Doc's bridle as they slowed. "I'll take him for you, Miss Ella."

Cale jumped down. "Good man, Ty. Hold on a minute."

He turned with outstretched hands, a much more inviting proposition than stepping down in her weakened state. Effortlessly, he lifted her from the saddle and set her on the ground, his hands lingering at her waist until confident of her balance.

She brushed at her skirt and shifted the satchel strap. "I seem to be saying the same thing over and over."

He held her gaze with a hint of concern. "What's that?"

"Thank you."

His grin mimicked his nephews, and he tipped his hat brim. "My pleasure, ma'am."

There it was again, that true cowboy trait that turned her insides to marmalade. Oh, how she would miss hearing those words.

Rather than weep at the thought, she gave each boy a quick hug and, with Cale's offered elbow, made her way to the back of the house and up the porch steps.

Helen burst out the screen door, arms wide. "Land sakes, it's good to see you."

The woman's hearty squeeze nearly pressed tears from Ella's eyes.

Drawing back, Helen cupped each shoulder in a palm and swept her gaze from Cale to Ella. "You here for good?"

Ella choked on her own breath, covering her sudden coughing fit with her hand.

Helen gave her back a good slap and ushered her inside.

"Let's get you some lemonade and a bite to eat. You, too, Cale, after you take that satchel to the boys' room. You are staying the night, aren't you, dear?"

The dimple stitched Cale's cheek in spite of his seamed lips, and he ambled off with her satchel. Dropping into a chair at the familiar table, Ella lightly fingered her cheeks and forehead. She'd not brought a hat for the long ride, and her sun-kissed skin would no doubt pay the price.

"To answer your question, yes. Mr. Thorson and a few others are coming out tomorrow to film scenery, and I'll return with them." She pushed the depressing fact to the farthest corner of her mind.

"So we've got company again. That means cookies, pies . . ." Helen set a lemony drink before her.

"No—they won't be here that long. Please, don't put yourself out."

A hand deflected the comment. "Cookies and pies are my specialty. How else do you think I bribe those three little hooligans into doing what I tell them?"

Genuine laughter eased the tension in Ella's shoulders, and the lemonade cooled her dry lips. The sense of *home* nearly overwhelmed her. Such a foreign impression compared to what awaited her in Chicago.

Helen moved a pan to the front of the stove. "I'll heat these beans for you, and I've got cornbread to go with them." She joined Ella at the table, dabbing her brow with her apron hem. "So tell me what you've been doing since last you were here. Anything exciting?"

Ella pressed the back of her hand to her wet lips, which sent Helen after a napkin and gave her time to phrase an answer. "I did some riding."

One brow cocked over all-seeing gray eyes that traveled from blouse to riding skirt to fancy stitched boots and back again. "Do tell."

Exactly what Ella didn't want to do. Thank goodness she had washed her face at the hotel. There would have been no ducking kohl-rimmed eyes and powder on one's collar. "How have the boys been? Has the bear returned?"

A heavy *humph* announced the woman's frustration. "They'll be bear bait for sure if they don't stay closer to the house. But for all my harping at them, the bear hasn't shown his hide since the last time you were here." She mopped her forehead again. "Did Cale tell you about the hunt?"

"Was it successful?" As soon as the words left her lips, she knew the question was misplaced if Helen was still warning the boys to stay close to the house.

"From what Hugh said, they lured it down to a pond on the Crossett place night before last. Staked out a bucket calf, poor little thing. But shooting in the dark didn't win any prizes, and the bear got away." She chuckled. "So did the calf. Lord, musta been looking out for the little fella."

A chill crawled up Ella's back as she imagined the sacrificial animal. One for the many? Is that how cattlemen viewed the situation? It gave her pause to think that Cale would agree to such terms. He seemed a kinder sort. Hugh, on the other hand, did not.

As if in confirmation, he banged in through the screen door and stopped abruptly.

The skin on Ella's neck crawled beneath his needling stare. "Hello, Hugh."

Helen stood. "Coffee? Sit a spell and visit. Ella's here for a day or so."

He swore under his breath.

If this were her father's parlor, the man would be escorted from the house. But this was *his* house. From his look of disgust, he wanted to do the escorting.

He turned and slammed out the screen door the same way he'd come in, banging it against the outside wall.

In the face of such disrespectful rudeness, Ella was embarrassed for Helen.

Helen was anything but.

The coffee pot hit the stovetop as hard as the screen had hit the house. "If I didn't take to those three youngsters like I do, I'd leave that man to stew in his own juices. No kind of woman wants to live with that. And if he's not careful, he'll drive those boys off too."

Ella sipped her lemonade, marveling anew at how dissimilar the Hutton twins were. "He and Cale are so different."

"Cale came close to mimicking his brother after they missed the bear, tearing around here like his tail was singed." Helen returned to her chair with an unladylike grunt.

Ella swallowed a lemony chuckle, allowing the woman her indiscretion. She deserved much more than an exhausted groan in light of her surly employer.

"Didn't surprise me one bit that he took off for town this morning and brought you back. Truth is I was hoping he would."

Ella stared at her hostess, struck again by such plain speech.

Helen let out a laugh. "Don't look so shocked. You do that boy a world of good, and he deserves it." She finished her lemonade, set the glass on the table without making a sound, and gave Ella a sideways glance. "He's crazy about you, you know."

No, she didn't know. Yet the way he kissed her earlier . . .

"Would you stay on if he asked you to marry him?"

Ella swallowed around her heart, for it had climbed into her throat screaming *yes! yes!*

Surprised at such an irrational answer that she dared not declare, she fumbled with the buttons on her shirt. "I . . . well . . . he's not . . ."

"Mark my words. If he knows what's good for him—and I believe he does—he will by this time tomorrow."

~

Cale wanted her to see the sunrise. But not after the fact. See it before it arrived, as it slid along the horizon like molten gold. If they didn't leave in the next half-minute, it'd be too late.

Doc stomped a foot, relaying Cale's tension as they waited at the corrals. Barlow dozed, one back leg cocked, willing but not eager about a pre-dawn ride to the ridge.

The screen door shut. Cale squinted toward the house, picking out only the faint glow from the kitchen window. He'd lit a lamp and set it on a stump outside before he left, hoping it would draw Ella through the dark. Hoping it would draw her to him, the old moth to the flame trick. But he had a different ending in mind, not one that consumed the fluttering creature.

Doc turned his head. Cale stilled every muscle, straining to hear what his horse heard, and soon he caught the uneven footfall on dry ground. His pounding pulse was louder.

"Good morning." Her near whisper reflected her nature—not abrupt or loud or out of place, but gentle. Comprehending. Confident. She greeted Doc with a hand-rub along his head, and the gelding whiffled his pleasure.

"I'm glad you came." Cale gathered the mare's reins and led her away from the corral. "Barlow's ready for you."

He couldn't see Ella's smile, but he sensed it the same way he sensed rain on the wind and snow before the storm. A clear day before it arrived.

She stepped in next to him, her hair smelling like a flower. No hat. He was ready.

He handed her the reins. She grabbed a handful of mane. Getting on was her challenge, putting all her weight—what little there was—on her right leg as she slid her left foot in the stirrup.

He lifted his hands, ready to catch her if she wobbled, but resisted encircling her waist and lifting her up. The determination glinting in her eye yesterday still shone in his memory. She'd conquered something. He wouldn't take it from her.

With her right hand, she gripped the low edge of the cantle, gave a little hop, and pulled herself up.

He mounted Doc and handed her one of Jay's old hats that was waiting on his saddle horn. "You might want this."

Her breathy laugh tightened a cinch around his gut. "You think of everything."

He could only hope.

Turning away from the barn, he struck out on a southerly trail that led up to the ridge. Ella followed close behind. He'd prefer to have her beside him, where he could look at her, see her smart little chin and dark eyes. But unfamiliar with the country, she belonged behind him in the dark.

Reflexively, he reassured himself by touching the rifle sheathed beneath his right leg. His revolver rested against his thigh. Not that he expected trouble, but neither would he be unprepared.

Doc took to the loose shale like a big horn sheep, Barlow just as sure-footed behind him. The night slid by degree toward the western mountain peaks, stars winking out to gray in its wake.

At the top, he reined in and Ella came up beside him. Doc blew triumphantly and bobbed his head. Barlow pricked her ears to the east as if listening for the sun's footsteps.

Ella remained silent, her face trained toward the horizon where a russet thread pulled along its edge.

A wren sang out. Its cousins joined, and soon a chorus filled the cedars and pines around them.

A slow, fiery orange split the seam between earth and sky, and Ella's breathy *oh* cinched him again. A hot stain burned into his chest, and grateful that she couldn't see him clearly, he slid his right hand beneath his vest and rubbed the spot.

The fire bled to gold that bled to pink, and light broke through a low band of clouds, throwing spires into the sky.

"'If I take the wings of the morning . . .'"

Had he not been holding his breath, he would have missed her voice for the bird song.

She saw it. Really *saw* it.

How could he go forward from this place without her beside him? Without the one so unlike him who fit him so well.

~

For all its glory, Cale dreaded the other side of a double-edged sunrise. A display like this morning's nearly always promised an afternoon storm. Any other day, he wouldn't have minded. But this could be his last day with Ella. Unless he asked her to stay. And she said yes.

Helen had the kitchen smelling like coffee, hotcakes, and bacon when they returned from their ride, and before they finished eating, Tug announced approaching visitors. Sure enough, a dark green touring car rolled into the yard with Thorson and Pete.

If scenery was what they wanted, Cale had plenty to go around. Hugh had made himself scarce since learning the night before at supper that Thorson would show up this morning, so Cale saddled an easy-gaited horse for the director. He helped Pete get his camera strapped on behind Barlow's saddle, and then mounted Doc.

He led them to the cross-fenced pasture, a good close spot for what Thorson wanted. Distant mountains rose in the west. Meadows rolled under foot, and a nearby creek spun through clusters of spruce and juniper. And to the south, an aspen-flanked ridge where he had no intention of taking them.

"Keep the barn roof in sight, and you can make it back to the house without me." He tugged his hat down and reined Doc around.

Thorson looked off toward a stand of pine and rubbed the side of his face. "You sure that bear's not around here? I see you've got your rifle with you."

Pete's head swiveled like a barn owl's. "Bear?"

Quick to catch his error, Thorson waved off his concern. "Rumor is all. Heard it in town." He cut a sharp look at Cale demanding confirmation.

"Don't go off in the woods. If you hear a racket in the brush, jump on your horses and ride hard to the house."

Pete went white. "You're serious."

Cale almost felt guilty leading on the two city dudes. "Not likely you'll see a bear in broad daylight." He squeezed Doc.

"You're not going to just lea-ve us, are you?" Pete's voice cracked.

"Oh, stop your whining." Thorson hitched his trousers, as much as he could while sittin' a horse. "Hutton's not worried, and that's good enough for me. Let's get this done and get back to town. I want to check on tomorrow's train."

Cale yanked the reins and nearly set Doc on his heels. Not the news he wanted to hear. It took a minute for his pulse to find its way back to his brain so he could think clearly, then he reined around and up to Thorson. "I'll bring Ella back in the wagon later."

Thorson gave him a hard look. Cale waited, both barrels loaded with what he thought of a man who'd leave her to walk back from the rodeo.

Without a word, the director dismounted and, holding his reins, turned in a slow circle, taking in the view.

Cale took off toward the house at a lope.

CHAPTER TWENTY-FIVE

Regret ate at Cale's gut for not asking Ella that morning when they were alone. He paced the barn, jumpy as water on a hot skillet, waiting for Thorson and Pete to get their film and get gone. A westerly breeze cut through the open back doors of the barn, and white fluffy clouds bunched above the house in the east.

Tug laid in the alleyway, head on his paws, eyes following Cale like a pendulum clock. His ears perked, and Cale ran outside. Thorson and Pete were trotting in, looking none too happy.

Served 'em right for coming out here and spoiling his last . . . his *day* with Ella.

"Get what you came for?" He took Thorson's reins and looped them over the hitching rail.

"Plus a few saddle sores." The director climbed off his horse and flinched when he hit dirt. "I've ridden more in the last few weeks than I have in a year."

Cale could say the same for someone else in the company.

"Make that more than my entire life." Pete clambered down and unstrapped his camera. "But I have to say, you've got some of the best scenery I've ever seen."

He stopped short and gave a sharp laugh. "Get it? *Scene*-ry and *seen*?"

Thorson shook his head and held out a folded check. "Thank you, Mr. Hutton. You've made our trip to Cañon City quite profitable. I trust it was the same for you."

245

Cale stuck his thumb in the fold to catch a peek at the dollar amount. Might not be good manners, but he didn't want to have to hunt the man down to get what he'd been promised.

Satisfied and then some, he slipped the check inside his vest and offered his hand. "Glad to hear it. You're welcome to come again."

Thorson glanced toward the house, and Cale intended to bulldog him if he as much as said a word about taking Ella. But he merely pulled his hat off and rubbed his forehead.

Manners demanded he offer the man a cold glass of water or lemonade or whatever Helen had waiting inside, but he wasn't feeling particularly mannerly.

The back screen door creaked. *Dadgummit.*

"Mr. Thorson." Helen marched around the corner. "Take some lemonade with you on your way back to town. I'm sure you worked up a thirst, and Cale can fetch the jar when he rides in." She pressed a cloth-covered basket into the director's hands and gave it a quick pat. "Cookies too. Enjoy."

She nodded at Pete, cut Cale a quick look, and turned with a spry step. Thirty seconds tops, and the screen popped again.

Best entry-exit Cale had ever seen.

"Well, I've got chores to tend to. Thorson, Pete. Drive safely." He did his best Helen imitation and walked away, leaving both men standing under the pine tree, more than likely stunned by their quick send-off.

Glancing back, an ornery idea stopped him short. "If you see that bear on your way to town, be sure and send word back, would you?"

Pete hoofed it for their automobile. Thorson shook his head and ambled on after him, a hitch in his get-along slowing him some.

Cale busied himself unsaddling their horses—and saddling Doc and a shorter, stocky little paint mare. Barlow'd been out twice today. She deserved a roll in the pasture and an extra can of oats.

He tied a rolled blanket behind the paint's saddle, and his stomach rumbled. Hunger or anticipation. Maybe both, as he considered a quiet picnic with a certain bob-haired gal in fancy boots. He turned out the other two mounts and made tracks to the house.

At the washtub, he scrubbed his face and neck and hands, then combed his hair back with his fingers. Ella crossed in front of the window, a pitcher in her hands that she set on the table. He left his hat on a nail, rolled down his sleeves, and took a deep breath.

As he reached for the screen door, three tornadoes blew around the corner of the house, and he turned and blocked the door, arms crossed. "You know full well what Miss Helen will say."

"But Ty and Jay'll wash first and beat me out of sittin' next to Miss Ella. It ain't fair."

Cale bit his cheek and pulled a sober face. "No, they won't."

Hope lit the boy's face, and Cale almost felt guilty for the second time that day. "She's going on a picnic with me."

"Can we go?"

The question earned Kip an elbow from Jay. Ty snorted, and Kip hung his head.

"Next time." He hoped and prayed he wasn't lying to his nephews.

Having spent his deep, clear breath, he drew another and walked inside to a set table. Confounded Thorson waited too long to leave. Cale hid his disappointment behind a forced smile.

"Looks good." He pulled out his chair.

The boys blew in and jockeyed for position.

"Kip, you're here." Helen indicated one of two chairs on the stove side. "Ty and Jay, there."

They skulked around to the other side of the table as Helen and Ella took their places.

"Kip, would you say grace for us?"

His shoulders hunched into his ears and he wiggled his backside farther into the seat, then took Ella and Cale's hands and bowed his head. "Thank you, Lord, that Uncle Cale and Miss Ella didn't go on a picnic. Amen. And for the food. Amen."

Snickers burned Cale's ears. Without raising his head, he peeked at the women. Both were staring at him.

Not to be outdone by a six-year-old, he squared himself like a man and reached for the boiled potatoes.

"Thought we could take some cookies and lemonade out to the pasture and enjoy the breeze after dinner."

Ella hid behind her napkin doing a poor imitation of dabbing her mouth that didn't need to be dabbed and making noises in her throat. Choking on a laugh, he figured.

"That would be lovely." She winked at the boys so quick that he almost missed it.

His belly reared up and pawed.

Ty and Jay squirmed and giggled until a glare from Helen set them straight. She dished up a spoonful of greens for both of them, passed Ella the bowl and a look that said do the same for Kit. "Since it's such a nice day, I'll be needing your help, boys. I have three rugs that need a good beating."

Shoulders slumped and guarded looks volleyed around the table among the conspirators.

Cale made a mental note to bring Helen another bag of bonbons.

After dinner, Helen prepared a basket like the one she'd given Thorson, then hurried Ella out the door, whisking her hands like a broom. "You go on now. Have a good time."

Cale took the basket and planted a peck on the woman's cheek, ruffling her feathers considerably.

"Go on with you. And if you see that brother of yours, tell him I held him back a plate."

Cale would be more likely to see the bear than his brother, but he nodded his thanks just the same.

Ella had gone ahead to the corral and was rubbing the paint's head, its eyes half closed in delirium.

"Don't put her to sleep, or we'll be riding double out to the meadow."

Her cheeks went pink, which was his intention. "Is she as good as Barlow and Doc?"

"No one's as good as Doc."

She laughed that liquid sound, and it ran through him like a swollen stream.

"I do believe you are prejudiced, Mr. Hutton."

"No apologies." He tied the basket to his saddle bag with a latigo, checked the cinch and rifle scabbard. He'd ridden armed for more than a week. No sense stopping now, though he truly believed what he'd told Thorson.

Ella loosed the mare and mounted easily without his help. She seemed rested, and he itched to know her history, certain she'd grown up around horses, based on her easy way with them. Maybe she'd tell him this afternoon.

The fear and tension she'd carried their first day out in the meadow was gone. And in its place was a peaceful confidence that made her bloom like a wild summer rose.

He joined her, and they cut around behind the barn and rode west toward the green patch along the creek. Tug trotted beside them, a bounce in his step as he sniffed the air.

~

The colorful little mare was a delight with her strong, sturdy build and light step. Ella felt secure, well-mounted, safe enough to drink in the beauty around her. She'd forgotten to bring her camera along, but perhaps it was better to focus her heart this time instead of her lens. She'd likely not see this setting again outside of Thorson's moving pictures. And then only for fleeting moments at a time.

Today she intended to relish every minute, burning the images onto her mind's eye for review on the long train ride back to Chicago.

Her mood dipped on that note, and she squeezed the mare into a gentle lope, leaving the depressing thought behind. Cale stayed with her, holding Doc back in his long-legged reach. He could well outpace her, but she sensed a race was not the intention, though she wasn't certain of what his intention was.

She knew only that she trusted him completely and would miss him desperately—the man who had so roughly yanked her from certain injury or death, persistently prodded her to ride again, and subtly charmed her with his cowboy ways. Unrefined but strong, capable but caring, he had patched a hole in her heart whether he knew it or not.

Perhaps Nana had been right all along—life was a collection of mended tears and tatted edges. Wounds healed over and beautified in the process.

They pulled up at the meadow's edge, close enough to the creek to hear its lilting song. She swung down, took the old blanket he handed her, and snapped it out atop the cushiony green. She anchored one corner and he joined her at the opposite, setting the basket between them.

The spotted dog lay down not far away, his eyes on the basket as if he knew what was hidden inside.

Cale stretched his long legs out to the side and leaned on one elbow, obviously not as at home at a picnic as he was horseback or straddling a kitchen chair. He thumbed his hat up and a red mark banded the top of his brow. A strange urge prompted her to smooth it away and brush it with a kiss. Unsettled by the thought, she distracted her traitorous emotions by pulling a napkin-wrapped bundle of oatmeal raisin cookies from the basket and offering him one.

He took it with a smile and held it up in a mock toast before two bites left nothing but crumbs. She covered a laugh.

"Wha?" A full mouth limited his conversational abilities.

"You make quick work of Helen's fare."

A hard swallow, and he unscrewed the lid from a jar of lemonade. "Gotta get while the gettin's good."

His manners at the Denton the night of the rodeo had been impeccable, as if he dined out on a regular basis. Yet now he was a rough cowboy in a cow pasture. Much of him was a puzzle she wished she had more time to piece together.

She bit into a crunchy cookie, showering her lap with crumbs.

He chuckled. She lobbed the cookie at him, and he caught it and shoved it in his mouth with a little-boy grin.

Sitting up, he crossed his legs, a trick with his spurs, but he managed not to gouge the well-worn blanket. He palmed his mouth and focused on her as if he were framing a photograph, his smile trading places with an earnest appeal. "Can I ask you a question?"

He'd waited a long time to press beyond boundaries other than her reluctance to ride. By this time tomorrow, she'd be gone. The way she saw things now, she had nothing to lose other than his company. She folded her hands in her lap. "Ask away."

Surprise jerked his head to the side, but his eyes never left her face. Apparently he expected resistance, and rightly so. She hadn't been exactly forthcoming, but she believed she knew where he was heading.

"How long have you ridden?"

A faint sigh slipped out in gratitude for an easier query than she'd anticipated. "My father has always kept a stable of fine saddlebreds. I began riding lessons when I was three and competed from about twelve years of age until several years after boarding school." *When I met Charles and fell in love.*

No surprise reflected on the planes of his face. "I figured as much, you bein' from Chicago and all." He leaned back on his hands and studied the mountain behind her. His eyes narrowed. "My guess is you didn't come west with the moving-picture company because you needed the money."

She dipped her head in agreement, unwilling to volunteer too much.

"So this was just a trip to see how us roughneck ranchers lived." His razor-edged tone cut deep, and inwardly she drew back, ruing her earlier unguarded ease. She scrambled to gather as many stones as possible from her crumbled wall.

He jerked forward and grasped her hand, his eyes dark and bleeding regret. "I'm sorry. That's not what I meant to say. It's just that . . ."

A gray ring clouded the blue of his eyes. She'd not noticed it before.

Aching, she withdrew her hand, pulling in the corners of her soul and tucking them in around the edges. "Just what?"

He yanked his hat off and scrubbed a hand through his hair, then reset it with a hard tug. "What happened on Main Street? Why'd you freeze up?"

And there it was. The core of the matter that had somehow scabbed over in the last few weeks but was now torn open again.

She pulled a loose thread in the blanket and twisted it around her finger. "Fifteen months ago I was engaged."

His abrupt stillness drew her glance to find his jawline set in stone, his eyes suspicious.

"I met Charles at a horse show. We saw each other regularly for more than a year. He proposed, I said yes. The next evening we were on our way in his motorcar to a party at a mutual friend of our families. It was raining."

Round and round she wrapped the woolen thread until the end of her forefinger blushed a deep red.

"Storming, actually. The roads were dreadful. Charles was driving too fast. A horse ran across the road—"

The thread snapped.

Her eyes squeezed shut against the pounding hoof beats of her heart, and she didn't see or hear Cale move, but he was beside her. Pulling her into his arms. Stroking her hair.

"I'm sorry." His graveled voice raked across her bruised spirit and her hands clenched in her lap. In his haste, he'd pinned her arms to her side, effectively closing the breach in her wall. It was just as well. She did not want his pity.

He leaned back, cupping her shoulders in his large hands, searching her eyes for an open door. A window. Any crevice she might have left unguarded. Slowly his hands slipped to her neck, his thumbs stroking her jaw with a tenderness unmatched even by Charles. How could a man pull her in such opposite directions, so efficiently tearing her in two?

"Ella," he breathed. "You're not like any woman I've ever met. I know I'm not a polished gent like Charles or anybody else where you come from. But I see a kindred heart in you, and I want—"

The dog growled, effectively drawing Cale's attention. His hands fell from her face, leaving it chilled in the absence of their calloused warmth. He looked the direction of the dog's attention, and she followed his gaze to a fluttering stand of aspen hugging the mountain's base.

As swift as a serpent, he was on his feet, pulling her up and nearly dragging her to the mare. "Ride to the house. *Now.* As fast as you can. Then ring the triangle by the back door to call Hugh."

Stunned by his harsh movements and urgent orders, she remained rooted in place. "What—"

The dog leapt up, growling savagely, the hair on its back stiffening.

Cale gripped her around the waist, flung her into the saddle, and shoved the reins at her. Before she could take a breath, he jerked off his hat and slapped it against the paint's rump with a frightening yell.

The mare lunged forward. Ella grabbed the saddle horn. The dog raced for the aspen thicket, she at a right angle, away from the meadow. Fighting the horse's frightened pace, she pulled hard on the reins, slowing enough to whirl around.

Cale was already in the saddle, yelling at the top of his lungs. "Tug! Come!"

The dog ignored him.

Cale looked her way, the hard lines of his face chilling the blood in her veins. "I said *go*—now!"

And then she saw it. A charging brown shadow, crashing out of the thicket and seeming to roll across the meadow.

Straight for her.

CHAPTER TWENTY-SIX

With remarkable speed, the bear ran toward its nearest target—*Ella*. Again, her tendency to freeze had put her in grave danger.

Her tendency and his stupidity.

Cale pulled his Winchester from the scabbard and chambered a round. Riding fast, he wouldn't have a good shot, but the noise might startle the bear enough to distract it.

He fired. Tug ran in too close, lacking the wisdom of Crossett's hounds. The bear slowed, faced Tug, and swiped.

A sharp yelp tore Cale's gut as Tug flew through the air and landed hard. Cale fired again but missed. Free of the dog, the bear turned after Ella fleeing on the white horse.

Oh God, help me.

Rifle in hand, he spurred Doc into a dead run, closing the distance between himself and Ella. So did the bear. With a final desperate charge, he flanked Ella's mare on the right, jerked to a stop, and stood in the stirrups.

He had one chance.

Sighting the charging hulk, he released his breath in a slow hiss and squeezed the trigger.

Time stopped with the echoing report. The bear missed a step, stumbling to a knee.

Cale aimed and fired again.

It lurched onto its chin, the bulk of its body tumbling forward, rolling it over.

Cale sighted a third time, waiting for movement. There was none.

Pounding hooves from his left brought Hugh at a gallop, rifle in hand. He pulled up next to Cale, breathing heavily. They waited in silence several minutes, then eased their horses closer to the fallen beast.

"Nice shooting." Hugh gave him an honest nod.

A long, puffing wheeze emptied the beast's lungs, and its sides lay still, black beady eyes open in death.

~

Ella pulled to a stop at the house and jumped down, stumbling in her haste toward the triangle by the back door.

Helen stood in the yard with her hands fisted tightly against her ashen cheeks. "What happened? I heard rifle shots."

"Cale sent me . . . the bear—" Ella's lungs screamed for air. She grasped the iron bar and banged it against each side of the triangle, round and round until the warning sounded in one long, continuous call. Then dropping the bar, she fell into Helen's outstretched arms. "He said to ring the bell for Hugh."

"Oh Lord, help us all."

Ella stepped back and combed her fingers through her sweaty hair, pulling it off her neck. Three eager faces were plastered against the kitchen window, but she quickly looked away. The boys needed to stay inside, out of danger. She walked toward the pine tree, straining to hear the sound of a running horse. Another rifle shot. *Anything.*

Nothing.

She caught the mare's reins and patted her lathered neck. "Good girl." With a quick swing, she was up in the saddle.

"Don't go back out there." Helen's fright was palpable.

"I need to know if Cale is all right." A sob nearly broke from her dry throat. "Keep the boys inside. And maybe you should have the shotgun nearby, just in case."

The silence unnerved her. No birdsong or barking. No human voices. Nothing but the clanging triangle echoing in her ears.

She squeezed the mare into a trot and rode past the barn. She had to see if Cale was safe. Alive. *Please, God.* The words squeezed from her soul. Cale had put himself in harm's way for her. Even Tug . . .

Just beyond the nearest clump of juniper, the view opened up toward the meadow. Two riders approached at a slow pace. Two brothers. Relief broke from her lips in a cry, and she doubled over the saddle horn, racked by gasping sobs.

As they neared, she made out a form draped across Cale's legs. Her heart wrenched anew.

~

She was waiting.

Cale choked up at sight of Ella. Tug whimpered, and he stroked the old dog's back, just above three long red gashes in its side. "We're gettin' you home, fella. Won't be long now, and we'll have you wrapped up and lying on a quilt in the kitchen."

"She ring the bell?"

Cale cut a look at his brother, suddenly rigid and resistive. "I sent her."

Hugh's eyes narrowed and his jaw muscle flexed. "You were in the meadow."

Not a question. Cale kicked ahead, in no mood for a war of words on the heels of a life-and-death encounter.

Ella met him just past the barn, her face wet with tears, her eyes red. How could he ever forgive himself for endangering her? He'd been a fool to take her out to the meadow. And a fool to let Thorson and Pete out there without protection—all for a few more dollars. God forgive him. He'd let greed get the upper hand.

"Are you all right?" Her words were tight and fearful, and he ached to reassure her.

He reached for her hand and gave it a squeeze. "Right as rain."

Her welling eyes washed over him as Hugh rode up.

"We can drag the bear to the barn and pull him into the wagon bed."

"Get a couple of heavy ropes and that logging chain pa used for dragging trees. I'll take Tug inside and send the boys out."

Hugh huffed. "Yeah, they'll sure enough want to see this." He cut Ella a hard look without speaking to her and turned off to the barn.

Watching Tug, she covered a sob with her hand and her shoulders bowed.

Cale wanted to take her in his arms, but that would have to wait. She was a trooper, for sure. Toughest city gal he'd ever met. "Tug'll be on his feet in no time. We'll get his wounds cleaned, wrap him up tight, and make a bed for him in the kitchen where Helen can keep an eye on him."

She bobbed her head several times but kept her hand over her mouth.

"Are *you* all right?" Her silence worried him.

She nodded again and then shook her head, confusing him even more.

"He'll be fine, Ella. May have a couple of broken ribs, and I've got my doubts about his left shoulder, but we'll get him put back together. If need be, I'll get ahold of the vet."

The boys must have seen their dad ride in, for they were already skirting the horses and running for the barn.

Helen met him and Ella in the yard and held Doc's headstall while he climbed down with Tug. Ella took the reins and led both horses away.

"You got an old quilt you don't use any more?"

Helen held the screen door open. "Even if I don't, I'll find one that will do. Poor thing. He needs some pampering from what I can see. Let me get the water to boiling, and we'll take a look at those wounds. Looks like he may need stitches."

She filled her kettle and fed the fire, then hurried to her room. A thump sounded like her trunk lid hitting the wall, and within half a minute she returned with a quilt he hadn't seen before. She laid it on the braided rug and scooted them in a corner by the pie safe. Out from under foot but not out of sight.

Tug moaned as Cale knelt on one knee and set him on the quilt. That bear had nearly laid him open. A half inch deeper, and Cale'd be stuffing his innards back inside.

The screen door swung open and Ella walked in. She gripped his shoulder as she lowered herself next to him, and her strong fingers shot desire clear through him.

Hang it all, he didn't care if Helen *was* watching. Some things were too important. He turned and wrapped Ella in his arms and just held her. Where she belonged.

She drew a halting breath and twisted his vest front in her hands. "It wasn't Tug I was frightened for." Her whisper seeped straight from her lips and into his chest. "It was you."

Gratitude swelled up in him. He fought his own tears and tightened his hold. She melded against him, soft and yielding, as if she were made special for him.

Yeah. Some things were too important.

Pulling back, he searched her face for more, but she'd tucked her words inside again. All he saw was pain and fear—two things he wanted to banish from her life forever.

Helen brought a basin of hot water and some rags and shooed him out of the way. "Let us take care of this. If there's a bone needs setting, I'll call for you." She pulled up a kitchen chair and sat right next to Tug.

Cale stood.

"You get the bear?" She was already pressing hot cloths against Tug's wounds.

"Yes, ma'am. We got him."

"Go on, then. I'm sure Hugh needs you now more than we do."

We?

Ella doubted it on two counts.

She was beginning to believe she needed Cale Hutton more than anyone else possibly could.

And in the one glance she'd stolen on her mad race to the ranch house, she'd seen Cale—alone—standing in his stirrups, his rifle aimed at the charging bear. She shivered at the too-fresh memory.

Helen gave her a worried look. "The sight of blood turns many a head the other way."

Irritation wiggled to the surface, but Ella tamped it down. She wasn't given to swooning, and she'd be far better off if people stopped worrying about how she felt. "I'm fine."

Gently, she pressed Tug's short fur away from a long gash. "A horse of my father's once cut himself badly in a broken fence. I watched the vet sew the muscles and flesh back together. Tug needs the same."

"Well, I'm not the seamstress you are, dear, but if it bothers you to stitch him up, I understand."

She swallowed. "What will we do for his pain?"

Helen bent near the dog's head with a hushed voice. "Nothing that I know of, other than getting it over quick as possible. He's in a good deal of pain already. He may not even notice a few needle pricks."

Few? There would be many. Nana's teaching threaded through her memory . . . *it's the finest of stitches that hold the important pieces together.*

She retrieved her sewing kit from her satchel in the boys' room and washed her hands at the sink with soap and water. Threading her smallest needle, she cringed at thought of stitching the dog without dulling its pain. But this was not the outskirts of Chicago, and there was no vet at hand.

Helen pulled the quilt, dog and all, away from the wall and against the toes of her shoes. "I'll hold his head in case he tries to snip at you. But I don't think he's got much fight in him."

Ella took a deep breath and slowly released it, then took another and knelt to the task.

Mended tears and tatted edges . . . wounds healed over and beautified . . . O Lord, make it so.

The three long gashes closed easily, and Tug gave little resistance other than a whimper now and then. Helen cooed continually to him, rubbing his head and leaning close while Ella drew the edges together with her grandmother's needle.

She knotted and snipped the final thread with dainty silver scissors and leaned back on her heels, arching her back and neck. "Do you have any alcohol?"

Helen gaped.

Ella laughed.

"For Tug. To disinfect his wounds, not for me."

The woman clapped her mouth shut and pushed out of the chair with a grunt. "I knew that."

Returning from the dining room, she handed over a dusty whiskey bottle, half full. Ella drizzled a small stream along each seam, dabbing with a clean cloth as she went. Then she corked the bottle, set it on the chair, and straightened, sore from kneeling but grateful for her newfound strength. A month ago, she would not have survived the afternoon.

She gathered the bloody rags. "Where do you want these?"

Helen bustled over, took the rags, and dropped them in the basin. "Go lie down, rest yourself. I'll take care of supper and whatever else the men need, short of dressing out a smelly old bear."

Ella laid a hand on her friend's arm. "I can't lie down. Not until I check on Cale."

Helen's gray eyes glimmered, and she blinked rapidly. "You're the best thing that ever happened to that boy. I hope he knows it."

At the barn, the little mare's ears swiveled, acknowledging her approach.

"You up for one more jaunt?" She stroked the paint's neck and shoulders and checked the cinch, then climbed up. "You will have earned your oats tonight."

The mare tossed her head smartly and showed no hesitation at another trip to the meadow. Ella set her to an easy walk. No hurry returning to an animal that was no longer a threat.

Again, two riders approached from a distance, but this time, three little boys bounced along before them as if leading a victor's parade. She reined into a shady spot to wait. Their going was slow, and she soon saw why. Cale and Hugh were dragging the bear behind their horses.

The beast was enormous, and both horses threw their shoulders into the task, heads bobbing with each step. The men stopped at the back of the barn behind the farm wagon and it suddenly made sense.

She'd be riding to town with a bear carcass.

Reality came crashing down, scattering the surreal events of the day, pulling her first one way and then the other. The company was leaving tomorrow. Would they leave without her?

Did she care?

She doubted the men would make the trip today, so late in the afternoon. Perhaps they would wait until tomorrow.

"They got the bear!" Kip bounded up as Ella dismounted. "Pa and Uncle Cale got the devil bear!"

She'd not correct his assumption, that was his father's duty. But Helen would certainly correct his descriptive language.

"Where's Tug?" Jay stopped short and looked around, worry creasing his normally smooth brow.

"Come here, boys."

Ty reluctantly left his father and Cale to their chore, but Jay and Kip were beside her in a instant.

She bent at the waist and braced her hands on her knees. "Tug helped kill the bear."

Kip's eyes widened with awe. "He did?"

"What'd he do?"

"Where is he?"

She looked each boy in the eye and chose her words carefully. "He was hurt, but he's resting now in the kitchen."

Kip dashed away, but the other two remained.

"The bear clawed Tug pretty badly, but your Uncle Cale carried him home, and Helen and I stitched him up. We're all going to take the best care of him that we can. And we can pray for him."

Jay's eyes welled and he swiped at them impatiently. Then he threw his arms around her. "I'm glad you helped him."

Ty poked his brother in the shoulder. "Come on, let's go see."

Torn between unsaddling the mare or hurrying after the boys, she chose her closest responsibility—the horse she'd ridden. Memory of Mabel leaving her mount saddled, sweaty, and awaiting relief outweighed the image of three little boys and their faithful dog. Helen was with them. They weren't alone.

She hung the saddle on a low rack in the tack room and hunted a brush. The little horse had saved her life—along with Cale. And Tug played his part as well. But ultimately her thanks lifted heavenward.

Working the brush along the mare's back, she recalled her father's resentful send-off at the train station. He'd warned her that unimagined dangers lay ahead, that she was foolish to flee blindly into the unknown. Indeed, danger had found her in Cañon City, but the Lord had remained at her side, providing His promised way of escape from temptation as well as His promised protection.

Again, fate failed.

But what she hadn't expected in her quest for a change of scenery was a change in perspective regarding her father. And it was Hugh, of all people, who had opened her eyes.

He opened them farther as he came round the end of the barn and stopped short.

"You."

Her skin prickled. "Hugh."

"Why are you here?" His voice was heavy with blame, as if the entire situation with the bear was her fault.

She refused to defend her right to accept Cale's invitation. She owed Hugh no explanation. But neither would she cower.

She walked around the mare and continued her grooming. "Just giving her a good brushing before turning her out."

Hugh swore and cut through the barn toward the back. Within minutes, his voice shot out of the alleyway as if from a megaphone.

"She's turned your head, and you're not thinking about what you should." A brief pause, long enough for a man to spit. "I thought they were leaving."

Cale's response was quieter, beyond Ella's hearing, which made her feel like an eavesdropper. She should turn the mare out and go back to the house. Not linger there waiting for Hugh's inevitable darts.

"She's a city gal. She doesn't belong here."

The crack of breaking wood stilled Ella's hand and heart. She waited a beat but heard nothing more. After opening the pasture gate, she slapped the mare through, and rather than go back to the tack room, she set the brush atop a fence post.

The last thing she wanted to do was come between Cale and his brother.

Maybe Hugh was right. She didn't belong here. And the sooner she left, the better.

CHAPTER TWENTY-SEVEN

The cast-iron pulley busted through a board in the outside wall. Shoulder throbbing from his wrenching throw, Cale whirled to face his brother, hands fisted.

They'd come to blows in their childhood, as boys did. But not since they'd grown into men had Hugh driven him to such anger. It took every ounce of willpower he possessed to not tear into him and break his teeth for the things he said about Ella.

Both hands flexed and closed in rhythm with his pounding heart.

Hugh stood unflinching, quickly recovered from the shock of Cale heaving the pulley through the wall.

Cale debated praying for self-control or praying to win a long-overdue fist fight.

"You're gonna drive everyone away from you. You're not the only man in the world who's lost a good woman, but you're about to lose everyone else who cares about you. If you don't get a rein on your hateful tongue, Helen will leave. I'll move out, and your boys will hightail it well before they should."

He took a step forward, chin and voice lowered to rock-solid promise. "Ella's got more gumption than any woman in this county, and I intend to marry her whether you like it or not."

Hugh glared at him, his jaw so tight Cale expected it to crack. But his shoulders slacked a notch. Then his hands. His eyes dulled. He turned and left.

At least Ella was in the house and hadn't heard the bitter words.

Cale retrieved the pulley. They were finished with it. Maneuvering the carcass into the wagon had been easier than he'd expected.

The hole in the wall could wait.

He unsaddled Doc but couldn't find the brush he always used. The back of his neck crawled, and he walked out front. The paint mare was turned out, the brush on top of a corral post.

Ella.

Thudding horse hooves circled the barn and Hugh loped past on Shorty, headed who knew where. A distant rumble warned of a coming storm. Surely he wasn't fool enough to ride right into it.

Cale turned out Doc and made for the house, clawing through his head for what he'd say to Ella. The whole day had been nothing but interruptions on his intentions, and his gut ached nearly as much as his back and shoulders after helping pull the bear into the wagon.

His promise to Thorson echoed through him with the next roll of thunder. He'd promised to have Ella back today. But today had turned into early evening, and he wouldn't take her out in a storm.

And if the company left without her?

Temptation proved to be a sorry snake, inching up on him when he wasn't looking. If she missed the train, maybe she'd stay on. He'd made enough off Thorson that he could spare to pay for her extra week at the Denton. Maybe by then he'd convince her to stay for good.

Truth was, he needed Ella Canaday.

So did the boys.

He stood outside the screen door, watching them on their knees next to Tug, Ella in the middle with her arms wrapped around their slumped shoulders, her head bowed.

"Lord, please save Tug." She prayed so softly he had to strain to hear. "Please heal his wounds and help him rest and get strong enough to run and play again. And thank you for how brave he was today. How he alerted Uncle Cale to the bear."

A hornet-like sting hit his gut. She paused, and he took hold of the door handle.

"And thank you for helping Cale shoot the bear and keep us all safe."

His knees threatened to cut out from under him, and he tightened his hold. The hinges squeaked. Four faces turned his way.

"Uncle Cale!" Kip scrambled to his feet and pushed the screen open, his six-year-old arms doing what Cale couldn't seem to manage.

"You boys go wash. We're having an early supper after all today's excitement." Helen shot him a worried look. "Where's Hugh? Or should I ring the bell for him?"

Cale hung his hat on a peg, rolled his sleeves up, and then looked at his shirt and thought better of it. He needed a bath. His shirt and grimy trousers were smeared with dirt and blood and bear hair. And he probably smelled to high heaven. He just couldn't smell himself over the stew Helen had simmering on the stove.

"You can ring for him, but I doubt he'll hear it. He's on some errand." A near lie, but he wasn't about to make her and the boys worry.

Ella pulled herself up on a chair and smoothed her skirt, not looking at him.

He'd have to make do with the washstand in his room. "Helen, I need a kettle—"

"—of hot water. Got one right here for you." She gripped the handle with a folded rag and headed through the dining room door.

The boys banged outside, and that left him alone with Ella. Hugh's words had cut a swath across her face that she was trying to hide, and he regretted not beating his brother into the ground.

He took a step toward her.

She took a step back.

"Do I smell that bad?"

A weak smile flashed, then faded, and she shook her head. "No. I—I just think . . ."

"Don't pay any mind to Hugh. His mouth runs off ahead of him before he knows what he's saying."

She looked up at him from under her fringe, confirming that she'd overheard their argument.

"I want to talk to you, but I smell like that bear, and I need to clean up first."

She raised her chin and her hands went to smoothing her skirt again. "If you'll lend me Barlow, I can ride into town. I'll leave her in back of the studio with Jed's horse, Lucky, and tomorrow when you take the bear in, you can bring her back."

A rock dropped his gut all the way to his boots. "There's a storm coming."

She looked out the window, and her fingers curled into fists. No way would he let her ride out in it. It was a fool's errand and more so, given the storm that led to her accident and injury.

And the death of the man she loved.

It hit him full force. She loved Charles. Didn't matter if he was dead. There wasn't room in her heart for anyone else.

He shook his head. "It's too dangerous."

God saw fit to toss a lightning bolt close by and the boys stampeded inside. Ty reached for the inside door and slammed it shut, rattling the glass pane.

Ella stood shoulders hunched, eyes screwed tight, and both fists under her chin. His arms ached to pull her close, but he wouldn't soil her. "Ella."

Her eyes flew open.

"I can't let you ride out in that."

Another crash, and he took a step toward her. She didn't move away, but she curled into herself even though she stood on both feet. He could taste her fear.

Jay went to her and wrapped his skinny arms around her waist. "It's all right Miss Ella. We're safe in here. I'll take care of you."

Ty snorted like his father, and Cale realized the boys hadn't even asked after their pa. A sad state of affairs.

Helen sailed through. "Ella, would you please set the dining table. I believe you know where everything is. We'll use the good china."

The woman could turn the devil himself on his ear if need be. Her snappy order was his cue to leave.

As quick as the storm rolled in, dumping its load of water and roaring its head off, it rolled out. He didn't know what storms were like in Illinois, but here they didn't hold a grudge. Got in, got done, got out. Tomorrow the sky would be blue, the air fresh.

And Ella gone.

After a supper that loaded him down for a hard night's sleep, he followed Ella out to the porch, where she stood looking at the stars.

If things had gone differently, he'd be holding her close.

He stopped at the railing, a foot away. He couldn't erase what his brother had said—they weren't his words to take back. But he could speak his own if he could get 'em lined up right.

Lord, I could use a hand here. "Can you forgive me?"

Her head turned fast enough to swing her hair across her eyes. She fingered it back and stared. "Forgive you? For what— saving my life?"

He swallowed a knot in his throat and plowed ahead. "For putting you in danger. Taking you out there in the first place."

Her hands gripped the railing, pale in the half-moon's light. "You didn't know the bear would attack. And haven't you always said they don't strike during the day? How could you have known?"

He eased closer.

Her voice dropped to a near whisper. "If anything, I owe you my life."

Hope spurred all the way up to his shoulders.

"Tug and the mare too."

His pride took a hit, though she was right. It'd been a team effort.

She leaned on the railing and tilted her head back. "Look at those stars. It's so clear and bright, a person could walk right down the road and see where they were going."

"Promise me you won't."

She shifted her gaze to him.

He reached for her hand. "Promise me you won't sneak out and saddle Barlow tonight."

She almost smiled. "Now that you mention it . . ."

"I'll have to bring up all the saddle horses and sleep in the barn if you don't promise."

Moonlight glinted in her eyes, and her lips curved up at the edges.

He moved closer, raised his hand to her cheek, and thumbed the corner of her mouth. "Stay."

She slipped her hand from beneath his and dipped away from his touch, taking all her warmth and most of his hope.

He fought the image of the man she loved, the man she wouldn't let go of. And he fought the foolishness of the words that were busting through him as sure as the pulley smashed through the barn wall.

"I love you, Ella."

~

Ella's breath caught in her throat, too late to hide. Too late to act as if she hadn't heard his declaration. Her heart fractured, something she'd wanted to never happen again.

She had lost Charles. Now she would lose the only other man who had believed in her, who loved what she loved. Who apparently loved her in spite of her imperfections. She'd seen the truth of his words in his eyes today, felt it in his embrace. But she refused to come between him and his brother, and Hugh was clearly opposed to her. She was *city gal* and nothing more.

"I know you loved Charles."

Against her better judgment, she raised her fingers to his lips, and the act sent a jolt of longing through her. He gripped her hand and held it against his galloping heartbeat. Her own matched its desperate flight, but she fled in the opposite direction. She'd had enough family division to last a lifetime and refused to create more. The irony cut deep. It was Hugh's pain that illuminated her understanding, that prevented her from loving Cale.

"I'll not come between you and your brother. I'll not divide your family."

"You can't break what's already broken."

His other arm drew her against him, and he spoke into her hair. "Hugh's been loco since Jane passed—full of anger and hate and sharp edges. I warned him that he'd drive his boys away if he didn't get hold of himself."

She freed her hand and wrapped both arms around Cale, resting her head against his chest. Minutes passed, and his pulse steadied. His arms enveloped her, shielding her from every threat of harm other than that which lay at her very core.

Gently she pushed back and looked into his dear face. "That may be true, but he showed me something I couldn't see before I came here."

Puzzlement drew Cale's brows down, and his clear eyes, dark in the moonlight, grazed her face, searching for understanding.

She thumbed the crease at his forehead, rubbing it away, and let her fingers stray down the side of his unshaven cheek. He shuddered and tried to pull her to him again, but she braced her hands against him.

"Hugh showed me what was at the bottom of my father's very similar manner. Sharp-tongued. Abrupt. Unsmiling. For years I thought I had disappointed him. Let him down somehow, and I tried everything to make it up, to be good enough. And I failed."

"You could never fail."

She closed her eyes, steeling herself against his graveled voice. "After Charles's death, when I regained enough strength to walk unassisted, I answered a newspaper advertisement from Selig Polyscope for a seamstress willing to travel. I left against my father's wishes."

He brushed at her fringe, and his touch lit torches of desire across her skin.

"What's that got to do with Hugh?"

She drew a shuddering breath and backed out of his reach. "Hugh strikes out in the pain of losing his wife. He doesn't despise his sons or you or this ranch. He's suffering, unable to find healing for his wounds. When I see Hugh, I see my father, lashing out against everyone around him after my mother died. Like a wounded animal, he attacked those nearest him who sought to help."

Still Cale did not understand. His confusion clouded his eyes, and they darted across her face, frantically searching.

"I have to go back and make amends with my father. If I don't, he will die a ravaged and lonely man, in spite of his wealth and so-called friends. I have to make him see that he must let go of the pain and loss if he wants to live again."

"What if he won't?"

She fisted her hands against the possibility and drew a shuddering breath. "I will have tried."

Cale stood silent for a good while, staring out into the dark. An owl called, and hidden creatures skittered through the brush. The air hung heavy with the after-perfume of the storm.

When he spoke, his voice was low and soft, blending in with the night sounds. "How do you know this is what he should do?"

Her hands ached to touch Cale's strong arms, comb through his hair, frame his face. But she clasped them in front of her. "Because that's what I learned from you."

Shock displaced confusion, and he turned from the railing to face her squarely.

If she didn't speak now, she would lose her nerve. "You believed I could ride again and helped me do it. You believed I was valuable in spite of my limitations and helped me see that value. You risked your life to save mine. *Twice.* There is no greater gift."

He stepped forward.

As before, she stepped back. "How can I not offer the same to my father?"

His eyes glistened with unshed tears, but she would not be dissuaded.

One moment she stood firmly resolved, the next she was crushed against him, his move so swift she could not react. One hand cupped her head, and his breath washed over her hair and seeped into her soul.

"Come back to me, Ella Canaday. Promise me you'll come back and marry me. Be my wife and live on this ranch and let me show you every day why I love you."

Yielding to his embrace and request outweighed the uncertainty of what awaited her at home. The only thing she knew for sure was that regardless of what happened there, she could not deny this man who had reignited such hope.

"I will," she breathed into the soft chambray of his shirt. "I will."

Hugh had not returned by morning, at least that she could tell. Cale harnessed a heavy horse to the wagon and pulled up in front of the house. Helen and the boys made a sad send-off party, and Ella fought back tears as each one hugged her and begged her to return. She made no promises, other than the one she'd given Cale the night before.

Stooping to Jay's eye level, she laid a hand on his shoulder. "I know you'll take good care of Tug."

He swiped at his cheeks. "Tug's just like those three boys you told us about. He did the right thing and God saved him."

Tears threatened until she thought she would burst. *Lord, may he never lose his tender heart, in spite of what life—or his father—may bring.*

A final embrace with Helen, and Cale handed her up to the wagon seat. The satchel strap rested comfortably across her, a reminder to pick up her film at the paper.

The tarp covering the bear was little barrier against the odor and no help with the weight. The familiar ride into town took twice as long, and it was near noon by the time they reached Main Street.

With mixed emotions, she spotted the three touring cars parked in front of the studio and what looked like half the town gathered around them. The crowd divided like the Red Sea as Cale pulled up near the first automobile.

Thorson was first to the wagon, his face a familiar mass of disgruntlement. "You said yesterday, Hutton. I'm a day late leaving."

"Look here!"

Cale turned toward the back of the wagon, where several men lifted the edges of the tarp. As many women fanned their faces with their hands and grimaced.

"It's the bear!"

Three such small words, but what a commotion they stirred.

The company, Mr. Thorson, and everything else was soon brushed aside in deference to the "killer grizzly." Young and old alike reached to touch its silvery-brown fur and vicious claws. Ella shivered.

Cale climbed out of the wagon and reached for her. "I need to deal with these people."

She gladly gripped his broad shoulders as he lifted her down.

"I know." Reluctantly, she withdrew her hands and patted her satchel. "I'm going to pick up my film, get the remainder of my things from the hotel, and say good-bye to Clara."

Leaving the crowd behind, she crossed the street against what felt like a rushing current surging from the opposite direction. It seemed the entire town was on its way to see the bear, including the newspaper editor, who rushed out as she opened his front door.

"Pardon me, ma'am—oh, Miss Canaday. Your film is ready. Just check with my assistant, Priscilla. And it's on the house." He lifted his derby straight off his head and plopped it back down, then hurried on.

Behind the counter, Priscilla was craning her neck to see the commotion in the street, seemingly unaware of Ella's presence.

"I am Ella Canaday, and I left a roll of film for development a few days ago."

"Oh—yes." Priscilla gathered herself. "It's right here." She dropped behind the counter and popped up again like a jack-in-the-box. "Lovely pictures. You have quite an eye. Mr. Hall wanted to talk to you about running some of them in the paper, but I'm afraid another more current event has taken his interest."

She lowered her voice and leaned toward Ella. "Did someone really bring in the cow-killing bear?"

"Yes." Ella slid the large envelope into her satchel. "Cale Hutton shot the bear. Yesterday afternoon on his ranch, the Rafter-H."

Stunned, the young woman stared. "Really? How do you know?"

"Thank you for the prints. I do so appreciate it. Good day." She didn't have time, nor the inclination, to alleviate the girl's journalistic curiosity. The editor would learn all he needed while photographing the bear's remains.

People continued to flow like a stream toward the west end of town, including lunch patrons from the Denton. The dining room was empty, and Ella was selfishly glad. She pushed open the door to the kitchen.

Clara looked up and relief washed her face like a waterfall. "Girl, where've you been? You done cut ten years off my life worryin' over you."

Ella melted into her cushioned embrace and felt the familiar tug of tears. "I was at the ranch with Cale. He invited me out before the company leaves for Chicago." She set herself back and swiped at her face. "Which evidently is any time now."

Clara took a bundle from the back of the stove and pressed it into her hands. "This is for your trip. No telling where they'll stop and let you eat, or if there'll be a dining car with them fancy porters."

"Oh, Clara, you're the sweetest thing. But how did you know?"

"Done told you. I know everything goes on around here." Her hand swatted the air, then sneaked up to rub her eyes.

"I promise I'll write to you, but I must hurry. I can't be left behind, and I don't know what time the train leaves."

Clara glanced at the clock atop a baker's rack on the far wall. "You got a half hour. You best be going. But I'll be lookin' for your letter. I done heard about you ridin' across the river, and I wanna hear all about the ranch and that handsome cowboy o' yours."

With a final hug, Ella thanked Clara for the meal and left before she cried a river in the kitchen. She still had her things upstairs to pack and must send someone from the studio back for the sewing machine.

CHAPTER TWENTY-EIGHT

"Well, Hutton, what do you say?"

Cale tipped his hat forward at Thorson's insistence and rubbed the back of his head. Almost felt wrong selling the grizzly.

"Let him have it."

The graveled voice swung him around to his brother, swollen-eyed and worn around the edges. "The cattlemen can keep their reward money."

"Where'd you go?"

Hugh tugged his hat down, hiding his eyes, and lowered his voice. "Cemetery. Waited out the storm in the church and woke up this morning on a back pew." He wiped a hand across his face. "Did some talkin' with the Lord."

His brother left plenty unsaid, but Cale heard it all. He gripped Hugh's shoulder and turned back to Thorson with an outstretched hand. "Deal."

The crowd cheered.

"You'll be glad of it." Thorson pumped his arm and grinned. "He'll make a splendid prop for our moving pictures, especially since I plan to return next summer. Is there a taxidermist in town?"

"This ain't no *he.*"

Startled whispers and conjecture lifted around them, and Cale's stomach clenched. He and Hugh worked through the townsfolk to a wiry fella at the back of the wagon.

"Samuel Pearson, wildlife scientist and taxidermist," the man said. "You've got yourself a grizzly sow. About ten years old, I'd estimate, until I can get a better look at her teeth."

Thorson pushed through to Pearson, and the newspaper editor started taking pictures. Cale backed off. Hugh followed.

"You know what this means." Hugh ran a hand around the back of his neck.

"Mean's this probably isn't the end of things."

"Excuse me, please." Ella shouldered her slight frame past curious onlookers, wearing her satchel and a smart little hat, and carrying a canvas and leather bag.

She gave Hugh an uneasy look.

Cale took the bag, and with a hand at her waist ushered her inside the studio.

All the furniture had been shoved against the wall, and the empty cavern of a room mirrored what he already felt in his gut. He knew he had to let her go, but he didn't have to like it.

She pulled a large envelope from her satchel and handed it to him. "My photographs. I promised my grandmother I'd bring her back a *plethora* of pictures from my trip." She grinned at the fancy word. "So most of them won't interest you, but the photograph of the two cowboys at the rodeo is in there. You may have that one."

Based on the stack of black and white pictures, he guessed what *plethora* meant.

She was good. He looked carefully at each one, noting her clear focus and the way each told a story. Until he came to a photograph of himself he didn't know she'd taken.

They were in the meadow on her second day at the ranch. He was lunging Barlow, and she'd caught both him and the horse in the frame. She'd caught his heart as well. Stitched it up as tight as a new seam on one of those costumes she worried over.

He glanced at her watching him now, her cheeks pink with a shy smile.

"You can't have that one."

He shuffled through the remaining pictures, stopping at the first of what she'd taken at the rodeo. He tucked it under his arm and slid the rest into the envelope. "You're good enough to get a job at the newspaper."

Surprise made her dark eyes dance. "You think so?"

"Sure enough. In fact, the editor's out there right now. Why don't you go take a picture of the she-bear. Bet your grandmother would like to see that."

The dancing stopped. "*She*-bear?"

There he went again, puttin' his foot in it before he thought things through. He reached for one of her hands, hoping to soften the blow. "Would it have made any difference if we'd known? Would it have stopped her charging us, or kept her from robbin' ranchers?"

Her eyelids fluttered and she hugged the envelope. "No, I guess not. But doesn't this mean there could be cubs?"

His insides twisted at thought of her blaming him for orphaning a couple of bear cubs. How could he make her understand a cattleman's—

"If there are, won't they grow up to be the same threat?"

He nearly laughed outright but caught hold of it in time. Instead, he swept her up and swung her off the floor. "Not necessarily. Not every grizzly is a cow-killer. But I've gotta say, the way you think, you'll make a fine rancher's wife, Ella Canaday. A *fine* wife."

Ella cherished those three words almost as much as the words most woman crave from the man they adore—*I love you*. Something about *a fine wife* said Cale believed in her, a common theme in that cowboy's repertoire.

Her cowboy. Clara had been right all along.

She played them over and over in her mind like a movie reel that rocked in time with the train. Mabel and most of the company had ridden back to Chicago in a different car than Ella, but it was no matter. She would not work again with Selig Polyscope or any filming company. Mr. Thorson and the troupe were returning to Cañon City next year, but she would be busy at the ranch helping Helen "wrangle" three little Hutton boys, as Cale called it. Possibly serving up cookies and lemonade if the company came again to the Rafter-H.

Most importantly, she'd be loving her cowboy, an occupation that she believed would take up most of her days and all of her nights.

Anticipation danced through her as the train subtly slowed in its approach to Grand Central Station. Leaning to catch the city through the smoke-washed window, she saw it with new eyes—eyes that remembered the pristine mountain views of Colorado, open ranges, and clear skies. The hulk of a grizzly bear filling the bed of a ranch wagon, and an old farmhouse table covered with freshly baked berry and apple pies. Things she had never dreamed could change her forever.

Yet she was not the only one who had changed.

Apparently, her trip west had altered her father as well, for both he and Nana met her at the station, and he pulled her into an unsophisticated embrace in full public view. His eyes glistened when he set her back at arm's length, and he swallowed hard against uncharacteristic emotion.

"I've missed you, Ella."

"Come along, Patrick, you're blocking the way. Let me have a look at our girl." Nana's eyes brimmed, and she squeezed Ella with surprisingly strong but trembling arms.

Worry tripped Ella's heart, and she encircled her grandmother's waist as they walked to the platform to collect her luggage.

Ahead of them, Mr. Thorson, Pete, Mabel, and others from the company gathered their bags and trunks and set off. Only Mabel looked back, her expression unreadable but lacking her earlier scorn.

A black Hudson touring car with canopy awaited Ella's family at the curb, their former carriage driver behind the wheel. No surprise, really, for her father had spent every waking moment at the Chicago Automobile Show in February. She knew it was only a matter of time before he had the latest and sleekest motorcar available.

He helped her into the spacious back seat, concern wrinkling his brow.

"It's all right, Father. I'm doing much better. In fact I've ridden in several automobiles this summer, and I'll tell you and Nana all about it this evening." Though she doubted she would mention her first encounter on Cañon City's Main Street and the runaway horse.

Nana could not keep her questions at bay and talked nonstop all the way home, recounting her delight in Ella's few letters and descriptions of the Western countryside.

Feeling a bit guilty for not having written more, Ella mentioned how quickly the time had gone and how totally consumed she had been in her work.

"I met some marvelous people in Cañon City who I'm sure you would enjoy visiting with. And in my satchel, I have the photographs I promised you. But let's wait until after dinner, shall we?"

That evening, Ella dressed in a tulle lace tea dress for the formal meal, a most uncomfortable affair after growing accustomed to lighter *suppers* in split skirts and boots. In the drawing room later, her grandmother exclaimed over the photographs, her father a little less so, particularly over those of Cale lunging the mare and roping steers.

"What a handsome cowboy," Nana said, her eyes shining with anticipation. "Is there any particular reason you have several photographs of him? That is him at the *rodéo*, isn't it?"

It would take hours to share her experiences and new dreams with dear Nana, and during the next several days she did just that, including recently made plans for a fall wedding to be held at the little white clapboard church in Cañon City.

Nana's trembling hand gripped her own one afternoon, and a deep sigh preceded the woman's benedictive words. "The Lord has blessed you, dear, in answer to my prayers. I only wish I could meet the young man who helped mend your torn heart, but that is not to be."

Dark eyes as sharp and deep as ever belied the frailty Ella recognized in her grandmother's constitution. The advancing years were doing so quite rapidly.

"I cannot make the trip, my dear, but I will be with you in spirit," she said with a pat of Ella's hand. "Rejoicing in your decision to give love another go."

Ella added the promise to the string of Nana's pearls already adorning her soul.

Over the next few weeks, several letters traveled between Cañon City and Chicago, not only from Cale whom she did not expect to write at all, but from Helen who allowed the boys to include pictures they'd drawn for Ella's benefit.

Cale's bold script mirrored his broad shoulders and square jaw, free of embellishment but full of purpose. He wrote of the rustlers' arrest—the two arguing men she had photographed at the rodeo, and he thanked her for her part in solving the case. They'd been caught selling beeves, as he put it, to a Cripple Creek butcher who verified that the brands had been "run"— which meant changed, he explained.

Helen's letters were full of plans for the wedding and questions about what Ella wanted in the way of flowers and bridesmaids and the flavor of cake that Clara had insisted she bake.

Ella promised to write Clara herself.

Were a couple hundred people too many for the big "feed" at the ranch after the wedding, Helen wanted to know. Based on reaction to a recently released Selig Polyscope flicker including a certain river-crossing episode, plenty of folk wanted to come. Including Cale and Hugh's sister Grace.

Did you know, Helen wrote, *that Cale's grandparents, Caleb Hutton and Annie Whitaker were married at the church? His folks as well, Whit and Livvy. You'll be the third generation, and I'm sure the grandest-looking couple of the bunch.*

The boys were fighting over who got to help do what, but Helen assured Ella that she'd find sufficient work to keep them occupied.

Hugh had come around to the idea of a wedding—somewhat—Helen offered, and Ella smiled at the woman's cautionary wording. However, the mention of the boys' father left her in awe at yet one more unexpected turn of events.

Rather, a turn of heart. Fate, she had learned, had no such power. Only love.

The force of it sent her to her father's study one afternoon, praying for courage and grace.

He invited her to join him on the green brocade settee near a window, the first time she could remember him doing such a thing. There, he took her hand in his. "I love you, Ella. You are the image of your mother, and that has made it hard on me. But I had no right to make it hard on you."

Stunned by his admission yet eagerly accepting the love she had craved, she threw her arms around his neck. "I love you too, Papa."

The childhood endearment tightened his arms around her.

Bolstered by her earlier prayer and her father's seeming change in demeanor, she shared what she had witnessed in Hugh Hutton.

Her father's jaw and the grip he held on her hand tightened somewhat, but he remained receptive. And when they left his study later, he was not nearly as stiff as before. He would always be somewhat reserved and formal—it was his way. But over the next several weeks, he softened by degree, and assured her that he would be on hand for the wedding.

~

In early October, Ella arrived a second time at Cañon City's Denver & Rio Grande station.

The scenery had changed.

Autumn gilded the cottonwoods along the Arkansas River and swept the sky a brilliant blue. The train slowed to a hissing stop, and she gathered her satchel and smoothed her skirt, craning her neck for a view of the platform and a certain cowboy.

Quickly she picked him out of the crowd, a head taller than most of the people milling about, tugging his collar, taking his hat off and putting it back on. As nervous as she had ever seen him.

Gripping her satchel strap in one hand and the iron handle beside the door in the other, she took the steps down to the platform only to be caught up by two strong arms that squeezed the laughter from her.

"You have a way of sweeping me off my feet without warning, Mr. Hutton."

The dimple stitched, so close to her face that all rational thought fled.

"Something I intend to do every day for the rest of my life, Mrs. Hutton-to-be."

Right there in front of everyone who cared to watch, his lips captured her breath and every quivering nerve ending she owned.

They broke from the kiss when three cheering little boys bounced across the platform, Helen in tow, attempting to scold them into submission while dabbing her eyes with a hankie.

Feet at last on the planks, Ella hugged all four of them, realizing that never before had she felt so much like she belonged. She straightened and squeezed her own eyes tight against what threatened until hard, gentle hands framed her face.

I love you and *a fine wife* came to mind again, words from this cowboy's lips that she treasured above all others. And then his voice rose from deep in his chest, a tight, graveled whisper of another phrase that changed her perception of all that surrounded her and all that would surround her forever.

"Welcome home, Ella. Welcome home."

~ ~ ~

Thank you for reading Book 4 of
The Cañon City Chronicles series,
A Change of Scenery.

If you enjoyed Cale and Ella's story,

I would so appreciate a brief review on your favorite book site.

You might also enjoy reading The Front Range Brides series.
Start with the prequel, Mail-order Misfire.

**Receive a free historical novella when you sign up for my
Quarterly Author Update:** https://bit.ly/3b4eavB

ACKNOWLEDGMENTS

It takes many hearts, hands, and hours for a book to come to completion, and for this I am grateful. I'd like to thank advance readers Nancy Huber, Jill Maple, and Amanda Beck; my editor Christy Distler; and you, the readers, for allowing the Hutton family saga to continue with the fourth generation, Cale and Ella. But most of all, I thank our good and loving God for pouring His stories into me and allowing me to tell them.

Thank you for reading Inspirational Western Romance. If you would like to leave a brief review on your favorite book website or other social media, it would bless my boots off!

About the Author

Bestselling author and winner of the **Will Rogers Gold Medallion** for Inspirational Western Fiction, Davalynn Spencer can't stop #lovingthecowboy. When she's not writing, teaching writer workshops, or playing on her church worship team, she's wrangling Keeper the Cowdog and mouse detectors Annie and Oakley. Connect with her via her website at www.davalynnspencer.com.

~May all that you read be uplifting.~